WATER AND BLOOD

THE CHRONICLES OF TERRASOHNEN BOOK 2

N. K. CARLSON

ALSO BY N. K. CARLSON

Novels

Shadow and Sword

The Smelly Gospel

The Things that Charm Us

Anthologies

Phantoms

Published in the United States by Creative James Media.

www.creativejamesmedia.com

978-1-956183-88-7 (trade paperback)

First U.S. Edition 2023

For Haley,

"The light shines in the darkness,
and the darkness has not overcome it."

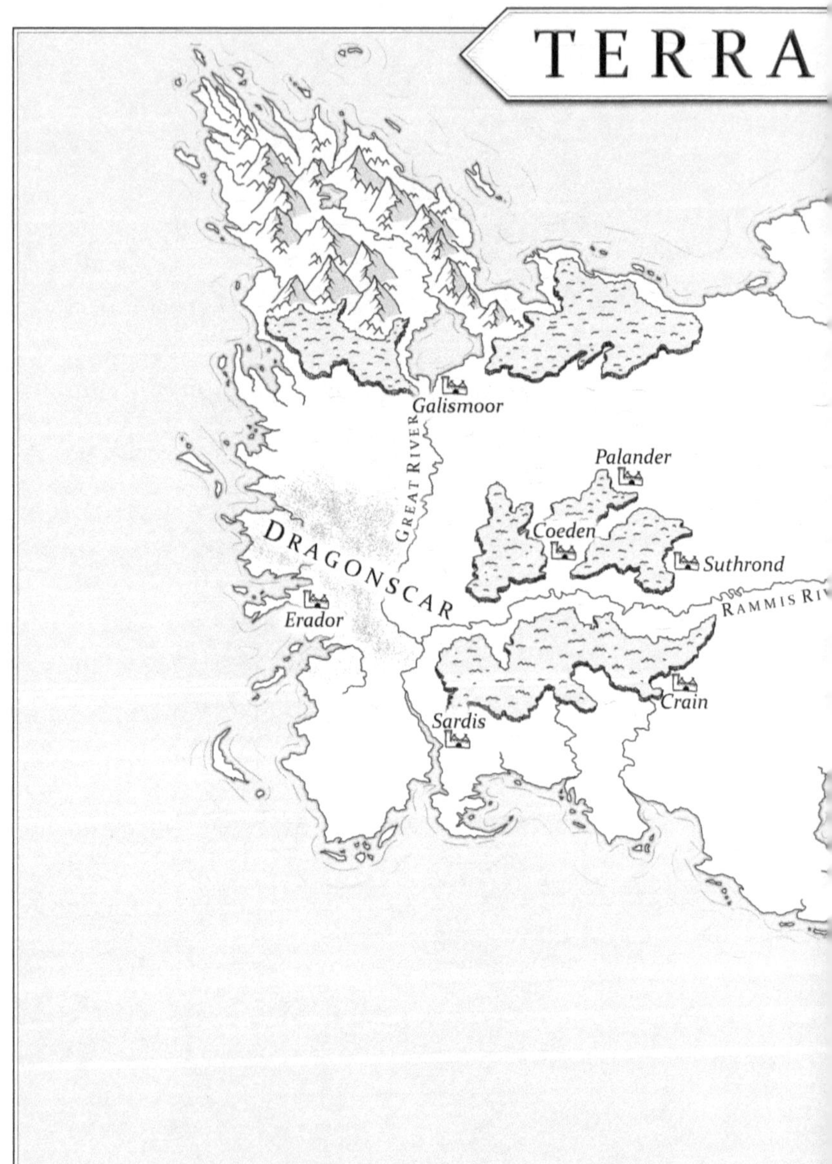

TERRA
Galismoor
Palander
Coeden
Suthrond
GREAT RIVER
DRAGONSCAR
Erador
RAMMIS RIVER
Crain
Sardis

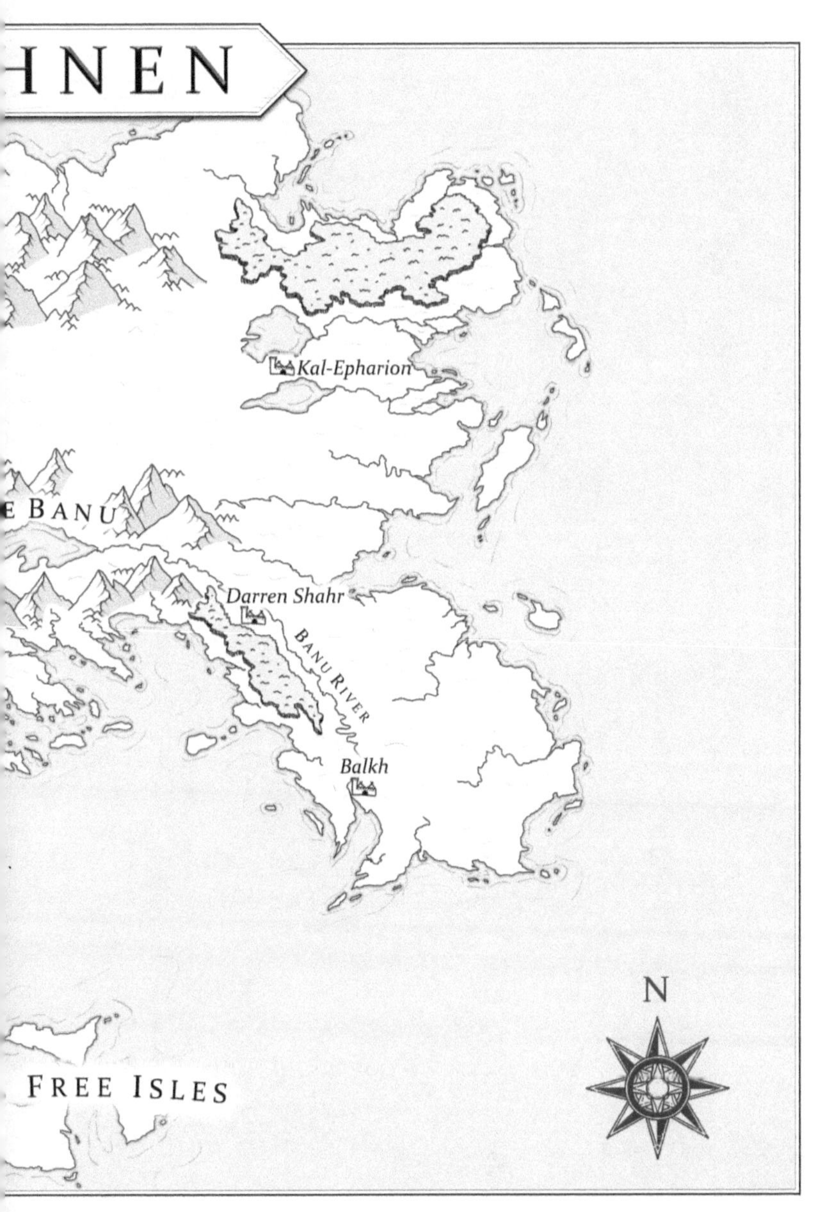

HNEN
Kal-Epharion
E BANU
Darren Shahr
BANU RIVER
Balkh
FREE ISLES
N

1

His shirt clung to his back with sweat as he walked beside his horse, one hand on the reins as a gentle guide. Not that the horse needed much of a firm hand, as the horse was well trained to stay with its fellows. In front of them, uncomfortably close, were the hindquarters of another horse. Reith attempted to slow down to put some more room in between them, but his horse took the lead and pulled him gently by the reins.

The smell of sweat and horse dung overwhelmed all his other senses to the point that Reith began to forget who he was and where he was going. He shook his head to clear his mind and struggled to form coherent thoughts against the onslaught of foulness on his nostrils.

It was the second day after Reith, Vereinen, Ellamora, and Dema had escaped the Elven Capital of Sardis. With them were Prince Romulus, Lord Myon, Brauron, and Aytos. The eight of them, three humans and five elves, made for an interesting assortment, the likes of which were seldom heard of in Terrasohnen. Conspicuous to the eight travelers were those who were not with them. Ellamora's uncle, Cassius, Dema's brother, Kydar, and several elves, whom Reith did not know their names, had all fallen on the flight from the city. Their absence haunted the group like ghosts and felt tangible. Reith blamed himself for Kydar's death. He had gone back in a desperate charge to protect his master, Vereinen. If they had simply escaped, perhaps Kydar might not have died.

The leader of the group called for a halt, but it took Reith several seconds to register this fact. He stood stupidly, holding the reins still as his horse nosed around for some grass to eat. He snapped to and discovered that they were in a small clearing in the forest, with room enough for horses, humans, and elves alike.

"Let us rest awhile and refresh ourselves," Prince Romulus said in a commanding voice.

Reith drank heartily from the waterskin hanging on his horse's saddle. Stepping away from the horses brought a breath of fresh air that revived him and made him more alert. The others sat below the trees in the shade. Though the whole group sat together, there was a clear order to the seating arrangements. On one side sat the elves of Sardis, on the other sat the humans. Whether she was conscious of it or not, Ellamora had sat neatly between the two groups.

Reith eased himself to the ground next to Dema, who stared blankly down at a piece of grass. He wished he knew what to say. Her grief was beyond tears. The previous night, Reith had heard her crying herself to sleep and felt helpless. His own grief for Kydar, his friend, was great. For Dema, the loss of her brother was beyond words.

"What is our travel plan?" Vereinen asked, his map of Terrasohnen rolled out on a rock in front of him. Romulus and Myon shifted closer to the chronicler and inspected the map.

"We are here," Romulus said, pointing to the Southern portion of the map, squarely in the middle of the elven territory. "In two days we have traveled perhaps forty miles. And we are heading here," he said, pointing to a point on the map further East. "The port city of Amisos." Reith leaned over to look at his master's map and saw that Amisos was the eastern edge of the elven lands, located alongside a massive bay that took a large cut out of the southern part of Terrasohnen. On the other side of the bay, Vereinen had written, "Dwarven Lands" in his neat handwriting.

"From Amisos, we must gain passage to the Free Isles," Romulus pointed to a small grouping of islands off the southern coast of Terrasohnen. "No elven ship would go from Amisos directly to the dwarves."

"It's a pity, the discord between our races," Myon said, sorrowfully. The old elf stretched out his legs in front of him as he spoke.

"Do we have to go via sea?" Vereinen asked. "Or could we go across land?" Reith could just make out the hint of nervousness in his master's voice. He had never been to sea, and he assumed that Vereinen had never either. He himself had seen the sea for the first time mere weeks earlier, as he stood on the Cliffs of Erador, the ancient, ruined city. His hand went instinctively to the hilt of his sword, which he had found there.

"No, see here," Romulus said, pointing to the map. "The mountains that separate the lands come all the way down here. We would have to travel so far north, and through the mountains. It would take several weeks more."

Vereinen nodded, resigning himself to the upcoming sea voyage.

"But before we take to sea," Myon said, "we must cross this land before us. It is a hard land. Few live there. Soon we will leave the trees behind us and the grass will turn to dust and sand. The desert awaits."

"It will be hard going, with very little water for several days," Romulus explained. "But we won't hit the edge until tomorrow."

After a few more minutes of rest, Romulus called for the company to depart. Soon they were picking their way through the forest, leading the horses on foot because of the low hanging tree branches above them. The single file walk was unfriendly to conversation, the miles felt longer and time seemed to move more slowly.

The sun fell from the sky behind them, and the trees cast long shadows. Presently, Romulus called for them to set camp for the evening. Within minutes, a fire was started in a clearing and Brauron and Aytos were sent to find a nearby water source, which Romulus assured them was nearby. Reith sought out Dema, who sat quietly by the fire.

"Hey," he said, sitting down next to her. The smell of the fire brought comfort to him. She stared into the flames.

"Hey, Reith," she said, the firelight glinting on her eyes. He stared into the fire, remembering how it had consumed Kydar's body as the God of Light took him away. The experience was one he was not soon to forget.

"How are you?" he asked her, still looking into the dancing flames.

"I'm here," she said softly. Reith didn't know what to say, so he said nothing.

"I still don't understand," she said after a pause. "He was here, and now he's not." There was another long pause before she continued. "Everyone is gone. Mom, Dad, now Kydar. Everyone's gone and I am the only one left."

Reith felt her anguish deep in his bones because it was his anguish too. His parents were dead, his town also destroyed. He looked over at Vereinen, who talked softly with Myon. *At least I have Vereinen.*

He turned his attention back to the girl beside him. Every square inch of her looked defeated and crushed by the world. She stared vacantly at the fire, but her focus was miles away. She turned her head to him, looking up from piercing brown eyes deep as the sea and sharp as a sword. He lost himself in those eyes.

"What?" she asked.

"You have me," he said finally. "I will be with you."

"Promise?"

"I promise."

"What a silly promise to make," she said. "You don't know how much time you have left. You don't know the day or the hour."

"Only the God of Light knows."

"You believe that? You believe *in* that, I mean?"

Reith thought back on all the things he had seen and experienced in the short weeks since fleeing from the Gray Man at his hometown of Coeden. His thoughts went to the grove of fruit trees and the stream near Erador, the ruined city, where he had first heard the Voice. *Save them. Serve them. Fight for them. Then find me.* He thought too of the temple in Crain, with the Lore Master, Ellyn and her lessons about the God of Light. But all of that was nothing compared to the burial of Kydar, with the flash of light and the body taken.

"Yes, I do believe it," he said. "I have seen many strange and wonderful things, strangest of all being Kydar's funeral. I can't explain it. But the only thing that makes sense is that it's true."

"I suppose that's faith, then," Dema said. They lapsed

into silence before Dema spoke again. "The world sure is a scary place if it's true. Dark Powers and Shadows killing people. How do you fight a Shadow? How do you fight something eternal?"

"I suppose that's where the God of Light comes in," Reith said.

"Still makes me nervous. If he's so good and powerful, why are there such terrible things happening to people?"

"I don't know," Reith said. "But I aim to find out."

The fire burned low and there was silence in the camp except for the rustle of the trees in the wind and the occasional footstep of whoever was on guard duty. Reith lay near Dema on one side and Vereinen on the other, surrounded by the two humans he most cared about in the world. If he expanded his circle, he did care about Ellamora, who was beside Dema on the other side, and Laneras, Ellyn, and Pallin in Crain, and Heth, Trigg, Titus, Tara, and Lara, and the other humans from Suthrond. His world now was much bigger than it was but also much smaller. Whereas before he had a whole village that felt like family, now those he cared for were few and far between, with what seemed to be the whole world between them.

And it all came back to the Gray Man, or Solzar, as Vereinen said he was called. He still hadn't had much time to process all he had learned in the past few days, how Vereinen and Solzar had been close, close as brothers, before Solzar became the Shadow he was today.

He heard Vereinen's familiar soft snores beside him, a sound he was intimately familiar with, having lived with Vereinen before Solzar had destroyed Coeden. He had nearly given up hope of ever finding Vereinen again before they had met in the most unlikely of places: the dungeon of Sardis.

Reith knew that Vereinen blamed himself for the rise of Solzar as a Shadow. Vereinen said he had unknowingly passed along secret knowledge of Shadows and the Dark Powers that Solzar had used to transform himself from simple man to a man empowered by evil and ancient Dark Powers. While Vereinen had seen the study of Shadows as a mere academic study, Solzar had sought the Dark Powers as a means to power and revenge against those who had wronged him and his mother.

Still, in the quiet of the night, with the sound of snores all around, Reith could not blame Vereinen. He knew his master's heart to be pure. Vereinen had no idea just how powerful the Dark Powers were, and had probably underestimated them, perhaps even doubted that they were real. And if Reith had heard about them a year ago, he knew he would have had the same reaction. Now, he knew better.

He was wide awake and turned over to try to find a more comfortable position. Tomorrow would be a terrible day of travel if he did not get sleep tonight. His foot brushed against his sword, which lay beside him. He glanced down at it. The moonlight glowed off the hilt, which was the only part of the sword exposed to the light. It shimmered and shone, and perhaps by a trick of the moonlight or by some magic in the sword itself, it appeared to dance of its own accord.

The Gray Man had said the sword was the key to unlocking a source of ancient power. Vereinen had told him that the restoration of Terrasohnen was locked away, but that the key was lost.

And now Reith was sure that the sword he had found

in Erador was this infamous key. *What power would it unlock? Where is the lock?*

Then the words came to him. "Find me."

He sat up and looked around. The words were audible, clear as day. It was the Voice. The Voice he had heard in Erador. He looked around, wondering if the Voice was near.

Just as he was about the lay back down, the Voice said again, "Save them. Serve them. Fight for them. Then find me."

The hair on the back of his neck stood on end and he got goosebumps, as if someone had bent down and whispered in his ear. No one else stirred in the camp, but he saw the guard on duty pacing away among the trees, keeping watch. He thought it was Romulus.

His heart raced. He took deep breaths trying to calm down. He was shocked no one stirred, but then again, he wasn't entirely sure the Voice wasn't just in his head. Still, the Voice sounded clear as day, though like always, the meaning was almost entirely unknown.

I don't know where to look for you, he thought forcefully, as if casting his thoughts into the world around him, his mind yelling into the void.

As he had expected, the Voice did not answer back. *The Voice just seems to pop in from time to time to remind me of what it had said before. Too bad I have no idea what it means.*

He lay back down, all hope of getting a good night's sleep slipping away from him like water in a hand. He reached out absentmindedly and held the hilt of his sword. Just then waves of sleep washed over him and he knew no more until morning.

.They spent most of the next day in the saddle, as the trees began to thin, which gave them room to sit astride their mounts without fear of branches. The distance between them and Sardis grew more quickly. At their lunch break, Romulus even supposed they would leave the forest behind entirely that evening.

As the trees continued to thin out, space became available to ride side by side, rather than single file. During the first such opportunity, Reith found himself beside Ellamora. Ellamora was tall and fair, filled with the grace of her race. In the days since Sardis, she had been distant with the group, which Reith supposed had to do with her Uncle Cassius' death in the escape from the city.

"Care for a sparring match tonight?" Reith asked, probing Ellamora's mood. Ellamora had taught him, Kydar, and Dema much about sword play on their trip from Crain to Sardis, and Reith was eager to put his skills to the test again.

A small smile flitted across Ellamora's face. "I hope you are ready to be humiliated in front of these witnesses," she said, with her usual playful fierceness. "I would hate to see you disgraced in front of the Crown Prince of the elves."

"Oh, but that means nothing to me," Reith replied. "He is not my prince. It should be you who fears humiliation."

"May the best blade win," Ellamora said with steel in her voice.

The sun rose high in the sky, and as the morning turned to afternoon, their shadows began to grow in front of them. After a break, Reith realized with a start that he was riding beside Prince Romulus, all his earlier bravado with Ellamora forgotten.

"Reith," Romulus began, looking over at Reith from his own horse. "Tell me about yourself."

"I … uh," Reith stammered, caught off guard by the directness of the question.

"My apologies," the prince said. "Let me tell you what I know of you, and then you can fill in the gaps. You are an orphan, who lived with Vereinen, the Master Chronicler, and studied under him as an apprentice. As such, you are learned in history, or at least human history, and you have certain proficiencies in reading, writing, and geography. You are handy with the bow and have been for some time. When Solzar attacked Coeden, you fled, following directions Vereinen had left you in a note to go to Erador, where you procured that fascinating sword you wear, but you are not nearly as proficient in swordplay as in archery. There in Erador, a Voice told you save others from Solzar, which brought you to the human town of Suthrond, which had previously been destroyed by Solzar. You tracked the survivors south, to the banks of the river that divides our two lands. You joined them and brought them across the river into the realm of elves, finding refuge in Crain. When there was an uprising in Crain, you traveled to Sardis to petition the King, with Ellamora as your guide and Dema and her brother Kydar as companions. Do I have your story correct?"

"Yes, you do," Reith said, and then hastily added, "Your highness." He also made note of Romulus' comment about his proficiency with a sword for later use.

"Oh, none of that," Romulus said, laughing. "It appears I have left that life behind me. You and I are now brothers on the road. Call me Romulus. So tell me, Reith, what else should I know about you? If we are to travel together and face certain danger, I would like to know as much about you as possible. I shall, of course, return the favor."

"Well, you seem to know all there is to know of my story," Reith said. "You are well informed."

"Reith, I think you severely underestimate how interesting you are. For one, all that has happened to you makes you extraordinary on its own. But secondly, what interests me is your sword and the Voice. What exactly did it say?"

"Save them. Serve them. Fight for them. Then find me," Reith recited, the words etched in his memory. "Do you know what they mean?"

"It seems to me that there is a progression, with each command following the other. You have already saved the survivors of Suthrond from Solzar by taking them across the river. You either have served them or are serving them by coming to Sardis and now seeking help from the dwarves. Either way, it seems that battle is in your future."

"Battle?" Reith said, turning sideways to look at Romulus. "Are you serious?"

"Deadly," Romulus said, shaking his head sadly. "Peace seemed to last only as long as the races remained separate, but that peace meant only the absence of war. My hope is that we are on the brink of an age of cooperation and fellowship like in the olden days. But our path to that world is a dark one. Many oppose it. My father, for instance. Any potential unity among the races is a threat to his power in the elven realm."

"But you think it will come to battle?"

"That is all but assured, Reith," Romulus said. "I hate that it would happen in our days, but we can fight with the hope that our struggle is for a better world, a world of true peace and harmony."

"So, if a fight is coming, what then? What does *find me* mean?" Reith asked.

"I have no idea," Romulus said. "I have a suspicion

that the Voice belongs to a Guardian of Light, or even the God of Light. You have a destiny, Reith."

"Why me?"

"All chosen by the God of Light for one task or another ask that question. It is beyond our wisdom. The God of Light has purposes and plans we can know nothing about. He has written the story of Terrasohnen on the world, and we are following along as best we can, though the ending is hidden from our eyes. But as for your question, I do not believe the God of Light calls someone unless he purposes to accomplish something in and through them."

"So you think I will be successful in whatever this is?"

"I don't think it, I believe it. I have faith in the God of Light. I think he or someone speaking for him is speaking to you, so I trust that he will be with you."

"Easy for you to say," Reith said, "You're not the one facing fighting and finding."

"Perhaps not finding, but certainly fighting."

They rode on in silence for a few minutes.

"You promised to return the favor," Reith said. "Tell me about you."

"I am Romulus, firstborn son of King Koinas, heir to the throne of the elves. My mother died seven winters ago. I am the only remaining child of her and my father. He shall be furious that I have gone, but it is for the best. I was raised in the palace of Sardis and had the greatest tutors in history, mathematics, law, military strategy, astronomy, jousting, archery, and swordplay. As prince, I felt a great concern for my people, that all would be treated with fairness and justice. I have taken an interest in hearing the grievances of my people against one another and against the crown, which I did my best to decide equitably. I know rulers do not choose their monikers, but Romulus the Just has a nice ring to it. I hope to live up to it. And now, I am afraid that the greatest threat to the kingdom and my people is my father, and so I am on this quest beside you, fleeing from his wrath to a foreign land to beg for aid."

"Sounds bleak," Reith said, not really knowing what to say to the prince.

"It's not as bleak as one might think. The God of Light is with us. We saw that at the funeral pyre for Kydar. And when the God of Light is with us, who can oppose us?"

True to Romulus' prediction, at late afternoon, they found themselves at the last of the trees. Before them, scraggly grass and low bushes were the only vegetation.

"We are at the edge of the desert," Romulus said, declaring the obvious. "Let us camp here in the shelter of the trees, where we know water is nearby." They had crossed a stream about a half hour previous. "Come, let us go back to the stream and set our camp there. In the morning, we can drink our fill, and the horses too, before our journey through the desert."

Once camp was set, branches that resembled swords were cut from nearby trees and Ellamora and Reith stepped front and center, their sparring match to be the entertainment for the evening.

"Bow to your opponent," Romulus said, and Ellamora and Reith gave each other curt nods. "And fight!"

Ellamora's stick whirred through the air in an upward arch toward Reith's left ear. He ducked and the makeshift blade passed over his head harmlessly. The force of Ellamora's blow caused her to turn away from him slightly, and he lunged forward, aiming a backhand slash at her exposed side. She backhand parried his blow and regained her stance facing him. They traded blows for a minute, neither gaining an edge. To try and gain the edge, Reith began to attack harder and harder, but Ellamora calmly turned aside each blow. He was tiring and knew he was lost if he did not do something to turn the tide soon. After a particularly intense flurry of blows, he spun out and away from her. The bait was taken. Ellamora pressed her advantage, thinking he was withdrawing for a break. He was ready. He stopped his spin halfway around and quickly changed direction, spinning back the other way. She realized her mistake too late. Her stroke was in the wrong place at the wrong time. He dodged her feeble attack and landed a soft blow on her back as she passed. She stumbled and fell to her knees, defeated and breathing heavy. Reith grinned and basked in the applause from the assembled onlookers.

"What a move, Reith!" Dema said proudly. She knew how far he had come in just a few short weeks.

"Superb!" Vereinen exclaimed.

"Excellent, excellent," said Myon.

Ellamora stood, tossed her sword away, and shook hands with him. "That was a pretty cool move," she said. "But I'll be ready for it next time."

"Care for another match?" Romulus asked. He was holding Ellamora's discarded branch. Reith remembered Romulus' comment about his sword play skills and eagerly accepted, hoping to prove Romulus wrong.

"Give me a minute," Reith said. He went to the stream and plunged his face in, wiping away the sweat that poured down his face and drank deeply. Soon he was ready again.

"Bow," Romulus said, in a low voice. They did and Reith sized up his opponent as Ellamora had taught him. From what he knew of Romulus, he would be a master. *Maybe he will be overconfident.*

"And fight!"

Romulus did not attack as Ellamora had, instead he stayed back waiting for Reith to make the first move. Instead of attacking, Reith began to circle around, trying to gain an edge on Romulus' off hand. Romulus kept pace and soon Reith was on the opposite side of the makeshift sparring ring.

Romulus looked relaxed, comfortable. *Well let's change that.*

Reith swung a forehand blow at him, not up high but down at his shins. Romulus jumped back and caught Reith's branch with his own downward blocking swing. The move surprised Romulus, as Reith had hoped it would, and Romulus took a step forward to balance himself. This time Reith did a full spin to get to the side of Romulus and attacked his right shoulder. Romulus reset himself and blocked the blow, but Reith had jumped to the side to get behind Romulus and struck again. Romulus blocked again and spun himself to face his foe, but Reith was ready. He spun back to where he had just been and swung hard at Romulus' ribs. He heard a satisfying crack and his hand vibrated with the force of the blow. Romulus staggered to his knees, holding his left hand to his side.

"I yield," he said with a groan. The clearing reverberated with appreciation for Reith's skill again.

"How did you get so good?"

"I thought I wasn't proficient in swordplay?" Reith asked mockingly.

"I shouldn't have said that," Romulus said with a pained grin, still massaging his ribs.

There was nowhere to hide from the hot desert sun. The shade of the forest had been taken for granted and Reith missed it now that there was no barrier between his skin and the sun. They did not spend their entire time riding but spent about half of their day walking beside their horses to give them a slight break in the heat. They saw no water source and were on strict rations.

"There are oases throughout the desert," Myon said at one of their breaks. "We'll see them soon."

Once the sun was high in the sky, they talked little as all their throats were parched. Reith was glad that the sun was out of their direct line of vision. He had spent most of the morning with his head down, though the sunlight gleamed off the sand and hurt his eyes.

With the sun now setting behind them, the heat continued to grow. Around midafternoon, Romulus called for a lengthy halt to rest until the temperature grew less oppressive.

"Come, let's travel for another hour and see if we can find an oasis."

They traveled until it was no longer prudent to because of darkness. They set camp, all of them tired, thirsty, and grumpy. Even after his ration of water, Reith was ravenously thirsty.

The full moon rose over the desert and the temperature mercifully dropped to tolerable levels. In the distance, an animal howled.

Reith drew the first watch, which he was to share with Dema. They did not have much opportunity to talk as they each circled the camp on opposite sides. Every so often they heard distant howls, but they seemed to be getting farther and farther away from the camp. They kept the fire going in between their loops with the pile of brush the group had cut upon setting up their camp.

Reith froze as the hairs on the back his neck stood on end. He notched an arrow and peered into the darkness, willing his eyes to see the invisible thing that his senses told him was there. He felt Dema approaching from his right.

"I think I heard something," he hissed.

She pulled her bow and notched an arrow but said nothing. He was thankful for her silence. His ears strained trying to catch the sound of anything approaching. All of a sudden, a pair of yellow eyes materialized in the darkness, silently walking toward them. As it came near them the shape of a huge dog became visible in the firelight. It let out a terrifying howl.

"Wolf! Desert wolf!" Dema yelled.

2

———————

Startled by Dema's shout, the wolf jumped forward, but soon fell with an arrow in its neck from Reith's bow. He soon had another on the string.

Whether it was the wolf's howl or Dema's shout, the camp was roused. Bows and swords were drawn ready for action. More wolves approached as Romulus took charge.

"Dema, Ellamora, put more brush on the fire!" he yelled, as he sent an arrow into a nearby wolf. Myon's bow twanged as he sent an arrow hurtling toward another. Brauron and Aytos had their swords out, and the wolves kept their distance from the blade which gleamed in the firelight, now blazing high from the efforts of Dema and Ellamora. Its light spread farther out from the camp allowing the defenders to see their attackers.

A sharp snarl rumbled through the air behind Reith, and he whirled, loosened his sword from its scabbard and got the blade up just in time to stop a lunging wolf in its tracks. The hot breath of the wolf hit his arm as the sword plunged in. He drew his sword from the beast and looked around for the next one.

He saw it in an instant. The others had been distracted by other wolves and had somehow parted, leaving an open lane from the outside of the camp directly to the fire in center. Ellamora was bent over, picking up some brush to throw on the blaze, ignorant of the danger behind her.

"Ellamora!" Reith shouted as he sprang into action, leaping forward. He drew his sword back behind him and reached up to clasp the hilt with his left hand as well as his right. He reached the wolf just as it reached Ellamora. His sword came down with his whole weight from his lunge. The wolf's jaws were open an inch from Ellamora's neck when Reith's sword sliced through the wolf's neck. He fell in a heap on top of the wolf and blood poured over him.

"By God, Reith!" Romulus said.

"I'm fine," Reith said, panting with effort from the short battle against the beasts. "It's not my blood."

He looked around to see the carnage. Dead wolves lay around the camp. Their whole party was standing except for Brauron, who appeared to have suffered a bite or a slash on his right forearm. Aytos leaned over him, tending to the wound. Everyone appeared all right, though shaken.

"Why did they attack?" Dema asked.

"Desert wolves are prone to attack camps," Myon said. "It rarely happens though because these lands are rarely inhabited, but there are stories. They need to eat, same as any other creature."

A howl rose in the distance and they all froze. When they realized it was far off in the desert, they relaxed.

"Well, I don't think I will be able to sleep after that excitement," Romulus said. "Shall we depart in the night, and save ourselves the heat of the day? Maybe we can find an oasis to refresh ourselves."

The plan was agreed upon, and they packed up their camp. Reith retrieved his arrows from the bodies of the wolves littering the desert floor. At last, they were ready to leave. They left the fire blazing behind them, a beacon in the night to any who may be watching, but in the desert the chances of another sentient being seeing it were remote. Everyone was glad to be rid of the corpses that littered the ground where they had so recently been asleep.

By the light of the moon and the stars they rode. The horses were surefooted, even in the dark, and their going was smooth. Their eyes adjusted to the night rather quickly away from the fire, and they could see a long way off in all directions in the moonlight.

Reith used a small amount of water to wash the blood from himself, though he still felt sticky and gross in the aftermath. *Who knows when I'll be able to take a proper bath again?*

A few hours before sunrise, they saw a small group of trees looming over the surrounding desert and turned that way. To their immense relief, they found a small spring at the base of the trees and they all drank deeply. Reith used the water to rinse himself clean, though he did avoid plunging himself in, despite desiring to do just that. He didn't think the others would appreciate it if he got wolf's blood in the small spring.

They rested and set a guard of four. Romulus, Ellamora, Aytos, and Brauron were placed on guard and Reith happily lay down on his bed roll. In seconds it seemed, he was asleep.

***

The sun was up when Reith awoke. He found that nearly everyone was awake already, except Ellamora who had gone to sleep when Myon had woken up early in the morning. The trees provided a strange fruit, which was yellow and juicy. They spent an hour eating, drinking, and staying in the shade of the tree. Myon and Romulus decided it would be best to travel for a few hours, camp for the rest of the day, and then travel again by nightfall. This way the whole company would be awake for any dangers in the nighttime and they could spend the heat of each day resting.

The sun felt even hotter today after the refreshing morning at the oasis. Before they had departed, Reith had soaked himself nearly completely in the cool water from the spring, but within minutes he was bone dry again.

He managed to take a short nap when they stopped just after noon. Very little was said in the afternoon. All were tired and thirsty and Brauron was sore from his wolf wound.

With about two hours left of daylight, Romulus called for them to begin their journey again.

"If my calculations are correct, in two or three days we should be in Amisos." This thought cheered them all as the desert was making them all weary.

Near sunset, they came across another oasis, though they did not stay long. They drank until they were satisfied, filled the water skins, plucked some of the yellow fruit, and began again. The night grew chilly as it seemed that the air could hold little of the sun's heat on its own. In the distance wolves and other unnamed creatures howled and roared, as if frustrated by the elves' and humans' presence by the oasis. Soon they were on their way again and the howls and roars faded into the blackness.

At dawn, the sun peaked over the top of mountain peaks in the distance and they formed walls from north to south. Reith saw they were heading toward the southern edge of the range.

"We are getting close," Myon said. "Those mountains

are the eastern border of the realm of elves. We will find Amisos at the end of the mountain range."

Their course was corrected by the mountains, so they now traveled slightly south in addition to their original eastward trek. The sun was in their eyes for the morning, so when it finally rose higher than the peaks, they were surprised to find the peaks bigger than they had appeared at first light. *We are making good progress.*

A little after noon they again stopped, but they did not have the fortune of finding an oasis. Water was in short supply and tempers were short. There was unnecessary snippiness when anyone spoke, and soon the company grew silent, each lost in their own thoughts.

Reith took this time to reflect on what lay ahead. *Amisos, sea, the Free Isles, the dwarves,* he mentally recited. Each step in the chain seemed more and more unreal to him. He had dreamed of seeing the world while studying history and maps with Vereinen, but he had never dreamed to see some of these lands. In his wildest dreams he had supposed he would travel the kingdom of humans, visiting the various towns and cities, particularly Galismoor and Kal-Epharion. And yet here he was, perhaps a score of miles from Amisos, another elven city, and the sea. He drifted off into sleep with thoughts of a sea voyage playing in his head.

As the sun set behind them, they again set off on their journey. No wolves or other animals disturbed them, though at sunset, they came to a stream flowing out of an oasis in the same direction they were going. The direction it took was a bit more south than they had been going, but the decision was made to follow it in the night so they were guaranteed a water source near at hand. The horses sure did appreciate it.

Almost imperceptibly, the air grew steadily denser and

vegetation grew thicker and ever taller. And then the first breath of salty air drifted through the night and Reith knew they were near the sea. Soon they reached the top of a bluff and the land before them unrolled like a scroll. There stood Amisos, a city smaller than Sardis but still quite grand in its own right, but two miles on. They saw it in the light of a thousand torches in the streets, candlelight in windows, and the glow of the moon overhead. Beyond Amisos lay the sea.

"We shall stay here the rest of the night," Romulus declared. "In the morning, we will send a small party in to survey the situation. I think it should be Myon, Brauron, and Aytos. I would be too recognizable and the humans would be too conspicuous."

"Can I go?" Ellamora asked, stepping forward. "I think I could be of some assistance."

Romulus looked at Myon, who nodded. "All right, the group will be Myon, Brauron, Aytos, and Lady Ellamora. The rest of us shall find shade where we can and wait. But for now, let us sleep. I will take first watch. I think we are safe with one guard this close to the city. No fire tonight though. We don't want to alert anyone to our presence."

They set up their makeshift camp, and Reith settled down beside Vereinen and Dema. He was weary from their journey through the nights and resting during the day. His body was not adjusting well to it. He was asleep within seconds, and his hand held loosely to the hilt of his sword.

It felt like no time later that he was shaken awake. The sun was barely over the horizon of the sea, and already the air was warming. It would be another hot day. Myon, Brauron, Aytos, and Ellamora were all preparing to head into the city. They decided they would loop around the city and come to it from the southern edge, which was the usual way travelers by land would arrive. The southern reaches of the elven kingdom were friendlier to travelers, as they were grasslands, not deserts.

"Now one more time, what is your story?" Romulus asked Myon, making sure all the details were correct.

"We have traveled to Amisos from Sardis, seeking to charter a vessel to the Free Isles. We three," indicating himself, Brauron, and Aytos, "Will be going under our own names. Word from Sardis should not have come about us yet. Ellamora, shall be my niece. We will sell our horses in the city to raise more funds for ourselves."

"Good," Romulus said. "Charter us a ship and have it meet us down the coast, out of sight from the city in two days' time. We shall stay here today and tomorrow. If you have any difficulty in procuring the ship, send one or two of you out to meet us here. On the morning of the day after tomorrow, we shall break camp early and make for a spot down the coast about ten miles or so."

With the plan agreed to, Ellamora and the others said their farewells.

"Best of luck, Ellamora," Reith said, giving her a quick hug. She moved over to hug Dema too.

"Thank you," she said. "This is quite exciting."

"Keep a good head," Romulus said to her. "Be smart, be safe."

"I will be fine, as long as I am with Myon, Brauron, and Aytos," she said with a smile.

They soon left, traveling due south, leaving the humans and Prince Romulus by themselves.

"And now we wait," Romulus said.

They stayed on the bluff during the day, keeping an eye on the city. To their left the foothills of the mountains rose, each hill leading to another taller hill, until the hills blended seamlessly into the mountains, which towered high above the world. Reith supposed it would be virtually impassable. When he made the point aloud, Romulus and Vereinen agreed with him.

"There is a pass far to the north," Vereinen said, "which is the only way to reach the dwarven kingdom by land. These mountains are nearly impenetrable, and few have lived to tell the tale of passing through them."

Reith contemplated where he was. On one side was the desert, safely traversed. To his left, the mountains, looming and impenetrable. Before him and to his right, the sea, vast and deep. These things were all so foreign to his life a short while ago. He missed the trees of Coeden. This world was beautiful and strange to him, and it did not feel like home. All of a sudden, he felt a foreboding sense of danger coming at him from all sides. His head was on a swivel, looking to and fro at imaginary dangers on all sides. *Stop being silly*, he told himself. *You're perfectly safe here.*

The moment of panic left him, but the sense of danger did not. While he was indeed safe at the moment, there was danger ahead, coming for him. He gripped his sword tighter, ready for anything that would come his way.

"Vereinen, what do you know about the Key of Terrasohnen?" Reith asked, his hand and mind on his sword.

Vereinen looked up from polishing his leather bag. Romulus and Dema also stopped what they were doing to look at him.

"Not too much, I am afraid," Vereinen said slowly.

"Why does the Gray Man, I mean Solzar, why does he want it?" Reith asked. "He has the Dark Powers on his side. What more could he need?"

"I don't know if it is a matter of his need or if it is our

need," Vereinen said. "Whatever the Key unlocks is said to bring about the restoration of Terrasohnen. That is the opposite of what the Dark Powers want."

"So you don't think he wants to use whatever the Key unlocks?" Reith asked.

"I think if he can bend that power to his will and the Dark Powers' will, he would. But I don't think it would work that way. Wills are hard to be broken."

"What do you think it is?" Reith asked.

"That, I am afraid, I do not know," Vereinen said, shaking his head sadly. "I have only come across two sources that talk of the Key at all. One is the text I read in our house shortly before Solzar attacked. The other I read years ago. It was in a secret library in Kal-Epharion, a secret chamber that only I had discovered in the thousand years since it had been built. Neither source said exactly what the key was to unlock."

"There may be more information in the Free Isles," Romulus said, cutting into the conversation. "It is said their library is the grandest in all Terrasohnen. Many of the ancient texts of Erador were evacuated there, saved from the Dragon War."

"I guess they didn't need to move them," Reith said. "The library at Erador was almost completely intact, as if the dragons ignored it, or some magic protected it from them."

"I would not be surprised if it were some spell," Romulus said. "The ancients were well versed in magic. Many walked closely with the Guardians of Light and received some of their wisdom in those days."

"It has been a lifelong dream of mine to travel to the Free Isles and visit their library," Vereinen said longingly. "I just wish we had more time there."

"You never know," Romulus said. "We may have

trouble finding passage on a ship to the Dwarven coast city of Balkh. From my understanding, only dwarves sail back to Balkh from the Free Isles, and only elves sail to Amisos. We might be there awhile. But it's still preferable to those," he said, gesturing up at the mountains.

"What happens if we can't get on a ship to Balkh?" Dema asked, finally joining the conversation. "We can't just give up."

"No, we can't," Romulus said. "We will cross that bridge if and when we come to it. Worst case scenario, we commandeer a ship of our own."

"Ah, saving the world through piracy," Vereinen said. "What does the King's Justice say about that?"

"No comment," Romulus said with a wry smile.

"Have you ever been to the Free Isles?" Reith asked Romulus.

"Oh, no," Romulus replied. "As Crown Prince, it was always advisable to remain in our kingdom. One never knows what trouble one might encounter abroad. My father's arm was not so long as to snatch me back. Though I am afraid now he has stretched out his arm too far." His face darkened. "So no, I have never left the land of elves. As soon as we land on the Isles, I will be out of my kingdom for the first time in my life."

That night, Reith took first watch. All was quiet. He watched the moonlight dance upon the waves of the sea, entranced by its beauty. The moon somehow seemed closer here.

He slept well into the morning. The others let him be, as they had nowhere to be that day. The shadows cast by the sun were short when he finally stirred into wakefulness. It was a hot day so he plunged himself into the stream, basking in its cool flow. When he got out, he dried himself under the hot sun and watched the others. Romulus and

Dema were in a shooting match, which Romulus was winning handily. Vereinen had his maps spread in front of him, studying them. As much as he would have enjoyed the shooting match, he decided to be a student again.

"I am here to learn again, master," he said to Vereinen as he sat down beside him.

Vereinen smiled at him. "Welcome Reith, what do you want to learn today? Perhaps geography? History? Mathematics?"

"Why not geography?"

"Alas, you have chosen the subject that I am not well-versed in. Perhaps you even know more than I do. I think I will need to make a new map, one that accounts for the new places we are going."

"It's very exciting, isn't it," Reith said. "Did you ever dream you'd see this much of Terrasohnen?"

"Only in my wildest dreams," Vereinen said. "Though I never imagined the calamity befalling us that is the reason for this journey of ours. No, I wish we could be in these lands in peaceful times."

"No one remembers the peaceful times," Reith said. "They're not in any of the history books."

"No, they are not, and I am starting to think that my vocation as chronicler is contributing to that in a negative way. Throughout history, the peaceful times have been the most prevalent. But history has its eye on the wars and intrigue, the famines instead of the harvests, the deaths instead of the births. Most people are born and die under the banner of peace. But we don't keep those stories."

"Maybe we should," Reith said.

"Maybe we should," Vereinen echoed.

"All my life I wanted to be part of a great adventure, a story bigger than myself," Reith said. "But now that I am in one, I long for the good old days of studying, hunting, and town life. All those things are gone."

"Gone for now," Vereinen replied. "But not gone forever. Everything is being made new again in Terrasohnen. Your experiences in Dragonscar are the sign of things to come. Streams now flow in that thirsty land. Trees grow heavy with fruit. And spring seems to be contagious, from what you say of the seeds planted from that fruit. You have left a trail of newness behind you as you have traveled about Terrasohnen."

"But what difference does that make?" Reith asked. "The Shadow is growing stronger. The world is in mortal peril."

"It makes all the difference in the world. Life and light, healing and restoration, these are the things that fight back the Shadow. Never underestimate the power of planting a tree where once there was none."

"I still don't understand," Reith protested.

"You will someday," Vereinen replied. "When you are an old man, you will remember this conversation and acknowledge I was right."

"I hope I live that long," Reith said.

Before dawn, Reith was woken by Romulus, who had taken the last watch of the night. Together they roused Vereinen and then Dema. Dema nearly connected Romulus' face with a flailing right hook, so startled she was at being awoken, but he managed to dodge the blow.

"Oh, my goodness, I am so sorry," she said, when sufficiently awake to realize what had just happened.

"Don't worry about it," Romulus said, grinning.

"Better to come out swinging against an attacker in the night than not."

They gathered their few belongings and mounted their horses. The moon was hidden behind clouds, so they traveled in near complete darkness for many minutes. Reith could just make out the shapes of Romulus, Vereinen, and Dema ahead of him. To their left, Amisos was visible because of the torches that lit its walls. They made good time and were past the city before the sky began to lighten in the east, over the sea. It was still too dark to see if any ships were on the water.

Romulus led them through the wilderness around Amisos down toward the coast. The sky continued to grow lighter and Reith could see waves crashing in the distance through the early morning gloom. They came to a road, which Romulus hurried them across, for fear of being seen or heard. It wouldn't be the end of the world if they were caught, but it was always better to be safe than sorry.

The desert sands changed to rocky ground. At last they found themselves on the beaches south of the city. Reith could not tell how far away the city was, but he knew that anyone watching from the walls would barely be able to see them, even if the watcher knew they were there. Under the light of the newly rising sun, Romulus urged his horse to a trot and the rest followed suit. The smell of the salty air was strong, and the sound of the waves crashing was rhythmic. At times, it seemed like the horses were intentionally timing their trotting to their rhythm. Reith could have continued like this all day, but soon it was time to stop. Romulus found a good spot to wait for the ship the others should soon be bringing them.

They unsaddled the horses, who wandered around looking for a place to graze, but were unsuccessful, as the beach was only sand and rock. They sat and waited.

Romulus set about gathering driftwood and kindling. He set these up into a small pile, ready to be lit when the ship carrying their friends came into sight.

Reith hadn't been worried about this part of the plan, but now as they waited, his stomach was uneasy. So many things could have gone wrong. *What if word from Sardis beat us here and the others were arrested? What if they couldn't charter a ship? What if they already came by here this morning and were continuing South?*

The tension and dread mounted all morning. Reith could tell he wasn't the only one with these thoughts. Romulus looked worried and stressed, as did Vereinen. Out of all of them, Dema looked to be the most at ease with her situation, but Reith supposed this was more to do with her ability to mask her feelings, particularly in the wake of Kydar's death. Only the horses seemed unperturbed.

"There's a ship!" Reith said excitedly, pointing to a ship out on the sea sailing south. The others rose expectantly, looking in the direction Reith pointed.

"How can we know for sure?" Vereinen asked. "We don't want to give away our position if it isn't them."

"If it is them," Romulus said, "they will sail as near the shore as they can. Let us watch." He hovered over his wood and kindling, ready to strike it ablaze at the first sign it was their friends.

The ship continued along its course and the breeze from the north guided it southward. Reith could see it had two sails, one near the front of the ship and one near the back. He saw sailors scurrying about on the deck attending to the ship, which gave him some idea of its size. It was not a large ship, but it seemed big enough for the eight of them and a crew.

"I don't see any of our people," Vereinen said, the worry evident in his voice. "Could it be a trap?"

"I don't know," Romulus said, hovering over the not yet started fire. "What do you two see?" he asked Reith and Dema.

Reith squinted to try and get a better view of the ship's deck. The elves he saw looked nothing like Myon, Brauron, and Aytos, and there was no sign of Ellamora.

"If it was them," he said, "we would see them on the deck looking to the shore. I don't see anyone looking our way."

"I don't see any of them," Dema said.

"We should hide," Vereinen said. "Just to be safe."

They slowly scrambled up the hill away from the beach. They crouched behind some boulders, less exposed than they had been. If anyone from the ship saw them, they didn't care, and the ship was soon far down the coast.

"I hope we were right about that," Romulus said. "It would be a shame to waste time with our ship making its way south without us."

With the ship gone, they again resumed their positions on the beach. Romulus sat near his future fire, and Reith and Dema practiced sparring with some driftwood branches. The afternoon wore on. They saw a few ships head out to sea, away from the city, going eastward, but none that sailed south past them. No one spoke it, but they all wondered how long they would have to wait and about whether they needed to make a secret trip into Amisos to see what had befallen their friends.

An hour before sunset, another ship came into view. This one was smaller than the previous one, but not by much. It had a single mast in the center of the ship with a sail. Several oars were seen swirling into the water propelling the ship forward from holes in the side of the ship.

The sun was directly behind them, making it easier to see the ship and its passengers. Like before, there was movement on the deck as sailors went to and fro pulling ropes and getting the ship ready to sail.

"It's Ellamora!"

All four of them shouted it out simultaneously. Ellamora was clearly visible on the deck at the front of the ship, her hair shining in the late afternoon sun. Romulus eagerly lit his fire, and soon smoke rose from the flames. They all waved clothing over their heads to attract more attention. They were soon spotted and after a flurry of activity on board, two small rafts were sent off, each manned by three. As they got nearer, Reith saw that Brauron and Aytos were each in separate rafts with two unknown elves who were rowing. Romulus kicked sand over their fire, and they all said a quick farewell to their horses. There would be no taking them further. When Dema had expressed concern about this point earlier, Vereinen had pointed out that more likely than not, some farmer would find them and take good care of them.

The rafts scraped the beach and came to a rest.

"Ahoy!" Brauron said to Romulus. "Hop in and we will get back. We need to move quickly before it gets too dark."

Brauron extended a hand and helped Romulus and Dema into his raft, while Aytos helped Reith and Vereinen into his. It was a tight fit with five on each raft. Aytos knelt in the front of the raft and Reith and Vereinen sat in the rear while the two elves in the middle rowed. They rowed facing backward, so Reith and Vereinen were face to face with them. Their skin was dark from many days under the sun. Their arms were powerful judging by the ease with which they rowed and the speed at which the raft cruised through the waves. There were no pleasantries exchanged, though Reith found himself being studied closely by the two elves.

The ship loomed large ahead of them. When they got close, Aytos grabbed hold of a rope and held them steady. A rope ladder was let down for them, and Vereinen climbed it first with great effort. Reith followed him up. He scrambled onto the deck and saw several elves standing around watching them. Before he could even look for Ellamora or Myon, one of the elves stepped forward.

"I am Captain Naftis," he said. "Welcome aboard *The Mermaid's Fortune.*"

3

C aptain Naftis wore a long red jacket over a white tunic, black pants and knee-high boots. His face was angular, and he had a small, pointed beard. A curved sword hung at his side.

Reith and the other newcomers introduced themselves. Just then, Reith was enveloped in a big hug from Ellamora. She soon let go and similarly embraced Dema.

"I missed you two," she said, breathlessly. "It's been too long."

"It's been two days," Reith replied, though inwardly he was happy to see her too.

"Tell us about Amisos," Dema demanded.

"There will be time for that later," Myon said, stepping forward. "Captain Naftis wants a word with you four."

"I've never had humans on board before," said Naftis, appraising the newcomers. "According to old sailor tales, humans are notorious landlubbers."

"What?" Dema asked.

"Landlubbers. Dry land people. Non-sailors if you will. Anyway, as I was saying, I ain't never had humans before on my ship. There are a few things you should know. First, this side," he pointed to the side facing land, "is the starboard side. And this," he pointed to the left side of the ship, out to sea, "is the port side. Got it?"

The newcomers nodded.

"Good. Remember those two things and we will have no problems. Oh, and one more thing," he said, leaning forward. "The captain's word is law. My word, my law. Cross me and it will be the last thing you do."

The humans and Romulus looked nervously at one another. Then Naftis and the other sailors burst into wild laughter.

"I'm only teasing," Naftis said when the laughter subsided. "But seriously though," he said, and the smile left his face, "if I give a command, you'd best be obeying it." The smile returned to his face. "Crew, full speed ahead!"

The sailors jumped to work, moving about the deck and unfurling the sail to catch the wind. Naftis went to the higher deck at the back of the ship and took the wheel.

"Come, let me show you around," Ellamora said to Reith, Vereinen, Dema, and Romulus. She walked toward the back of the ship, and Reith saw there was a trap door in the deck. Ellamora opened it and scurried down the ladder to the darkness below.

Reith and the others followed. Their eyes took a few seconds to adjust to the dark. There were some windows which let in small amounts of light and a few candles, but it was rather dark. There were benches and oars for rowing and large barrels of what Reith assumed were supplies. Hammocks filled the available space, strewn between the various timbers of the ship.

"Our hammocks are in the very back," Ellamora explained. "The captain sleeps above us in his cabin. The rest of the crew sleeps in the other hammocks. If we ever have to row, that happens down here."

"Tell us about Amisos," Dema said. "I want to hear all of it."

"Well," Ellamora said, sitting down on a hammock and rocking slowly back and forth, "there's not too much to tell. The morning we left you, we came into the city and found a tavern to stay in. The tavern keeper was quite helpful in pointing us toward the docks and suggested who we might hire to sail us to the Free Isles, so we went and inquired of a few captains. But everyone was either not leaving port for a few weeks or had no room for us. So we went back to the tavern that night, rather discouraged."

"At least you got to sleep in a real bed," Reith said.

"Well, yeah, that was pretty nice," Ellamora said sheepishly. "The next morning, we again went out to the docks and talked to a few more people. But again, we were frustrated. Just about the time we were going to go back to the tavern, this ship, *The Mermaid's Fortune*, sailed into port. Myon had a feeling and waited for it to dock. Then he walked right up the gangplank and spoke to Captain Naftis. They went into his cabin and a few minutes later they came out with a deal. Naftis had to sell his goods, but still promised to sail the next day, today. So, we waited around the tavern all day until mid-afternoon when one of the sailors came to fetch us. And here we are. Now tell me about you."

"Well," Reith began, "there's not much to tell, really. We waited around until early this morning when we traveled to the beach."

"And slept on the hard ground," Dema said.

"Well, those hammocks don't look half bad," Ellamora said. "They'll be better than the ground."

"Any idea how long it will take to get to the Free Isles?" Reith asked.

"Captain Naftis said it takes about a week," Ellamora replied. "A week at sea sounds lovely after all we've been through."

That night, Reith settled into his hammock. It was quite comfortable, and he gently swayed side to side with the rocking of the ship in the waves. Snores from sailors and the others began to reverberate around the wooden hold of the ship. Soon he drifted off into sleep.

When he awoke, it was still dark and the world was spinning. It felt like the deck was violently tipping back and forth as if there were a storm raging. He fell from his hammock and landed hard on the ground. He tried to stand, but he was too dizzy. He crawled forward, under and around the other hammocks. He found the ladder and heaved himself up the deck. Somehow, he pulled himself up to the railing and was violently ill over the side of the ship. As he wretched, he remembered Naftis' lesson and realized it was the port side of the ship.

When his vomiting ceased, he gradually became aware that there were others on deck with him. Footsteps sounded behind him and he looked around. He was still dizzy and had a difficult time focusing on Captain Naftis' face in the moonlight.

"Drink," Naftis said, handing Reith a brown jug. "It's the drink of choice for all sailors."

Reith took the jug and took a swig. The liquid burned his throat, but he soon started to feel better and took another sip.

"That's rum," Naftis said. "The finest beverage in all the world."

"It's helping," Reith said, taking another sip. He finally was able to focus on Naftis' face.

"Should help you sleep too," Naftis said. "There's no shame in pukin' your first time on a ship. Even some of my lads started out that way. Sit here for a while, get used to the motion of the ship, and then you can go back to bed."

"Thanks," Reith said gratefully. "I appreciate it."

Naftis left him to go tend to the ship wheel and Reith sat against the side of the ship watching the sailors. There were two others on deck along with Naftis. Every once in a while, they pulled on some rope or another and adjusted the sail.

The moon was bright and reflected off the water to magnify its light. Even the stars seemed to provide more light than usual. The night was cloudless and the breeze remained steady from the north. The air was cool and felt good on his face. He enjoyed being on deck so much that he waited considerably longer than he needed to recuperate from his ordeal before going back to the ladder down into the hold.

He climbed down slowly and at the bottom waited for a few minutes for his eyes to adjust to the gloom. The light of a candle illuminated the space and gradually his eyes were able to pierce the darkness. He picked his way between hammocks and around barrels. He was amazed he had been able to traverse this space in his earlier state.

He climbed into his hammock, none too gracefully, and was soon rocking back and forth to the gentle swaying of the ship in the waves. This time it did not bother him. The rum felt like fire in his belly, warming him and keeping his head from spinning again. He shut his eyes and listened to the sound of the water and the snores of the others in hold.

Reith woke up the next morning feeling even better than he had the night before. The rum had done wonders for him. He looked around and saw that he was alone in the hold. Sunlight streamed in though the small windows. He got to his feet, and the ship felt steady beneath him. He climbed the ladder to the deck and saw that Myon, Vereinen, and Captain Naftis were in a discussion toward the front of the ship. Nearer at hand were Romulus, Ellamora, and Dema who were eating some bread. Aytos and Brauron sat a little way away from them. He sat next to Dema, who offered him some bread, which he gratefully accepted. He didn't realize until now just how hungry he had been. *Throwing up the entire contents of your stomach will do that to you.*

"How are you feeling?" Dema asked him, concern etched on her face. "We heard from Captain Naftis …"

"I'm fine now," Reith said. "Starving actually."

"Here, take some bread," Romulus offered.

"Thanks," Reith replied. "What are they talking about?" he asked, gesturing with the crust of bread toward the front of the ship and the ongoing discussion.

"Intel gathering," Romulus answered. "Myon wants to learn all he can about the Free Isles and the dwarves. Vereinen was curious too."

"And you're not curious?"

"Oh, I am indeed," Romulus said, and then he lowered his voice to just above a whisper. The other three leaned in close to hear. "But right now, I am a nobody. It's best that my identity remains a secret, for now."

Later, Reith found Vereinen and asked him about the conversation.

"Oh yes, Naftis has been to the Free Isles many times. He's actually from there, you know. Got into sailing as a crewman and eventually bought his own ship."

"What did he say about the dwarves?" Reith asked.

"Well, you see, even at the Free Isles, the races remain separate, according to Naftis," Vereinen explained. "Each goes about their own business."

"If they are so separate, how do they maintain their peace? Surely they must fight about things."

"The Isles are run by a parliamentary government. Each race gets half of the seats of the parliament. They must get along and compromise."

"So will we be able to charter a ship to the land of the dwarves?" Reith asked.

"We'll see," Vereinen said. "Naftis wasn't so sure it would be possible. It will take strong convincing that we are telling the truth for a dwarf captain to take us on. But we must try. The dwarves are our only hope in stopping the spread of the Shadow."

"And what if they don't help us?"

"I'm afraid that they too would fall to the Shadow's power in the end. Maybe they can be persuaded."

The rest of the day, Captain Naftis took it upon himself to teach his passengers how to sail. He explained the various ropes and rigging and how the sail worked. When the wind shifted, he showed them how they could catch it and zigzag across the water to continue moving the direction they wanted to go. He let each take a turn at the wheel, and Reith quite enjoyed his time there, though there was not much to do, with the wind steadily pushing them southward.

Dinner was bread, cheese, and grapes. All in all, Reith's first full day at sea was quite pleasurable.

It was not to last. That night the wind began to pick up, and the waves as well. By morning, the wind had shifted, coming instead from the east instead of the north. This pushed the ship toward the shore, which they kept in view on the horizon to the starboard side. Naftis and the crew worked hard to keep the ship going south, but the land to their right continued to grow as they drew nearer.

Rain began to lash the deck and the wind began to howl even more ferociously. The deck of the ship pitched up on one side and plunged down on the other. Then in the span of a second, the two were reversed.

"Go to the hold!" Naftis shouted to his passengers. "We will drop anchor and wait it out!"

The sailors rushed around the deck as quickly as they could and pulled down the sail. The large metal anchor was released into the sea, and its splash was lost amid the chaos. Reith dropped to his knees as the deck seemed to rush up to meet him. He crawled to the ladder then down to the hold. Below deck, he found that Dema, Ellamora, and Vereinen had all made it safely in. Right behind him came Brauron, Aytos, Myon, and Romulus. Romulus closed the trapdoor and the sound of the storm was muffled. Flashes of lightning occasionally lit up the room through the small windows in the sides of the ship, but even in the daytime, it was dark below deck. There was not much to do except wait it out. Occasionally sailors would come down for a drink and a brief respite from the storm, but soon they would be replaced by another sailor and would return to the elements.

All day the storm raged. Reith felt very sick, and he wasn't the only one. It seemed all of them were miserable below deck. Despite the rain, Reith wished he were on deck if only for a breath of fresh air.

Presently he realized that it was even darker than it had been. Night had fallen. Naftis stumbled down to the hold, exhausted and soaked through. He collapsed to the floor and Ellamora brought him water, which he drank with thanks.

"How is it out there?" Myon asked. "Is the storm growing any lighter?"

"Hardly," Naftis said, before gulping down more water. He shook his head violently like a dog shaking dry. "I hope by morning it will blow over."

"Are we in any danger?" Vereinen asked.

"No, we are safe for now," Naftis replied. "Our anchor is holding us steady. We are simply staying put and letting the storm batter us. It's not pleasant, but it beats being pushed around without anchor. The worst thing is we lost a day of sailing time. Should have enough provisions, but not as much as we'd like."

True to Naftis' word, as the night wore on, the ship gradually settled down as the waves subsided. One by one, sailors and passengers alike took to their hammocks and drifted off to a well-earned sleep.

After the storm, the wind was nearly non-existent. Each sailor and passenger took turns at the oars below deck, pulling the ship forward through the sea. It was hard, monotonous work. It was hot below deck, as there was very little movement in the air to dry the sweat that so easily formed. Reith's back and shoulders ached from the exertion, and his hands were soon rubbed raw by the wood of the oar. His shirt was soaked with sweat when he was finally relieved from duty.

He climbed to the deck and fell in a heap to the ground and lay there, completely spent. Someone handed him water, which he eagerly drank.

"Wind should pick up again tonight," Naftis said, surveying Reith in his pitiful state.

"It had better," Reith said.

"It's good for you, Reith," Dema said, walking over to them.

"You haven't had a turn yet," Reith said. "Just you wait."

"I bet I can row better than you," Dema retorted.

"Now, now," Naftis said.

"There's a ship!" The cry can from directly above them. One of the elven sailors was in the crows nest, a spyglass to his eye, peering toward the horizon.

"What colors?" Naftis called up to him.

"Too far away to tell, Captain."

"Let me know as soon as possible," Naftis said.

Reith rose from the deck and stood up, straining his eyes to try and see the ship in the distance, but all he could see were the waves.

"Come on," Dema said, and she took his hand and pulled him forward to the front of the ship. She climbed up onto the rail and held on. "I think I see something," she said, pointing. Reith could not see what she was pointing at, but he kept staring. About a minute later, he saw a dark spec on the horizon that he guessed was the ship.

"The flag is red!" the sailor in the crows' nest yelled.

Naftis swore loudly. He jumped down to the deck and shouted into the hold below. "Easy now, we've got company from a red flag. Wait for the signal."

"What's a red flag mean?" Reith asked.

Dema shrugged.

He looked around the deck for an answer. The elven sailors on deck looked tense.

Then he saw Myon emerging from the hold. "What is the meaning of this?" Myon asked Naftis. Myon was sweaty and it was evident he had just ceased rowing.

"The Red Fleet," Naftis said grimly. Reith and Dema walked over to them.

"What's the Red Fleet?" Dema asked Naftis and Myon.

"The Red Fleet," Myon began, "has been a thorn in the side of the elven kingdom for years."

"They are a savage bunch of pirates and smugglers," Naftis said. "They rule this sea and every ship on it."

"Would they attack us?" Reith asked.

"Most definitely," Naftis said. "Especially once they see that it's my ship."

"And why is that?" Myon asked grimly.

"Let's just say me and the Red Fleet don't exactly see eye to eye. It would be best for all of us if we were able to sail past them."

"What does that mean?" Myon asked impatiently.

"I sort of owe them a lot of money," Naftis said. "And they are not happy with me. They said they'd kill me and my crew if they caught me without the money."

4

"Let me get this straight," Myon said, his anger rising. "You owe money to the Red Fleet, the band of ships that patrol this part of the sea, and you didn't think to mention that when we hired you?"

"It didn't come up," Naftis said, sheepishly. "You didn't ask."

"How do you plan on getting us out of this mess?" Myon asked.

"Well, the goal is to not get boarded at all," Naftis said. "If we can outmaneuver them, I think we will be able to sail freely and not worry about them."

"And if we can't outmaneuver them?" Myon asked.

"Improvise! But it won't come to that. I need everyone on the oars below. We need to row at a steady pace until we are near them. Then I'll turn the wheel sharp, and we will go out to sea and give it our all and get past them. By the time they get turned around, we should hopefully be well away."

Reith and the others clambered down the ladder to the

hold and took positions on the rowing benches. They soon found a rhythm, which they kept to, propelling the ship forward.

"By the God of Light, we had better stay well away from those pirates," Romulus said as he rowed.

"Are they really that bad?" Reith asked.

"Murderous thieves, the whole lot of them," Romulus said. "Cruel as can be. They sell their captives into slavery, if they leave any alive, that is."

An icy cold feeling rushed into Reith's stomach. They kept rowing, oblivious to how close they may be to the approaching ship of the Red Fleet. The minutes passed agonizingly slow, and still they rowed on.

"Pick up the pace a little, but not all out just yet!" Naftis called out from above.

They rowed slightly faster now, and the ship lurched forward with the weight of their renewed efforts. The only sounds now were the oars in the water and the grunts of some of the sailors rowing.

"Prepare to go fast," Naftis called. "Thirty seconds left. Twenty. Ten. Five, four, three, two, one, now!"

Every muscle in Reith's body screamed as he gave it his all on the oar. As one, the rowers rowed in unison, a perfectly choreographed dance. He felt the ship veer sharply to the left, heading for open sea. Above the sound of rowing he heard shouts, and he deduced they must be coming from the Red Fleet ship, which must be quite near them. He pulled even harder on the oar and felt the others do the same, as the ship picked up speed. He felt like he would break at any moment, all his energy was spent and every muscle was in a frenzy of agony. If he stopped he knew his body would refuse to start again. He gritted his teeth and kept going, pulling harder and harder.

He heard another rower falter behind him, and then saw Vereinen stop rowing in front of him. The ship began to slow ever so slightly.

"Keep going!" Naftis screamed from above. But it was no use. They had no more to give. One by one, the rowers stopped, and collapsed exhausted to the ground. Reith feebly tried to keep going, but it was no use. He seemed to have lost control of his arms, and they flopped down beside him, useless. He had no concept of time anymore, and simply waited for his body to be his own again.

Presently, he became aware of voices on deck. He could make out Naftis' but had no idea what he was saying. Other voices spoke to Naftis. He managed to sit upright and make his way to a standing position. A few of the others managed this as well. Before anyone could move, a voice called down to them through the trapdoor.

"Come up, one by one, hands up. You try anything, and we'll kill you."

Reith looked around at the others. He saw terror in their eyes.

"Trust me," Romulus whispered, and he went up the ladder first.

One by one they ascended the ladder to the deck above. When Reith arrived on deck, he saw that a second ship, slightly larger than *The Mermaid's Fortune*, was pulled up next to them and the two were tethered together by ropes. Naftis stood slightly apart from the rest of the sailors and passengers on *The Mermaid's Fortune.* Several hardened looking sailors from the Red Fleet kept a close eye on him, and drawn swords were in their hands. All told, there were twenty or so members of the Red Fleet occupying their ship, with more besides in their own ship. The odds were not good if it came to a fight. The Red Fleet must have felt good about their odds as they didn't bother searching and disarming their prisoners. Reith's sword hung at his side, though he saw that his comrades were unarmed.

The leader of the Red Fleet ship was a tall elf, taller by a few inches than any elf Reith had seen. He had broad shoulders and his arms were covered in scars, as was his face.

"Naftis," he said, in a voice that hissed like a snake. "I will give you one chance, where is my money?"

"I told you," Naftis said nervously, "I'm working on it. I'll have it for you."

"Oh, Naftis," the scarred elf said, "I have heard that from you so often. You are out of chances."

"I'm doing this job, and then I'll have your money for you," Naftis said, a whiney plea in his voice.

"What job is this?" the scarred elf said.

"These are my passengers," Naftis said, pointing out Reith and the others.

"And who might you be?" the scarred elf asked. "Are you paying Naftis well for the privilege of sailing aboard *The Mermaid's Fortune?*"

"We are but travelers to the Free Isles," Romulus said. "We want no trouble with the Red Fleet."

"Well, unfortunately for you, trouble with the Red Fleet follows closely in the wake of this one," the scarred elf said, indicating Naftis.

"Please, Juraz, give me a chance," Naftis pleaded.

"You have had too many chances," Juraz hissed. "I should have killed you the last time we met. Now, down to business."

He reached for his sword, but someone stepped forward next to Reith and spoke.

"I wouldn't do that," Romulus said.

"And why should I listen to you?" Juraz said with a sneer. "You're nothing and no one."

"You're wrong." Romulus stood right beside Reith now. "I am Prince Romulus, heir to the throne in Sardis."

Juraz stared at Romulus in disbelief.

"You're joking," he said finally.

"You wish," Romulus said, "but I speak the truth. You will disembark from our vessel and continue on your way. So long as I am on this ship, you shall not harm Naftis."

"Well, your *highness*," Juraz said with the most sarcasm he could muster. "I don't see how you can enforce your will upon me. I see no armies, no navy here to rescue you. The Red Fleet bows to no king!"

"You shall bow to me," Romulus said. Then in one smooth motion, he unsheathed Reith's sword, spun in a full circle and brought the glittering blade whirling around and sliced through Juraz' neck. Before Juraz' body hit the deck, he grabbed Juraz' curved sword from its sheath and twirled back toward Reith, handing him the bloody sword.

"To arms!" Romulus called out.

Reith and Romulus plunged into the nearest members of the Red Fleet, cutting them down where they stood. Naftis, his sailors, and the other passengers reached for whatever weapon they could, even if it was just bare fist. Brauron punched a foe over the railing into the sea below, and Aytos wrested a sword away from another and kicked his chest forcefully, sending him crashing down into the sea as well. Several members of the Red Fleet escaped to their ship. Reith rushed to the railing and cut *The Mermaid's Fortune* free of the ropes binding her to the Red Fleet ship. He turned and saw the rest of the Red Fleet members on board were either dead or disarmed. The two ships drifted slowly apart.

"Let them go," Romulus said. "They may jump and swim for their lives." The remaining members of the Red Fleet needed no prodding. One by one, they plunged overboard in graceful dives. The bodies of the dead were thrown unceremoniously overboard. A breeze began to blow from the north.

"By the God of Light," Romulus said. "A blessing in the wind."

"Unfurl the sail, boys!" Naftis said. It wasn't long before *The Mermaid's Fortune* was rapidly putting distance between it and the Red Fleet ship.

"Good work," Reith said to Romulus.

"I had hoped my words would disarm the situation before a sword was required," Romulus said. "Praise the God of Light you kept your sword at your side. It truly is a magnificent blade."

"Thank you for all that," Naftis said, walking over to them. "Your highness," he added with a small bow. "I had no idea."

"It was best that you had no idea," Romulus said. "We are in terrible danger." Romulus proceeded to tell Naftis the story of Solzar the Shadow poisoning King Koinas' mind and how the arrival of humans in Sardis caused the situation to escalate.

"Even now my father's troops are marching for war. We must reach the dwarves and secure their help if this crisis is to have any hope of a happy ending."

"You have my word that we shall travel with great haste to the Free Isles," Naftis said. "If I can be of any assistance, my ship is yours to command. I owe you after Juraz."

"How did you end up owing the Red Fleet money?" Romulus asked.

"Well I, uh, put in a bit of work for them. Shipping their goods and such to and from the Free Isles. Truth be told I had to abandon a shipload of cargo when I neared Amisos once. A military ship was going to board me and check my holds. Quite valuable stuff I dropped overboard too. Juraz was none too thrilled."

"Well, now your work with them is over," Romulus declared. "If you are true, I shall see to it that there is no warrant placed on your arrest and you shall have amnesty for any past crimes you may or may not have committed."

"My Prince, thank you," Naftis said. "Long life to your majesty."

"I hope so, Captain, I hope so."

The breeze came steadily from the north the next two days. Sometimes it oscillated between the northwest and the northeast, but the constant was a nudge from the north ever southward. Reith was glad. He never wanted to see another oar again. After their sprint away from the Red Fleet, he had been sore for days. The following morning after their adventure, he could barely get out of his hammock. Myon and Vereinen were worse. Vereinen stayed in bed for the entire day, unable, or unwilling, to leave the comfort of the hammock. Reith had to bring his food to him.

Dema was subdued in the aftermath of the short battle with the Red Fleet. When Reith and Ellamora tried to talk to her about it, she went silent.

"She's thinking of Kydar," Ellamora said to Reith when they were alone. "And I don't blame her. I keep thinking about Cassius. The sight of blood ..." she said before trailing off.

That night, Reith could hardly sleep. He kept thinking of the elves he had struck down in the fight. They had seemed surprised at his blade's kiss as they fell dead before him. He wondered if they had families somewhere who were waiting for them to come home. The thought made him sick. *But what choice did we have?*

His insomnia was so strong that he gave up and decided to go on deck and watch the stars. One of the sailors was at the wheel and another one was on the deck when he arrived. He nodded at them, and they nodded back, each content to let the other mind their own business.

He saw a figure standing at the front of the ship and walked slowly forward until he saw it was Dema. She was looking up at the stars, apparently lost in thought. He joined her. After a few minutes of silence, she spoke.

"I can never get over how bright the stars are out here," she said. "Even in Suthrond, the stars were never this bright."

Not knowing what to say, Reith stayed silent.

"Kydar and I would watch the stars," Dema continued. "Back home, before, well, you know." She paused at the memory of the destruction wrought by the Gray Man, that Shadow, Solzar. "When we were little, he said that they were little fires set by angels."

"Is that so far off?" Reith said. "After everything we have seen, everything we have learned about the Guardians and the Dark Powers, Shadows, and the God of Light, it doesn't seem nearly so ridiculous."

"No, I suppose you're right," Dema said thoughtfully.

"Dema, I am so sorry about what happened to Kydar. I feel like it's my fault."

His words swept over the waves, spreading out and filling the world with their weight.

"It's not your fault, Reith," Dema said after what seemed like hours to Reith. "And even if it were your fault, I forgive you."

Her words of grace engulfed him, and he felt brand new, like he took a drink from the stream by the trees at Erador. He wrapped her in a one-armed hug. "Thank you," he whispered into her ear.

They had long since left the coastline behind them. Naftis had informed them that they had left the bay and were now in open sea, making straight for the Free Isles. The wind grew stronger as they left shore behind, and it pushed them even faster toward their destination.

"The God of Light must desire our swift passage," Myon declared one night as they rushed forward.

On the morning of the seventh day after they set out from Amisos, the sun rose to reveal a landmass in front of them.

"The Free Isles," Naftis declared, though no one needed his declaration. From this great distance, the isles peaked over the horizon, giving a tantalizing hint as to their size.

Naftis and the other sailors had given them some description of the Isles, namely that there were three of them, Klotha, Lakeces, and Antropa. The three were nearly perfect triplets, arranged in a triangle with Klotha to the West, Lakeces to the North, and Antropa to the South. The parts of the Isles facing each other sloped gradually down to the sea. The outward facing parts of the Isles were staggeringly high cliffs. This arrangement meant that the Free Isles were nearly always protected from attack. Defenders from the cliffs could throw rocks and shoot flaming arrows from relative safety while attacking ships were forced to sail between the Isles to find a harbor. This natural fortification was why the Isles had always been free and never part of either the Dwarven or Elven Kingdoms.

As *The Mermaid's Fortune* approached the Isles, what at first had been a single mass rising from the sea, clearly divided into two islands, Klotha and Lakeces, with the third, Antropa hidden from view.

The rock of the cliffs was dark, nearly black. With no point of reference, Reith had a hard time discerning just how tall the cliffs were. And yet on and on they sailed, and the Isles loomed ever larger. It soon became clear that the Isles were each as tall as the mountains near Amisos had been.

Naftis steered the ship for the gap between Klotha and Lakeces. He told them his aim was the Port of Antropa, which had the largest market of the three Isles. As they neared the gap, Reith saw large stone fortresses constructed on top of each cliff overlooking the narrow strip of sea between Klotha and Lakeces.

The gap between the Isles was perhaps two hundred yards wide. Using this measure as an estimate, Reith guessed that the cliffs were at least five times taller than the gap was wide. The sun was nearly overhead, so they did not sail under any shadow as they entered the gap. Inside, the world opened before them. The cliffs on their left and their right gradually sloped down parallel to each other and the sea. Ahead of them was the bright green sloping plain of Antropa, which rose skyward out of the ground.

"Look!" Dema said, pointing to the cliffs on their right. Reith looked up to see a white goat perched precariously on the cliff. Then he saw another and another and realized with a start that dozens of goats had managed to find footholds on the sheer face of the rock.

In between the Isles, small boats were going to and fro carrying passengers, animals, and goods from one Isle to another. These small boats were nearly flat, and evidently their owners were not afraid of waves swamping them, as the Isles protected their terrain from any such wake. The water was nearly as smooth as glass, and the only disturbances were the ships themselves.

Gradually the port towns of Klotha and Lakeces came into view. The buildings were constructed from stone and wood, and wooden docks jutted out into the open water between the Isles. The small ships were docking there, and as *The Mermaid's Fortune* sailed along, dockworkers and those in the other boats began to call out greetings to the ship and her crew. What struck Reith was how colorful the clothes were. Vibrant shades of red, blue, and green were ubiquitous among all the folk of the Free Isles. He looked eagerly for a dwarf but was slightly disappointed to see only elves.

They were now squarely between all three Isles. The gaps between Klotha and Antropa and Lakeces and Antropa diagonally went away from them, and they could see open sea beyond. Before them was a large town set on Antropa. Its buildings went from the sea up toward the top of the cliff. There was not much green on that Isle, as buildings covered most of it. At the very top was a gigantic fortress made of stone. Gaps between the buildings showed that roads zig-zagged all the way to the top. At the docks were many of the small, flat boats, and three or four larger vessels, about the same size as *The Mermaid's Fortune*. One ship towered over them all, nearly three times the size of *The Mermaid's Fortune*. To Reith it looked like a military ship, not a cargo ship.

Naftis brought the ship gently into the docks, and the sailors pulled the sail down. Dockworkers were there, ready to help them. The sailors and the dockworkers threw ropes back and forth, securing *The Mermaid's Fortune*. Reith watched them closely and then with a start realized he was looking on dwarves for the first time in his life.

5

The dwarves were not as he had imagined them. Based on descriptions he had heard in stories back in Coeden, he had thought they would be considerably shorter than the average human. While the elves were slightly taller on average than a human, the dwarves were slightly shorter, and stockier, with shorter arms and legs. Some of the dockworker dwarves had long beards and some had shorter beards, but all had facial hair of some kind or another. The sound of their voices, which he heard as they called out to one another and to sailors, was harsher, and there was an accent on their voices that was raspier than the elegant sounding speech of elves or the common accent of the humans of Coeden. Though he realized, as he reflected on it, that everyone else probably thought he had the accent, and not them.

The gangplank sat between the ship's deck and the dock. Naftis descended it first and greeted a dwarf by name. They had a short discussion and then he called out for the passengers to come down to the docks, which they did.

After a week at sea, the dock felt sturdy beneath their feet. Naftis and the dwarf were walking toward the land by the dock, and Naftis beckoned them to follow. The sailors and the dockworkers continued to bring *The Mermaid's Fortune* to rest. As Reith walked, he came close to several of the dwarves. He tried to avoid staring, but he could not help stealing glances at them. They hardly seemed to notice him at all until they realized he was a human. Then their heads swung around to gawk. Reith noticed that Dema and Vereinen were receiving similar attention.

At the end of the dock, a road opened which ran parallel to the water. Facing the water were many huts and shops, selling anything from food to clothing to ship goods to things Reith had never seen before in his life and had no guess as to what they may be. Some of the shops were staffed by elves and some by dwarves, all dressed in bright colors. In moments, Reith took all of this in as the group halted at the end of the dock.

"Right," Naftis said. "This is Kazor." He gestured to the dwarf. "Kazor is dock master of Antropa, and I have asked him to take you to the inn, which he has kindly decided to do."

"Is this where we leave you, Naftis?" Myon asked.

"Nay, tis but a short goodbye," Naftis said. "My crew and I will stay for a few days. We'll probably drop by the inn for a pint most nights. I reckon we'll see each other several times before either of us departs."

"Thank you, Captain," Romulus said.

"No, thank you, my prince," Naftis replied. "For taking care of the, uh … unpleasant situation." With that, Naftis turned and walked back down the dock toward his ship, which was beginning to be unloaded of its cargo.

"Welcome to Antropa of the Free Isles," Kazor said,

with a raspy, harsh voice that nonetheless was full of warmth. "If you'll follow me."

He led them to the right, down the road in front of the water, past several shops and stalls, and a few docks, until they reached a road that sloped diagonally up the hill back toward the center of Antropa. He took them up this road, and they passed several more shops, some larger than the ones down by the water. The buildings here were two or three stories, and some even had stairs going down to a lower level built into the ground itself. Because of the slope of the Isle, the roof lines did not match up, and it looked from the street like giant stairs ascending the hill. Most of the buildings had first floors made entirely of stone and then it looked like wood for the second and third levels. Reith wondered about the source of the lumber, as he hadn't seen any trees on any of the Isles.

They soon came to a building that had stairs going down to a lower level of stone, and two levels made of wood rising above the street. A sign above the door at the bottom of the stairs depicted one of the goats Reith had seen on the wall of the cliff earlier.

"This is the Mountain Goat," Kazor said. "Finest inn on the Isle. The proprietor, Mr. Borden, will see to it that you get good rooms and good food and drink."

"Thank you, Kazor," Myon said, and handed Kazor a coin, which disappeared into one of Kazor's pockets.

"Pleasure is all mine," Kazor said. "Naftis said you will be looking for passage on a ship. Tomorrow, come down to the docks, and I will speak to you about that."

"Thank you again for your helpfulness and hospitality," Myon said. Kazor gave a small bow and left, returning to the street.

One by one, they filed into the tavern. The room was dark, and as it was mostly underground, the windows were high up on the wall and at street level. The room was long and narrow. Along the left was a bar, behind which a jolly looking dwarf stood, wiping a glass with a rag. There was a large, open fireplace on the far end with a roaring fire flickering light on the stone walls. There were tables and chairs laid out in no discernible pattern. Apart from the tavern keeper, the room was empty.

"Hello," Myon said, striding forward to the bar. "Are you Mr. Borden?"

"Aye," the tavern keeper said, and he put down the glass he had been cleaning. "How can I help you?" His eyes searched the faces of each of them in turn, though incredibly quickly. He seemed to linger slightly longer on the faces of the three humans.

"Kazor, the dock master, told us you could provide us a place to stay and food to eat while we are here in Antropa."

"You heard correctly," Mr. Borden said with a smile. "How many rooms?"

Myon and Mr. Borden began to haggle, but Romulus stopped paying attention to them and instead strode across the room and took a seat at the table nearest the fire. The rest followed, leaving the business matters to Myon. A few minutes later, after silver had changed hands, Myon and Mr. Borden returned to the rest of the party.

"Everything is settled," Myon said. "Mr. Borden has promised to graciously provide for our needs while we are here."

"What can I get you to drink?" Mr. Borden said. "Our house made ale is the best of the Free Isles. And I can bring out some snacks as well. Dinner will be served beginning an hour before sundown."

A round of ale was ordered, and Mr. Borden brought eight mugs, a loaf of bread, and a hunk of white cheese to them. Aytos took to cutting the bread into pieces, and Brauron did the same with the cheese. When all were served their food and drink, Romulus raised his mug.

"To us," he said.

"To us," they all answered. There was a clink of glass all around and each took a sip. The ale was dark, strong, and bitter, and reminded Reith of the coffee he had drunk in Sardis.

"We have a few hours until dinner," Ellamora said. "Can we explore a bit?"

"I don't see why not," Romulus answered. "Stay together and don't cause any trouble."

"Is there a library in the Free Isles?" Vereinen asked.

"I believe so," Myon said. "You could ask Mr. Borden."

Vereinen rose to ask the tavern keeper and soon returned with the good news, and a hand drawn map. Reith, Dema, Ellamora, and Romulus all decided to accompany Vereinen to the library, while Brauron, Aytos, and Myon stayed put in the tavern. They were soon out on the street again, climbing up to higher levels of the city. After a few hundred feet, the road reached a crossroads. They could either turn down and to the left, or up and to the right.

"Further up," Vereinen said after consulting the map. So, they turned right and continued up the slope. As they climbed through the city, they encountered fewer and fewer people on the roads. It seemed that most of the commerce and business happened lower in the city, nearer the docks. The buildings looked more and more residential as they continued. The higher they got, the nicer the buildings looked.

"Do you know anything of the library here, Romulus?" Vereinen asked as they walked.

"Little enough," Romulus said. "My tutors taught me

about the Free Isles, but mostly in a historical and military sense, of how they have remained unconquered for generations. All I know is that the library is said to have the oldest materials of any library in Terrasohnen."

Vereinen, practically bouncing, was giddy with excitement. "I have seen the libraries of Galismoor and Kal-Epharion, and those are old and ancient libraries. I can't even imagine …"

"Vereinen, you have to go back to Erador," Reith pointed out. "The library is preserved there!"

"It is all too wonderful for this chronicler," Vereinen said.

They encountered another crossroad, and after consulting the map again, Vereinen took them on the left road, which went farther up.

"It's near the top," he said.

They continued on. Reith and the others could see the fortress at the top of the Isle rising over the houses and buildings. One more turn and they found that the road opened on a large, flat semicircle. Around the ring were two tall buildings, one on the left and one on the right. Between them, a road led to the fortress gate beyond. The two front buildings were grand, four stories high apiece, built of elegantly carved stone. A lawn stretched out in front of the two buildings.

"Mr. Borden said the library is on the left," Vereinen said, pointing to the corresponding building. Sure enough, Reith saw that "LIBRARY" had been carved into the topmost stone across the front of the building. The other building had "COLLEGE" carved into it.

Vereinen led the way toward the library. They stayed on the road rather than take the shorter way across the immaculately kept lawn. There were three steps leading up to the library, they hesitated as the black door loomed before them.

"Here we go," Vereinen said, and he pulled the door open. Its hinges creaked with age and they all stepped across the threshold into the library of Antropa. The sight took their breath away.

Though the building was stone, it was elegantly paneled with dark wood. The bookshelves matched and reached up high toward the ceiling. The entire building was open, and the shelves were at least thirty feet high. Around the edge of the room were three levels of balconies with more shelves. Sunlight streamed through large, ornate windows along all the walls. Reith saw that the ceiling even had a large stained-glass window, which he quickly realized was a depiction of the Free Isles as seen from above. The few patrons they could see paid the newcomers no mind. Vereinen confidently stepped forward, and Reith could tell it took great restraint for the chronicler to not run forward.

Vereinen followed the signs on the ends of the shelves to the history section. There were great leather-bound books and ornate scrolls. Vereinen ran a finger along the spines of the books as he slowly walked past. Pure joy radiated from the master chronicler, and Reith could hardly contain his own. Vereinen took books and scrolls from the shelf and was soon laden down with a stack, which he took to a table to peruse. Romulus wandered off, briefly saying he was going to try and climb the stairs to the upper levels before he left. Reith decided to keep exploring. In the silence of the library, he and the others dared not speak, as if the sound of voices would awaken a watcher and draw scrutiny. He beckoned to Dema and Ellamora to follow them, which they did.

They passed through the shelves, making a large circle

of the room. Reith saw dozens of books he wished to pick up and read, but something kept drawing him deeper into the library. He had a feeling that he was looking for something, but he did not know what it was. They pressed on, and soon found themselves nearing the back wall of the library. Reith was just about to turn to loop back around the other side of the library when he stopped. There in the corner, nearly invisible, was a small railing. Beyond the railing was a gaping hole, with stairs leading down. There were perhaps twenty stairs he could see before the floor of the library obscured the rest. There was a torch mounted to the wall. He beckoned again to Dema and Ellamora, who exchanged a look of apprehension. He beckoned more vigorously, and they shrugged. He edged around the railing and stepped down. After a half dozen steps, he could see further down the stairway by the light of several torches lighting it. The stairs ran parallel to the back wall of the library and appeared to go from one side wall to the other. At the end of the stairs, was a small flat landing, and a torch mounted to the wall. Between him and the torch were perhaps a hundred steps, and four torches mounted on the walls. They were spaced nearly perfectly so that the light from one nearly met the light from the other. But in between it looked like a few feet of pitch darkness.

He felt compelled to continue down, and so he did, walking slowly by the light of the torches, and a little more swiftly in the shadowy places between torch light. The footsteps behind him told him Dema and Ellamora were following.

They soon reached the bottom of the stairs, and Reith saw that the landing extended to the left, and then stairs began again going down, in the opposite direction they had just come.

"Reith, wait," Ellamora's anxious whisper cut through the air like a knife. He felt her hand on his shoulder and turned to look at her.

"What?" he asked.

"Where are we going?" Ellamora whispered.

"I don't know. But aren't you curious?" Reith asked.

"It just doesn't feel right," Dema said.

"I feel like we need to go on," Reith said, not understanding their lack of curiosity.

"And what if we get lost?" Ellamora said.

"Look, there's no way to get lost, not yet anyway," Reith said. "There's only the staircase, nothing else. Let's go see what we can at the bottom of this flight. If you don't want to continue, we can come back."

Ellamora and Dema looked unsure, but eventually they nodded their assent. And so the three of them descended one stair at a time. It seemed to them that the end of the staircase was never coming any closer, no matter how far they walked. The distance between torches seemed to stretch longer and longer each time, and Reith had another strange feeling, that something didn't want him to continue down the stairs. He felt the two in his gut, struggling for supremacy within him, but the will to continue won the day.

He felt a hand take his and turned to see Dema had grabbed it, and she was also holding Ellamora's hand. The three of them continued, bound together. After what seemed like several minutes, they reached the landing. This one turned right, but instead of stairs, there was simply a long passage, running back the direction they had just come. In the very middle of the passage, flanked by two torches, stood a double set of wooden doors. At the other end of the passage was another torch on the wall, and what looked like another passage leading off to the side.

Reith realized they were at least a hundred feet down below the surface of the library, deep within the rock of the Isle.

"Shall we continue?" Reith asked his companions.

"Something within me feels we must," Ellamora said. "But another part says to turn and run."

"I feel that too," Dema said. "But I think we must go on."

"Come on, together then," Reith said. The three grasped hands, with Dema in the middle. They walked slowly down the passage toward the door.

There were no torches in this passage except the ones at either end and the two on either side of the door in the middle. Between the torches, darkness lay thick and heavy. And though the darkness tried to conquer the three of them, they did not turn back. The two torches ahead were their lighthouse, their beacons of hope. They soon found themselves before the double doors.

"I'll go first," Reith said. He leaned against the right door, and pushed his shoulder gently into in, and then more forcefully. The door was heavy and hard to open, probably due to lack of use, but it began to swing open, inch by inch.

Firelight flickered and a beam of light came through the gap between the doors, first narrow, then growing in width until it disappeared in a general glow of firelight. Reith saw that a room as large as the library above was here below it, nearly it's mirror in every respect. Torches lit the walls instead of windows. Wooden benches lined the room instead of shelves. A center aisle stretched before them between the benches and led to three steps up to a raised dais. On the dais was a table, and in front of the table stood a cloaked figure, with its back to them.

Reith's heart skipped a beat in his chest at the sight of

the figure. He heard Ellamora and Dema gasp beside him. He was about to turn and leave when the figure spoke.

"Welcome to the Shrine of Antropa, Reith, son of human, Dema, daughter of human, and Ellamora, daughter of elf."

6

R eith, petrified with fear, stood rooted to the spot. The figure on the dais turned toward them and raised its hands to lower the hood covering its face. Reith now saw that it was an elderly dwarf, with a long silver beard and a bald head.

"Come, son and daughters," the old dwarf said. "There is nothing to fear here except that which you bring with you." Reith had no idea what that meant, but he deemed it foolish to run, though he greatly wanted to. He took Dema's hand in his right hand and Ellamora's in his left. Slowly, they marched forward toward the old dwarf. As they walked, the old dwarf spoke.

"I can read it in your faces that you are afraid and full of questions. Fear not, for you shall find answers here."

As they walked closer, Reith saw that the table on the dais was a dining table, and on it were golden pitchers, silver chalices, and platters of fruits, vegetables, and bread. Tables were set around it. The old dwarf sat down at the head of the table and held out a hand for them to sit. There were three seats set out, one on the opposite end of the dwarf, and one on either side of that one, so that none of the three would have to sit very near the dwarf. Reith took the seat opposite the dwarf, with Dema to his right and Ellamora to his left. They say uneasily, near the edge of their seats, ready to run.

"Please, make yourself at home," the dwarf said. "There is food here for refreshing your strength. I hope the conversation will be equally refreshing for your minds, your hearts, and your souls." The dwarf poured wine from a pitcher into three chalices, which he placed in the middle of the table near enough to Ellamora and Dema so they could reach them. They each grabbed one, and Dema took a second one which she passed to Reith.

"First, let us drink. This wine reminds us of the blood the Maker poured into all living things, granting us life. Let us drink and remember." The dwarf tilted his cup back and sipped. Reith quickly sniffed the wine, and took a very small, cautious sip. Dema and Ellamora did the same.

"And now, let us eat of the fruit of the vine, which the Maker causes to grow in season for our sustenance." He took a bunch of grapes from a platter on the table and placed them on a golden tray. He plucked one grape for himself, and passed the tray to Dema, who took a grape. The others followed their lead. When all had a grape, the dwarf popped his in his mouth and chewed slowly, his eyes closed in apparent contemplation.

"And finally, let us eat of the bread, for in bread we join the Maker and make something from that which has been given to us." He took a loaf of bread and broke it in half, and then each half in half. He placed three pieces on another golden platter and passed these to Ellamora. When all were served, he took a bite of his loaf. Reith and the others did the same.

He couldn't explain it, but Reith now felt at ease. He

realized he had been holding tension in his back and shoulders, but he took a deep breath and released the tension. He felt his body relax and he sank back all the way in his chair. He saw Dema's and Ellamora's posture do the same.

"Now that the ceremony is over, you may eat and drink freely," the dwarf explained, and he himself took bread, fruit, and vegetables for his plate. Reith eyed the food with hunger, and soon was helping himself to the various options before him.

"What is this place?" he asked, as he settled in again to his chair.

"You are in the Shrine of Antropa," the dwarf said. "This is a holy place set apart for worship and communion with the Maker."

"And who are you?" Dema asked. "And how did you know our names?"

"There is much I need to tell you," the old dwarf said. "And so little time in which to tell it. My name is Onias, and I am the High Priest of the Shrine. As to how I know your names, fear not, it is not from sorcery or magic. I just happen to be friendly with a certain dock master."

"How did you know we could come?" Reith asked, still perplexed at that part of the mystery.

"I heard the call," Onias said simply.

"What call?" Ellamora asked.

"The call that you certainly felt which compelled you to come here," Onias said. "Reith felt it most strongly at first, but the call grew in you, Ellamora, and Dema too. The call is strong, oh yes, it is strong. I also felt the resistance, the power holding you back, the one telling you to flee."

Reith, Ellamora, and Dema gaped at Onias.

"I see that there is still much confusion for you. Let me

start from the very beginning. At the very beginning of time, there was the Maker. He had always been, always is, and always will be. He fashioned the world with his hands and brought everything into being."

"Is the Maker the same as the God of Light?" Reith asked, curious.

"I suppose you could say that," Onias said. "The God of Light and the Maker are the same, but the God of Light is not the Maker and the Maker is not the God of Light."

"You speak in riddles," Reith said, shaking his head. He had no idea where this was going or if they were simply listening to the ravings of a mad man.

"Riddles to us, they may be, but we may hope for understanding one day."

"So the God of Light and the Maker are different but the same," Reith summed up. "It is clear as mud to me."

"As I was saying," Onias continued as if their theological digression had not happened. "The Maker created everything, including dwarves, elves, and humans. But the Maker also made the Guardians, spirit beings to protect and watch over the world."

"I've heard this before," Reith said. "From the elves."

"Yes, it is one and the same story. The Guardians are who drew you to this place."

"Then the Dark Powers tried to keep us away?" Reith asked.

"You are catching on quickly," Onias said. "In my prayers, the Guardians revealed themselves to me and allowed me to hear their call to you and the Dark Powers' counter call. So, I set the table and waited. And here you are."

"But why?" Dema asked. "Why were we called here?"

"Because I know things that are essential for you to know as well," Onias said. "Great and wondrous things are at work in our land, but terrible forces prowl around looking to devour the innocent."

"What do we need to know?" Reith asked.

"A thousand years ago, when Erador fell, the Guardians devised a plan for the restoration of all Terrasohnen. They locked a great power away and hid the key in Erador. That key is in our presence today."

"So the sword is definitely the key?" Reith asked.

"Oh yes," Onias said. "The sword is the key for the restoration of all of Terrasohnen."

"What does it open? What power does it contain?"

"The Guardians wrote a scroll. A copy was made and sent to Kal-Epharion. The original is here with us. It tells of the plan the Guardians made at the end of the Dragon War." Onias picked up a scroll that had been sitting in front of him this whole time. He unrolled it almost to the end. He cleared his throat and read:

And then, when all seemed lost, a plan was formed in the valley of death. Hope was saved, and hope would prevail, even over a thousand years. For among the Guardians of Light was one wiser than all the rest. He spoke to his brothers and sisters. "Come, let us store up a power so great that when loosed, it will bring about the restoration of this whole land. Though the peoples are divided, not forever shall they be. Though the land lay in shadow, a new day shall come at last. Come, let us hide the key in this city, this city that was a monument to them. For even in this hour of despair, hope springs eternal."

The other Guardians thought this to be a good plan and followed the lead of the wisest among them. They crafted a key of such beauty and greatness, all who beheld it saw its power and might and even a glimpse into the wisdom of the Guardians. And in Dragonscar, they hid it, until such a day as when one worthy of reuniting Terrasohnen would rise from among his brothers and sisters and take the Key and unleash the Power within.

He finished reading and rolled the scroll back up.

"It appears that one worthy of reuniting Terrasohnen has arisen," Onias said. "Reith, for this purpose, you have been chosen. It is your destiny."

"But why was I chosen? Where is this power? What does it mean that the power will bring about restoration?" Reith asked in rapid succession.

"It is not for me to say why the Maker or the Guardians have chosen you for this task. But what has been revealed to me about you means there is no doubt."

"What do you mean?" Reith asked.

"The restoration of Terrasohnen has already begun," Onias said. "And it is by your hand that it is happening."

"What have I done?" Reith asked, utterly perplexed.

"When you were in Erador, you encountered a stream and a grove of fruit trees. You ate of the fruit and took some with you on your travels. Where you cast the seeds, trees sprouted. Even now, Dragonscar is blooming with new life for the first time in a thousand years. Across Terrasohnen, you have scattered the seeds of the Maker's blessings. The world is becoming brand new, and you have done it."

Reith thought back to the trees that had sprung up overnight in the wake of his journey. He thought too of the peaches he had given to Heth to begin a peach grove in Suthrond. The seeds of the fruit of the trees of Erador were being planted all over the world.

"Okay, I understand your point there. But where is the power? How do I unlock it?"

"I have no scroll of this information," Onias said. "But

it has been passed down through the ages, high priest to high priest. You, Reith, have heard a voice calling to you several times now, telling you to find it. Here is what you need to know." Onias closed his eyes and began to recite words he had learned by heart.

"A thousand years hence, there shall be war. Shadows will rise and the key will be found. When hope seems lost, the key bearer shall travel due North, across the inland sea, and follow the frozen river. At the Temple of Ice, the key bearer shall present the key and encounter the power of restoration."

Find me. The voice came once more to Reith's inner ears, and he felt it reverberate across time and space.

"What do you mean there will be war?" Ellamora asked.

"Alas, I do not know," Onias said. "I have these words passed down for generations, and that is it."

"Where is the inland sea? And the frozen river? And the Temple of Ice?" Reith asked.

"The inland sea is the lake on which Galismoor is built," Onias said. "It is said that at the northern most point of the lake, a river flows into it from the Northern Mountains. According to the tradition, the key bearer must follow the river to the Temple of Ice. I cannot give any further advice or instruction, for those lands are far beyond what my eyes have seen."

"So do I go there now?" Reith asked. He thought through the logistics of such a journey. Here he was at the southernmost point of the known world. To use his key, he must travel to the far north.

"No, not now," Onias said. "There will be war, but for now, you must continue the path on which you trod. You have heard a voice, and you must obey it."

"Fight for them," Reith said softly, repeating the

command he had heard to no one in particular. "Then find me."

"Exactly," Onias said. "There will be a fight, make no mistake. War is coming to Terrasohnen. It marches now, and the Shadow is at its head."

"Hold on," Dema said, "That prophecy says 'Shadows will rise.' Shadows, plural. Are there more?"

"Always the Dark Powers are seeking those who will do their bidding and invite them in. But alas, all I know of now is the one. Who is to say whether the Dark Powers have succeeded in corrupting other souls?"

"Well then why don't the Guardians do something about it?" Dema demanded. "If they are so powerful, why don't they fight the Dark Powers and the Shadows?"

"What makes you think they are not?" Onias replied. "Weapons in this war come in all shapes and sizes."

"What's that supposed to mean?" Dema demanded. It clicked in Reith's head and he answered before Onias could.

"The Guardians and the Dark Powers use people, those are the weapons," he said.

"Exactly right," Onias said, giving Reith a nod of approval. "This war is a war on two fronts. There is the physical war, with armies and swords, spears, and bows. And then there is the battle in the hearts and minds of all the peoples of Terrasohnen. Restoration and peace can be won in both spheres."

"Restoration, you keep saying that," Ellamora said. "What does that mean, exactly?"

"When the Dark Powers separated from the rest of the Guardians, a fracture occurred in the very fabric of the universe. People were drawn toward the fracture, which only made it worse. Things are not as they should be. Famine, sickness, even death are the results. Restoration means the world will be made new. The Maker is fixing the broken pieces and bringing beauty from ashes. Light casts out darkness."

Reith, Ellamora, and Dema were silent as they all thought of a world where hunger, sickness, and death were no more.

"Well, if that's not worth fighting for, I don't know what is," Reith said.

"The path before you is a dark and treacherous one, Reith," Onias said. "And yours too, Ellamora and Dema. The key bearer and his companions are susceptible to attack from all sides."

"Will it all work out?" Ellamora asked. "What if we fail?"

"Your steps have been guided thus far, and your steps shall be guided. No matter how dark the night, the light will always dawn."

"That," Dema said, "Doesn't seem like it answers Ellamora's question."

"There are no easy answers," Onias said. "But whether good or ill besets your path, know that you are not far from the hand of the Maker."

Reith felt a strange feeling in his stomach, and felt it bloom and grow throughout his whole person. He realized it was hope burning like fire within him.

"Now it is time for you to return to your friends," Onias said. "I know not whether we will meet again, but I leave with you this ancient blessing. 'May the Maker hold you in his hands, may his light illuminate your path, and his word cause the darkness to flee. So shall it be.'"

"Thank you, Onias," Reith said, and the old dwarf gave a small bow. Then he stood and raised an arm in a gesture of dismissal. Reith, Ellamora, and Dema rose from their chairs and walked the aisle between the benches toward the door. At the door, they paused and looked back. Onias was gone, though none of them had heard him leave.

"Let's get out of here," Dema said, and she pushed through the door.

"Right behind you," Ellamora said.

Reith took one last look, and again did not see the old dwarf. But he had the strangest feeling that a multitude of eyes were watching him. He shivered and walked through the door, out of the Shrine of Antropa.

7

Reith, Ellamora, and Dema walked down the passage, up the long staircase, turned and then walked up the next staircase back into the library. They blinked in the natural light cascading through the windows, which was burning orange with the sunset. They found Vereinen exactly where they had left him. Books and scrolls were strewn about, as if Vereinen had been trying to read several at once in an effort to soak up as much information as he could. Romulus was seated in a chair reading a book with his feet propped up on the desk.

"Where have you three been?" he asked when they approached the table.

"It's a long story," Reith said. "We will tell you on our way back to the tavern."

"Would you help me get these books and scrolls together?" Vereinen asked, and the three of them began to help the Chronicler pack up his research materials.

"I learned so much today," Vereinen said, showing them several pages of hastily scrawled notes as they left the library some minutes later. "I will have to return whenever, well, whenever our errand is complete. But tell me about where you three got off to!"

Reith took the lead in telling the story of their visit to the Shrine and their encounter with the High Priest Onias. Ellamora and Dema chimed in whenever Reith left something important out. Vereinen and Romulus held their questions during the telling of the tale. They wound their way down through the city, and were nearing the tavern when Reith finished telling all about the prophecy.

"There is much to ponder in this," Vereinen said, when Reith had finally stopped talking. They stood in the street outside of the tavern.

"What do you know of all of this?" Reith asked.

"I am afraid not much more than you yourselves know already," Vereinen said. "This is all wildly outside the scope of my profession. This is the realm of priests and clerics, not scholars. But if you want my opinion on the matter, it all rings true to my ears. Heed the Priest, Reith. There are great powers and forces at work in our world, powers greater than any of us ever imagined. We face the darkness and must boldly stride into it, for better or worse."

"I do not like the notion that war is coming," Romulus said, "but I am afraid we already knew it was. I had hoped somehow it could be averted."

"Why us? Why now?" Reith lamented.

"Only the God of Light, the Maker, knows," Vereinen said. "All there is to do is to do the best we can in the circumstances. It's up to the Guardians to protect and guide."

"We should talk to Myon about it all," Ellamora suggested.

"He will have good insight," Dema agreed.

They descended the steps into the tavern and pushed their way through the door. They stood for a moment in the doorway and their eyes searched the room for their friends. It was much more crowded now than earlier, as nearly every table had at least one person seated at it. Ellamora spotted Myon and the others first and pushed forward, leading the way across the crowded room toward the fireplace. They all eased into chairs and each was surprised at how much their legs were thankful for no longer bearing their weight. Nearly as one, they each contentedly sighed.

"Welcome back," Myon said. "How was the library?"

"Enthralling," Vereinen said.

"And thought provoking," Romulus added. He nodded to Reith, and Reith re-told the story he had just told Vereinen and Romulus, though with less help from Ellamora and Dema this time.

Myon's face went from good natured smile when they had arrived to thoughtful pondering to grim determination over the course of Reith's story. Like Vereinen and Romulus, he did not interrupt.

"By the God of Light," he said when Reith had finished the story. "We are indeed in troubled times. This makes our errand more urgent. We shall leave this place as soon as possible for the Dwarves, tomorrow if needed."

"Our hope is not yet lost," Romulus said. "It is not time for the key bearer to go North. But what troubles me, and it sticks out more in this listen of the story, Reith, what troubles me is that shadows will rise. It seems that Solzar might be but one of our enemies."

"Perhaps your royal father is another," Myon added quietly. "We saw the shadow rising within him. Did he lend himself over to the darkness to be used? Or is there still hope for him?"

"I hope that he has not gone all the way into the

darkness," Romulus said. "Is there any hope for one which becomes a shadow?"

"Hold on," Vereinen said, pulling his papers out of a pocket and spreading them on the table. "I think I read something about that and made a note about it. Yes, here we are," he said, picking up one of the papers and holding it close. "Separation of a person from the dark powers is only possible through death."

The words hovered over their table like a dark cloud.

"Well, I hope for your sake, my prince, that he did not become a shadow," Myon said softly.

They sat in silence for a few moments before Mr. Borden came over with a tray laden with eight bowls. He placed steaming bowls of stew on the table before each of them. He hurried off and soon returned with more ale. With food in front of them and drink in hand, the atmosphere at the table changed considerably for the better. Despite their meal at the Shrine, Reith, Ellamora, and Dema found they were all very hungry and all devoured their delicious beef stew.

As they were eating, a minstrel stood near the bar and began to sing while playing a small stringed instrument which Romulus told them was a lute. The minstrel was an elf, tall and fair, and his voice soared smoothly above the noise of the tavern. Soon all were listening and a few of the tavern patrons joined in, though with rather less skill than the minstrel. The ale flowed freely and all were in high spirits several hours later when the ministerial begged off. A loud cheer erupted from all the patrons, including Reith and the others who were quite enjoying themselves, for the minstrel to continue playing. Coins were thrown toward him and the change bounced on the wooden tables and the stone floor and gathered near the minstrel, who bowed and began strumming the lute one more time.

As they watched and listened, Reith had a strange moment of clarity. *This might be our last peaceful night in a long time, and certainly our last night in a bed for a long time.* The thought filled him neither with dread nor pleasure, but rather a sense of determination. *The path is dark, but the steps are guarded.*

When the minstrel finally finished playing, and refused the calls for an encore, Myon and Romulus decided it was time for bed, and the rest of the party followed behind them. They walked up two flights of stairs to the top floor, which was a long, carpeted hallway with doors leading off on each side. Myon pointed out a door behind which was the room for Dema and Ellamora. Myon and Romulus were in another room. Brauron and Aytos had a room together, and at the end of the hall was the room for Reith and Vereinen. They pushed open the door to find two small beds, a small table between them on which a candle stood burning. Vereinen took the bed closest to the window and Reith settled into the one closest to the door. He laid his bow and sword beside him on the ground, ready for action if the night called for it. The mattress was comfortable and the sheets smelled fresh, as if they had spent the day blowing in the wind on a line, which of course, they did. Reith's last thought as he drifted off to sleep was that Mr. Borden sure knew how to run a tavern.

The next morning, Reith awoke to Vereinen gently shaking him awake. Sun poured through the window of the room. Reith stretched and yawned. He had slept soundly and now felt refreshed.

"Come on Reith, up you get," Vereinen said. "They will be waiting for us downstairs."

A few minutes later, Reith and Vereinen joined Myon and Romulus at a table in the dining room. Mr. Borden brought them coffee and a platter laden with bacon, eggs, and toast. Reith piled the food on this plate and ate hungrily. He was halfway through his first helping of everything when Brauron and Aytos arrived and had began helping himself to seconds when Ellamora and Dema came down, looking sleepier than all the rest of them.

"Good, now we're all here," Romulus said. "Let's go over the plan of action for today. Myon and I have decided it would be best if the two of us went to the docks to find us a ship. Our goal is to leave as soon as possible, so you all will need to stay here at the tavern in the event we find a ship going to Balkh that will take us today."

The plan was agreed to, and Myon and Romulus finished their breakfasts and rose to leave. They departed having been wished luck by the rest of the party.

"How did you sleep?" Reith asked Ellamora and Dema when Romulus and Myon had left.

"I slept like a log," Dema said.

"Me too," Ellamora said. "I didn't realize how much I missed dry land and a real bed. Hammocks on the ship were fine, but nothing beats a bed."

"Well, if all goes according to plan, that will be the last night's sleep in a bed for a while," Reith said.

"I do hope they find a ship," Ellamora said.

They spent the rest of the morning sitting in the empty dining room drinking coffee, talking, and playing board games that Mr. Borden lent them. Time passed swiftly and soon Mr. Borden brought out a platter of sandwiches.

"Thank you so much for your hospitality, Mr. Borden," Reith said with a mouthful of sandwich. He received a kick under the table for his lack of manners from Dema who glared at him. He shrugged and continued eating.

"It is my pleasure," Mr. Borden replied. "It is what I am here for."

While they were eating, Romulus arrived.

"We got a ship!" he said triumphantly. "Myon is working out final details, but we will leave this afternoon."

"When do we need to go to the docks?" Vereinen asked.

"We will leave here in about an hour," Romulus said, helping himself to one of the remaining sandwiches. "We will be sailing on a dwarven vessel called the *Nighthawk*. Its captain is the dwarf, Lord Eynali. He has a crew of thirty dwarves at his command. He was initially going to leave tonight, but Myon and I convinced him to depart earlier than that." He rubbed two fingers to his thumb in a circular motion to convey what exactly had caught the Dwarf Lord's attention.

"What is the *Nighthawk* like?" Dema asked.

"It's bigger than *The Mermaid's Fortune*," Romulus said. "Bigger and grander. We shall be very comfortable on our journey."

"How long is it from here to Balkh?" Ellamora asked.

"Eynali said it would take us five days, depending on wind conditions. With a crew of thirty, oars out will be a more manageable proposition, so it should take no longer than a week, God of Light willing."

"I hope it is enough," Vereinen said.

"Make sure you have all of your belongings from your rooms," Romulus said. "We cannot keep Lord Eynali and his crew waiting."

Reith knew he had everything and there was no need to go back up to the room. Ellamora and Dema did go up, as did Brauron and Aytos. Mr. Borden came around and offered more coffee, which Reith gladly accepted. Brauron and Aytos were first to arrive, then Dema and Ellamora a few minutes later. Scarcely had Ellamora and Dema sat down when the sound of distance bells reverberated around the Isles. Mr. Borden sprang toward the door, wrenching it open and poking his head out. The sound of bells grew louder with the door open, and the six of them stood to their feet in preparation for whatever it meant.

"What's going on?" Romulus asked sharply as Mr. Borden bounded back into the tavern and stepped behind the bar. He dropped out of sight but quickly stood up holding a menacing looking crossbow.

"The fortress bells toll," Mr. Borden said grimly. "The Isles are under attack."

"Attack? Who? How?" Vereinen asked, but Mr. Borden was already out the door and racing up the hill to the fortress above.

"Come on," Romulus said. "To the docks."

They jogged through the streets of Antropa. Nearly the entire city was out in the streets now, and they jostled passersby as they went. Some, like Mr. Borden, were going uphill as fast as their legs could carry them. Others ran toward the docks, evidently aiming to board a ship and defend the Isles on the sea. Many carried weapons. Reith saw an assortment of crossbows, longbows, swords, spears, and even some mean looking clubs with spikes on them. There was an organized calm to the distressing proceedings, as if the Islanders were used to practicing for defensive military action, which Reith supposed they actually did.

They arrived on the main street that ran parallel to the docks and looked frantically for Myon. Everywhere they looked, elves and dwarves were jumping into the largest ships and hastening them for sailing. The jostling of the crowd grew worse and Ellamora was even knocked to the ground. She would have been trampled if Aytos had not grabbed her by the back of the shirt and lifted her up to her feet again.

"There!" Romulus said, pointing ahead. Now they all could see that Myon was standing atop something that placed him head and shoulders above everyone. He was looking for them but could not see them in the swell of people. They pushed their way forward and Romulus could almost touch him before he saw them.

"Thank the God of Light you are here," Myon said.

"What is going on?" Romulus asked.

"The Isles are under attack. A great fleet is approaching from the West."

Romulus swore. "That's my father's navy," he said, then he swore again. "What does Eynali say?"

"Come, speak to him yourself."

Myon led the way down the dock toward a ship that was indeed bigger and grander than *The Mermaid's Fortune*. It had three sails as opposed to the one of their previous vessel. Its paint looked new and altogether it looked much less shabby than Captain Naftis' ship. Myon and Romulus rushed up the gangplank to the deck, and the others followed behind cautiously.

"My Lord," Romulus said, striding toward a lordly looking dwarf. His beard was brown and braided, and on his head was an intricately carved silver helm. At his side was a sword, longer and thicker than Reith's. Reith guessed it probably weighed at least twice as much as his. His face was stern but not unkind.

"The Isles are under attack," Eynali said with a deep, hoarse voice. "I am afraid our voyage is temporarily postponed."

"What do you plan to do?" Romulus asked.

"Join in the defense of the Isles," Eynali said. "You and yours are welcome to join in and fight."

"We have to go now," Romulus said, "Unless you want to see Balkh and Darren Shahr overwhelmed."

"Darren Shahr is the dwarven capital," Vereinen whispered in Reith's ear, prompting the question that had in fact been on Reith's mind.

"We have to protect the Isles," Eynali said. "I am sorry, but that's how it has to be."

"Eynali, listen to them."

Everyone looked around to find the source of the new voice. It sounded familiar to Reith and he turned to see Onias the Priest standing in their midst on the deck of the *Nighthawk*. He had made no sound and his arrival shocked all.

"Priest Onias," Eynali said, bowing slightly to the elderly dwarven priest. "I have never seen you outside of the Shrine or the Library."

"Then your eyes are weak indeed," Onias said. "They see but do not perceive."

"What does the Maker will?" Eynali asked.

"I do not claim to speak for the Maker in this," Onias said. "I speak from my own wisdom and will. You shall go with these elves and humans. Take them to Balkh. I fear only evil will befall you if you remain here."

"Is it evil to lay down one's life for the sake of others?" Eynali replied.

"Eynali, Eynali," Onias said slowly. "The Key has been found."

Eynali froze, and then he took a step nearer to Onias.

"By the Maker," Eynali said softly. "Who knew that such a day would fall during our own?"

"Your way forward is clear," Onias said. "Sail with all your might. May the Maker bless the wind in your sails."

And with that, Onias turned and walked slowly down the gangplank and back toward the city.

"This changes everything," Eynali said. "Prepare to sail to Balkh!" he called to his crew. They continued their scurrying around the ship. "Come, friends," Eynali said to the elves and humans. "Welcome to the *Nighthawk*. We shall leave soon. When we are out to sea, we shall talk more."

Within minutes, the *Nighthawk* was pushing away from the dock and oars were dropped in the harbor. They sailed north through the channel they had come in by with Naftis. All around the bells of the fortresses rang out and echoed on the slopes of the Isles. When they pushed out to open sea, Reith gasped. Hundreds of ships were coming from the West toward the Isles. Already some defending ships were engaged in pitched battle. Several ships were on fire, though Reith could not tell whether they belonged to friend or foe.

"My heart yearns to attack," Eynali said. "It grieves my soul to turn aside. To the East!"

He turned the wheel away from the attackers and steered the *Nighthawk* around the northern side of the Isles. Wind from the West propelled them forward at a tremendous pace and soon they were well away from the Isles. Smoke rose in the air behind them, but they could not see anything other than the smoke and the large mass of the Isles.

The Sun set behind them, casting a long shadow in front of the ship, so it seemed that the ship was continually sailing into darkness. The first mate was instructed by Eynali to show the elves and humans their quarters.

"Come," the first mate, whose name was Rejnik, said. He opened a door that led under the upper back deck of the ship. "You will share three cabins," he said. "For the ladies," he opened the first door and gestured in. Ellamora and Dema stepped inside and Reith caught a glimpse of bunks in a small room. "And two rooms for the rest." He opened two more doors and left them to determine their sleeping arrangements. Each small cabin had two sets of bunk beds and not much else. There was a small window on the wall of the ship, but there was hardly room to walk straight through the room without turning one's shoulders to the side. Myon, Brauron, and Aytos took one cabin, leaving Romulus, Vereinen, and Reith to take the other.

Vereinen insisted upon a bottom bunk, protesting that his elderly frame could hardly climb up and down. Reith deferred to Romulus, who took the other bottom bunk. Reith chose the top bunk above Vereinen.

"This sure does beat Naftis' sleeping accommodations," Romulus said.

They made their way to the deck and watched the last of the sunlight fall below the horizon behind them. Then, one by one, they bid Lord Eynali and the crew goodnight and returned to their cabins.

It took Reith some time to reorient himself to the rocking of the ship to fall asleep. One night on land had reoriented himself to sleeping with no movement, and he had to relearn. He eventually drifted to sleep and slept soundly that night.

He awoke some hours later. The darkness outside the window was not quite so complete, so he knew that dawn was approaching. He yawned, stretched, and quickly determined he would not fall back asleep. *I think I'll watch the sunrise.* He rose and quietly left the cabin.

Very few of the crew members were on deck. Rejnik was at the wheel, and he nodded curtly toward Reith as Reith looked his way. Ahead of them, in the east, the sky was ever so slightly lightening. As the sky came to the west, it grew steadily darker until it was pure night on the western horizon. Reith went to the front of the ship and watched the slow progression of the sky turning from night to day. He was reminded of Ellyn, the Lore Master and Cleric of Crain, whom he had stayed with before Pryderus had run them all off. The prayer she had taught him came to his mind, and he found he remembered every word.

God of light, forever our guide, lead us on paths of peace. Shine on us so we may shine on your world. Illuminate our hearts with truth. May it be.

He silently prayed the prayer to the God of Light. As he spoke "may it be" in his heart, the first glimmer of sunlight appeared on the horizon, bathing the world in yellow, orange, and red. He watched as the light seemed to bounce from wave to wave before them and the sea glittered like a large, blue jewel. He turned and watched the transformation the light was creating on the formerly dark earth. His back was now to the sun, and he saw now a large shadow stretching from the western horizon to the top of the sky. His heart sank. It was a gigantic, billowing cloud of smoke rising from the Isles. The Free Isles had fallen.

8

For a few minutes, Reith stood, rooted to the spot in horror. The massive amount of smoke which was still growing larger could only mean one thing: the attacking elven armada had taken the Isles and set fire to them. *How could the Free Isles fall?*

It was like living in a nightmare. He thought of Onias, Mr. Borden, Kazor the dock master. *Were they safe? Was the library safe? And the shrine?*

He couldn't bear the thought of the library and shrine burning. *Vereinen is going to be so upset.*

Now that the sun was up, the ship began to stir. Members of the crew came on deck in ones and twos. All gasped in dismay when they looked behind them at the smoke. Eynali fell to his knees and wept when he saw it.

Vereinen was the first of the elves and humans to awake, and he joined Reith at the front of the ship.

"That poor library," Vereinen said, as upset as Reith had anticipated. "Oh, I hope it was spared."

"Me too, Vereinen," Reith said.

It was a solemn day on board the *Nighthawk*. There was

little by way of merriment or conversation of any sort, and the smoke of the Free Isles hung over them—a melancholy cloud. The smoke drifting their direction meant one good thing though. The wind was at their backs. They sailed on at a frenetic pace, and no sign of the elven armada could be seen behind them, which they took as a good sign.

The next day the wind remained at their back, and the smoke of the Free Isles had dissipated, which Reith guessed was because the fires had been put out.

In the middle of the afternoon, Lord Eynali summoned Reith to stand beside him at the ship's wheel. Reith climbed up and stood beside the captain, and they both stared forward at the shadow of the ship rushing over the waves before them.

"Reith, let us get acquainted with one another," Eynali said, his eyes still on the sea. "Tell me of your journeys and how you have come to be here in this place."

Reith launched into the story of the Gray Man's attack on Coeden and his flight to Erador. He told Eynali of finding the sword and of the trees and stream giving new life to Dragonscar. He told of the Suthronders and their adventures in Crain. He told of Pryderus' betrayal and their flight to Sardis. All through the story, Eynali listened intently. After Reith finished with his trip to the Shrine of Antropa and meeting with Onias, Eynali spoke again.

"Onias is a great friend of mine. It is taking all my will power to not turn this ship around and see what may have befallen him. But I know he would not want that."

"He was good to me, in the brief time I met him," Reith said, sorrowful over the fate of the old priest.

"It is only because of him that we are here together," Eynali said. "He said the Key has been found. I trust you know this."

Reith nodded, but then realized Eynali still wasn't looking at him, so he audibly replied. "Yes, I do."

"Long have I studied the faith of my people," Eynali said. "Never did I think I would live to see the day when the Key was found. Pray tell, what is the Key?"

Reith hesitated, not knowing whether to trust Eynali or not. Then he remembered Onias, and the old priest's trust in Eynali convinced him.

"It is my sword," Reith said, gesturing to the sword at his side. He hardly realized he was wearing it anymore, it was connected to his body, as if he had grown an extra leg or another arm.

Eynali finally did look to Reith, making eye contact first and then scanning down to the sword.

"May I see it?" Eynali asked.

"Yes, you may," Reith said, drawing the sword out, which gleamed in the afternoon sun.

"Take the wheel, keep us steady," Eynali said, and the two switched places. The wheel generally stayed straight, but with every jolt of a wave, it wanted to jerk, but Reith held it firm.

Eynali took the sword in his hands and held it up to the light. He inspected the hilt closely and lovingly touched it as a mother strokes a child's head. After several minutes of inspection, he took hold of the wheel with one hand and offered the sword back to Reith with the other.

"I have never seen it's equal," Eynali said as Reith sheathed the blade. "It is a marvelous weapon. And I believe that sword was made by dwarves."

"How can you tell?" Reith asked.

"We dwarves pride ourselves on our metallurgy and smithing. We know secrets of metal the other races do not possess. Your sword, the Key, it has all the signs of being the work of a dwarven master smith. I see it in the way the metal is woven together."

"What do you mean, 'woven'?" Reith asked.

"It's a term we use for weapons grade metal," Eynali explained. "The steel is melted, folded, and hammered in very precise ways to create a blade strong enough for the rigors of battle and fine enough to have a sharp edge. The way our smiths work with the metal is like how a weaver creates cloth. A woven dwarf blade is stronger and sharper than any other."

Reith looked at his sword with newfound appreciation, as if he could have appreciated it even more than he did before. *This sword is a wonder, and I am the one chosen to bear it?*

"Key bearer," Eynali said, growing solemn. "The path before you is one that will take you through darkness and shadow."

Reith understood that he spoke not a warning, but a simple fact of the future.

"I fear Darkness will try and overtake you on the way," Eynali added softly.

"The Gray Man is trying to find the Key," Reith said.

"Not the Gray Man," Eynali said. "The *Darkness*. The Darkness that is at work in the world. The Darkness is what is at work in the heart of every dwarf, elf, and human. The Darkness seeks to kill and destroy, but above all, the Darkness seeks to bend wills to its own. I fear the Darkness itself will try and claim you."

"How would it do that?" Reith asked, shuddering at the thought of the Darkness creeping toward him.

"The Darkness works in subtle and manipulative ways," Eynali said. "The Darkness will entice you down the wrong path. The Darkness may even try and entice you with something you think is good."

"What sort of good thing can be bad?" Reith asked, honestly confused.

"Good becomes evil when evil is used to achieve some seemingly noble and good end," Eynali said. "There can be no partnership between Light and Dark. So, beware, Reith. Watch out for Darkness. Keep its deceptions at bay. May the Maker guard you."

"I hope I am strong enough," Reith said.

"None are strong enough," Eynali said. "That is what makes the Darkness so powerful. Only the Maker is strong enough to cast out the Darkness. Ask the Maker for help, and the Maker will grant it."

For a long time, neither of them spoke. Eynali kept his eyes forward to the sea, and Reith didn't look at anything, so absorbed in his own thoughts was he. *Is this Darkness really inside me?*

Finally, he spoke.

"How will I know?" Reith asked. "I mean, how will I know the Darkness is trying to entice me?"

"The Maker will tell you," Eynali said simply.

"What?"

"Not audibly, but the Maker will speak to you."

"How do you know?"

"Because the Maker has spoken similar things to me."

"What do you mean?" Reith asked, completely perplexed.

"The Maker only speaks Truth and Love," Eynali said simply.

"So, if I hear Truth and Love, it's the Maker speaking?"

"Reith," Eynali said kindly, "I think you are over thinking this. The Maker has brought you safe thus far. The Maker will be with you the rest of the way."

"You're so confident."

"It's faith, Reith. It's faith that the Maker will always be who the Maker always is and who the Maker has always been."

"I wish I had your faith," Reith said.

"The first step toward that faith is wanting that faith," Eynali said.

The rest of the day passed swiftly. The wind stayed at their backs, and Eynali announced to the whole crew that they should be at Balkh much more quickly than they had initially guessed.

Early the next morning, just after sunrise, Reith was awoken by a shout on deck. He immediately sprang to wakefulness and jumped down from his bed and rushed to the deck. All the dwarven sailors were hurrying back and forth. They all looked grim. He looked around for any of his friends and saw Vereinen standing by the starboard side of the ship gazing out over the waters. Reith joined him.

"What is going on?" Reith asked the chronicler. "The shouting woke me up."

"Look," Vereinen said, and pointed out to sea. Reith followed Vereinen's finger and saw a long way off the sea was churning like a boiling pot of water. It was hard to judge distances, but Reith guessed it to be several hundred yards away from the ship.

"What is that?" Reith asked as the sea writhed.

"Trouble," Vereinen said. "Something stirs in the deep."

"What do the sailors think it is?" Reith asked, still confused.

"They say it may be some sort of monster," Vereinen

said. "But we really can't be sure. Whatever it is, I hope it stays far away from us."

Reith looked up to the wheel to see Eynali already determinedly steering the ship away from the churning, boiling sea, toward the port side. By now, the whole ship was awake with a flurry of activity. All were on edge.

Myon came over to Reith and Vereinen and asked questions like the ones Reith had just asked, and Reith took his turn answering. When Romulus joined them a minute later, it was Myon's turn to convey the peril. Dema and Ellamora arrived together and Reith explained to them the gravity of the situation.

"Might it be better if we set about rowing away?" Romulus asked, though of course none of them knew what one should do in a situation where some sea monster was a few hundred yards off from a ship. "Well, let me ask the captain." Romulus climbed up to the wheel and spoke briefly to Eynali. They saw Eynali shake his head and say something to Romulus, and then Romulus was coming back.

"Eynali said the oars would just draw the monster toward us," Romulus reported. "He hopes that we are as of yet undetected, but he is steering us away just to be sure. He also instructed us to remain as silent as possible until this danger has passed."

Everyone nodded their heads in understanding and agreement. Reith looked back out over the boiling sea. *Is it closer now?*

Eynali continued to angle the ship away from the disturbance in the sea, but with the wind at their back from the west, they were really only able to take a forty-five degree angle away from the danger. And still it seemed to Reith to be coming near them.

And then, all of a sudden, the churning in the waves

ceased. Reith looked around at his fellow travelers in relief, but then he spotted the dread on the faces of all the dwarves on board.

There were several seconds of silent dread before Eynali called out, "Battle stations!"

Everyone rushed to grab weapons. Reith went to his cabin and retrieved his bow and arrows, which were stowed there. He had his sword buckled to his side already. He took his place beside Vereinen, armed with a borrowed spear, and Ellamora, armed with her sword and bow. He strained his eyes for any sight of churning and turmoil in the waves, but he saw none.

"If we are attacked by the sea monster, the Leviathan," Eynali called out to the ship's defenders, "remember that it's weak points will be its eyes and its open mouth. No sword can pierce it's hide."

"But what exactly is a Leviathan?" Myon asked.

"It is a giant serpent of the seas that tears ships apart. It is Chaos. It is Darkness."

"Have you ever seen a Leviathan?" Myon asked.

"No, praise the Maker. And I still have hope that we do not. Perhaps that churning of the sea was a shoal of fish or a whale. Everyone remain vigilant."

The next few minutes were tense. Eynali turned the wheel so that the wind was directly at their backs, pushing them forward at the same breakneck speed they had been traveling since leaving the Free Isles. They all began to relax. Reith gripped his bow a little looser and began to grow restless.

Then something erupted out of the water on the port side of the ship. Everyone turned and saw a gigantic beast rising from the sea. It soon was as tall as the ship's mast, and sunlight shone off its green scales. It was a huge snakelike creature, thicker than the sturdiest of tree trunks.

Then it let out a blood curdling screech, and all on deck reflexively covered their ears. After the screech, it blew a ball of fire from its mouth into the air.

"You didn't mention it could breathe fire," Romulus called out to Eynali.

"I didn't know it could!" Eynali replied. "Courage, crew, courage. Fight for your lives!"

The giant serpent peered down at the ship and its crew. And then quick as lightning, it struck. Its mouth opened wide and row after row of dagger sharp teeth were displayed to the frightened crew. It dove at one of the dwarves, who managed to throw himself out of the way, just missing being eaten whole by the large serpent. Immediately other dwarves jumped in and began to hack at the outstretched neck of the beast. Their swords glanced off its scales, which were stronger than any armor. Reith drew an arrow and let it loose at the monster's eye, remembering Eynali's mention of its weakness, but the beast had already pulled hits head back and up and the arrow glanced harmlessly off the skin and continued to the sea.

Again, the serpent reared up and surveyed the ship before choosing a new target to strike. This time an unlucky dwarf was caught and dragged screaming from the ship. The serpent tossed its head back and they saw the dwarf flying away from the ship, where he hit the water with a splash. *It's playing with us,* Reith thought with an icy feeling of dread coursing through his veins.

The serpent reared back again, and Reith shot an arrow at its eye. The serpent must have seen it coming, for it dodged slightly and the arrow bounced off the side of its head. *I need to be quicker than it if I am to hit it.*

Again, the monster struck, but it missed its target, Brauron this time. Brauron cursed and tried to stab it as he leapt to the side, but his blow was hopeless against the armor of the serpent. Ellamora was also shooting arrows at the beast but was having as little success as Reith was. *I need to move,* Reith realized. *I can't get it from this angle.*

He looked back and forth, trying to find a spot where he could shoot at the monster. Then he looked up at the crow's nest. *That's it.*

As the monster struck again, Reith jumped forward toward the center of the ship. He pulled a dwarf to safety from the mouth of the beast, and they both fell to the deck. He jumped up quickly and made it to the center mast. He grabbed the rope ladder and began to climb. It seemed to take him forever. Screams from the sailors and screeches from the beast filled the air, but after what seemed like ages, he pulled himself up. He drew his bow and waited for the right angle.

The beast reared up again, surveying its prey, but it did not see Reith so high in the air. He sighted down the arrow and stilled his hammering pulse. *Like a shooting range.* And then he released the arrow, which hurtled straight into the unsuspecting eye of the sea serpent.

It howled in rage, a screech that sent him to his knees with his hands over his ears. The sea serpent writhed in agony, churning up the waters of the sea, and then it breathed fire into the air again. *It's done playing with us,* Reith thought. *And it won't fall for that trick again.*

He hurried to climb back down. The serpent still writhed in pain, but it seemed to be regaining its wits. It turned so its remaining good eye was looking up on the ship. And it saw him. For a split second, he was staring directly into the bright red eye of the sea serpent. And he saw into it, as if it were a window of a house. Behind the eye was a Shadow.

The serpent lunged for him, but Reith saw it coming.

He let go and plummeted to the deck, ten feet below him. His leg landed awkwardly and he felt pain in his ankle, but the serpent missed him by inches. He tried to rise to his feet, but his ankle would not support his weight. The sea serpent reared back and then struck again. He ducked, fearing for his life.

But then someone was beside him. Dema was there with a borrowed spear in hand. As the serpent lunged, mouth wide open, Dema hurled the spear into the open pit that was its mouth. The spear sank deeply into the roof of the mouth of the beast and stopped it in its tracks, just a foot from Reith's face. He felt the hot breath of the sea serpent on his face and a horrible smell nearly overwhelmed him. The serpent tried to screech again but the sound was garbled and strangled. It made a coughing like sound and blood splattered Reith, Dema, and the deck. Reith thought it tried to breathe fire, but nothing happened. Its head swayed and then it fell with a crash to the deck, splintering the railing of the ship.

Reith sat there, covered in blood and stared into the still open mouth of the now dead sea serpent, completely lost for words. Dema collapsed to her knees and pulled him into a tight embrace, not caring at all for the blood covering both of them. Then she began to sob.

9

———

Dema and Reith sat in their embrace for a long minute before they began to be aware of movement around them. Their companions and the remaining crew were gathered, all panting from their exertion. No one spoke.

There was a strangled cry from somewhere way off the port side of the ship, and suddenly the dwarves burst into action. Dema let go of Reith and the two rose to their feet covered in blood and tears. Reith's ankle throbbed, and he nearly fell over from the pain, but Dema grabbed his arm to steady him.

A small lifeboat was dropped into the water with two dwarves on it. Reith and Dema hobbled to the edge of the deck, looking out over the water. They saw in the distance a figure bobbing up and down in the water and sputtering. The lifeboat slowly made its way over to the figure and the two dwarves reached down and pulled someone up and laid them in the boat. Then slowly they made their way back to the ship. As it approached, Reith realized the sodden figure lying in the boat was Eynali. He was unconscious.

The two dwarves were hauled up to the ship with a rope, and then the whole boat was pulled up with Eynali still in it. He was too weak or too injured to hold onto the rope. Reith could see he was covered in blood and water, though he couldn't see where Eynali was wounded.

The crew laid their captain on the deck and began attending to him. They began to strip his shirt off him and then Reith saw the teeth marks where the sea monster had bit down on the captain. Small, jagged cuts ran around his torso. Evidently the sea monster did not bite down, but only meant to throw Eynali from the ship, perhaps to finish him off later. They washed and bandaged his wounds. His face was white and his breathing was ragged.

"Will he make it?" Reith asked Vereinen.

"We can only hope," Vereinen said.

The captain was placed in his cabin, and then a meeting of every able-bodied person was called for by First Mate Rejnik.

"We lost a few good men," Rejnik said. "Kenjar, Raxett, and Bann were lost to the sea monster. And the captain is in bad shape," the dwarf said solemnly. "That monster nearly killed him too. Would've if we didn't get the bastard first." He paused to collect his words. For a brief instant, Reith wondered if the bastard was Eynali or the sea monster.

"While he is out of commission, I'll be in charge. We will continue to sail for Balkh. Hopefully we should arrive in the next few days or so. And hopefully the captain makes it there with us. We need all hands on deck helping us move forward. We must go quickly."

There was a flurry of activity as the remaining sailors readied the ship for sailing. Reith was recruited to go below deck and row until the sails were ready again. When the ship lurched forward with the wind, Reith lay down his oar, sweaty and spent.

He still had blood all over him. His ankle throbbed with pain, but he didn't think it was broken. He hobbled back up to the deck and asked for some sea water to be scooped up so he could wash himself. The salty, cold water refreshed and rejuvenated him. The blood and sweat rolled off with the water, and the wind on his wet skin cooled him off.

The wind kept picking up speed from behind them, and soon Reith was dry as a bone. The ship sped forward with tremendous speed, and nearly everyone on board gasped in surprise at the change. It was as if some power in the world itself were propelling them forward.

Save them. Serve them. Fight for them. Then find me.

The words came unbidden to his mind. In his heart, Reith knew the wind and the words were connected. *You're pushing me on.*

The thought gave him courage. He looked around at the surprised faces of the crew and his eyes met Vereinen's eyes. His master smiled at him, and Reith beckoned him over. Reith shared his suspicions with his master, who nodded in agreement.

"Yes, I think you're right," Vereinen said. "It seems whoever is calling to you is willing you onward."

"Why though?" Reith asked. "Why me?"

"Because you answered the call, Reith," Vereinen said. "Many are called, but few take up the mantle. And you wear it well. I am proud of the man you are becoming."

The wind kept howling all night long, sending the ship frantically forward with great speed.

"We will see Balkh soon," Rejnik observed at dawn. "I hope for the captain's sake it is not too late."

Eynali had become feverish in the night, and Rejnik assigned two sailors to monitor him at all times. They used rags dipped in seawater to cool him down. The captain did not regain consciousness, however.

Later that morning, they saw another ship coming toward them, heading in the direction of the Free Isles.

"Ahoy!" Rejnik called to the ship as it approached. He told one of the crewmen to raise up a red warning flag and a white surrender flag.

"We don't have a flag for, 'Stop, the place you're going has fallen to the elves.' Maybe we should have one. Anyway, humans and elves, below deck please. It's best that you lot not be seen just yet."

The humans and elves complied, but below deck, all sought the small windows to see out.

The flags and the calling out attracted the ships attention, which dropped its sail. Oars poked out from below deck and it rowed to shouting distance from the *Nighthawk*.

Rejnik's booming voice called out to the other ship, and the humans and elves below deck heard him tell the tale of the fall of the Free Isles. They heard some return shouting, but it was muffled and indistinct. After some back and forth, the shouting subsided, and they saw the oars of the other ship again drop into the water. Just then, Rejnik came below deck.

"Trading vessel," he said to their unspoken questions. "Heading for the Free Isles. 'Course, they can't now. So, they are turning back to Balkh. They just left at dawn. We will arrive in the port in a few hours' time. Until then, I think it would be best if you lot stayed here below deck. There's no use in causing a panic or inviting unpleasantness upon ourselves. Not yet at least."

"What will happen when we reach port?" Romulus asked.

"I will send a messenger to Lady Keely, the governor. I believe she will come aboard to meet with us."

"And why do you think that?" Myon asked.

"Let's just say she and the captain go way back," Rejnik said with a sly grin.

As they approached Balkh, Reith kept an eye out the small window below deck. He began to see other ships, mostly fishing vessels with large nets. Here, the land seemed to jut out into the sea. As the land passed by, he saw that it opened into a large bay. Rejnik ordered the sail be lowered and rowing to commence. Reith took his place on the rowing bench and heaved at the oar. Unfortunately, he was no longer able to see out of the window.

Eventually, the order to cease rowing was given, and Reith slumped over in his seat, utterly exhausted and dripping with sweat. Dema and Ellamora were both sitting near him in a similar situation.

The ship lurched as it struck what Reith assumed to be the dock and he heard Rejnik yelling orders to dwarves. Their gruff, unintelligible shouts and grunts drifted through the window, and he stood to get a view of Balkh.

The ship was docked on its port side, which was the side Reith was looking out. The small window gave him limited perspective, but he saw that the docks jutted out from a walled fortress. He saw a large gate standing open and he could just catch the smallest glimpse of the street beyond. There were many dwarves on the docks. Some were holding ropes and helping the *Nighthawk* to dock. Others pushed or pulled carts loaded with barrels and crates of unknown goods, either to load onto a ship or to bring into the city.

There were several soldiers around, dressed in red tunics and brown trousers. They were armed, some with swords, but most were armed only with spears. The soldiers milled around rather aimlessly, there to keep the peace, but not strictly regimented. Reith wondered how many soldiers the city had, and whether it would be enough.

The wall is a good sign. They can seal off the docks and lock down the city.

Soon, he saw the gangplank lowered and a single dwarf descended from the ship to the dock and rush off toward the city. Reith couldn't remember this dwarf's name. Soon the dwarf was rushing through the gate into the city itself. The soldiers paid him no mind.

Rejnik returned below deck a few minutes after the dwarf left.

"Shouldn't be long now," he said, taking a seat on one of the rowing benches. "I sent my best man. He's going straight to the palace."

Rejnik went back up and Romulus paced back and forth. Myon sat with his fingers together. Vereinen, sitting opposite Myon, unconsciously mirrored him. Ellamora and Dema wore tense expressions, and Reith caught Dema's eye. Dema gave him a small smile, which warmed his heart.

He resumed watching out the window. The soldiers were casually leaning against the wall beside the gate, chatting among themselves. Suddenly one of them straightened and came to attention. The others followed his lead. The sailor was returning, and beside him walked a female dwarf who could only be Lady Keely. She was nearly as tall as the sailor and wore her raven black hair braided. Sunlight gleamed off a small ringlet of gold in her hair. A dozen soldiers fell into step behind her, lined up two by two.

The lady and her escorts walked up the gangplank.

"Where is he?" Lady Keely asked rather breathlessly.

"Right in here," Rejnik said. Reith heard the door of the cabin open and footsteps, and then the muffled voices of Rejnik and Lady Keely.

Reith strained to listen but he couldn't hear a thing. The others were inclining their ears upward as well. After several minutes, they heard more footsteps and Rejnik spoke.

"Come on up."

One by one they clambered up to the deck. Reith and Vereinen were the last to go up and Vereinen gestured for Reith to go first. He blinked in the sunlight as he stood on deck and his eyes met the eyes of Lady Keely. He was taken aback. He was expecting cold, penetrating eyes but he found her eyes were full of kindness. She smiled at him.

"Welcome to Balkh," she said gesturing her arms out wide as Vereinen straightened up. "I am Lady Keely, Governor of Balkh. You are my guests and shall fear no dwarf while under my care."

"A thousand thanks, your lady," Romulus said giving a short bow. "I am Romulus, Crown Prince of the Kingdom of the Elves."

"Well met indeed," Lady Keely replied. "Rejnik has told me some of your errand, but I should hear it all tonight, over dinner at my estate." She clapped her hands twice, and four of her soldiers hopped forward. "Take the wounded captain to the hospital," she commanded. "I shall want hourly reports on his condition."

The four soldiers bowed and entered the cabin. They emerged soon after with the prone form of Eynali suspended on a stretcher between them. They carefully walked down the gangplank and then hurried off as fast as they could without jostling Eynali too much.

"Come now," Lady Keely said jubilantly, "let us retire to my estate. I am sure you all could use some refreshment."

Four of the remaining soldiers led the way down the gangplank with Lady Keely close on their heels. Rejnik and Romulus fell into step behind them. Reith, Vereinen, and the other humans and elves came next, followed by the remaining dwarven sailors. Four soldiers brought up the rear.

The dwarves on the docks bowed to the governor as she passed. Some immediately went back to their work when she had passed, but others looked on with curiosity at the newcomers behind her. Upon catching a glimpse of the humans and elves, many jaws fell open in surprise.

At the gate, soldiers stood at attention as they walked through. Reith was surprised to find the wall was nearly twenty paces wide, so that the gate was a short tunnel that they walked through to reach the city itself. The tunnel opened into an open square with well-manicured grass crisscrossed by stone paths. Around the edge of the square were shops of every sort. He smelled roasting meat from a few and saw that others had window displays of clothing, tools, and other goods. The square was filled with dwarves going about their business. When they spotted the governor, these dwarves on the square reacted much as the dwarves on the dock did, humble reverence toward Lady Keely and surprise toward the elves and humans.

Reith expected the city to rise before him, but he was disappointed. No grand buildings towered over them. In fact, it seemed to him that most buildings were a mere single-story and a scant few were two-stories.

The soldiers led the party through the square toward one of the largest buildings. It was a two-story brick building with sizable, ornate windows and a black double door. The first two soldiers each grabbed a door handle and pulled the doors open and stepped to the side. The other soldiers took up posts beside the door and Lady Keely led the way into a large open foyer, with a spiral staircase leading up to the second floor. Reith paused and turned on the spot, his eyes drinking everything in. Dema bumped into him from behind and he almost fell.

"Sorry," Dema apologized.

Lady Keely had turned to the left and Reith saw that there was a sitting room with chairs and couches. Tapestries and paintings hung on the wall. Lady Keely gestured for them to take their seats. Reith chose a wooden chair on the far side of the room. Ellamora and Dema sat beside him on either side.

Lady Keely picked up a small bell from the table beside her and shook it slightly. It dinged and shortly after Reith jumped as a door he had not noticed opened behind him. Dema looked at him and nearly laughed, and his face flushed red. A servant stepped into the room.

"You rang, my lady," he said in a gentle voice.

"Yes, Phineas," the lady said. "May we have some tea? And can you inform the cook that we shall be needing lunch shortly."

"As you wish," Phineas replied, bowing and retreating through the door, which he shut with a snap.

"Now, to business," Lady Keely said. "Rejnik, your

man gave me some of the details, but now I must have the full story. If you will."

For the next few minutes, Rejnik recounted all their adventures since leaving the Free Isles, starting with the elven fleet. He spent a considerable amount of time on the sea monster, and lauded Dema and Reith's bravery. During this part of the story, all eyes turned toward him and Dema. His face turned red once more in embarrassment, and Dema awkwardly fidgeted beside him. He was grateful when Phineas returned with tea, so he hid his face in his cup as he sipped.

"These are strange tidings indeed," Lady Keely mused, when Rejnik had finished his story. "But it seems to me that we began in the middle of the bigger story." She made eye contact with each elven and human face in turn. "Who can give me the whole story, from the beginning?"

Eyes again turned to look at Reith.

"I think young Reith has been part of this whole story from the very beginning," Myon said.

"Very well," Lady Keely answered. "Begin your tale, Reith."

"What do you know of shadows, my lady?" Reith asked, knowing her answer would set the course of his story.

At the mention of shadows, Lady Keely stiffened, and her face drained of color. "They're ... they're a legend," she said. "A nightmare meant to scare children."

"*If* they are the stuff of nightmares," Vereinen replied. "But no, they are not a legend. They are very much real. And they are dangerous. Do continue, Reith."

"A shadow attacked and burned my village of Coeden," Reith began. "I would have been killed had I not been out hunting. I lived in Coeden with Vereinen as his apprentice. He is a chronicler. He managed to escape and left me a note to meet him in Erador."

"Erador?" Keely asked sharply. "Erador in Dragonscar? The ruined ancient city?"

"The very same," Reith replied. "I reacted just as you did. I was confused. But I went."

For the next hour, he recounted all his adventures to Keely, who interjected more than once with protestations and questions. He left out the part about the voice and the grand importance of his sword, though he did mention Solzar was looking for something in Erador. He spoke extensively of his time in Crain. He had to stop for a pause when he got to the part about Gwandoeth's death.

When he finished his tale with their arrival at the port of Balkh, Lady Keely sat in silence for several long seconds. Then she spoke.

"The elves are coming to Balkh?" she asked, looking to Romulus.

"Yes," he replied gravely.

"If Balkh falls, they can go all the way to Darren Shahr. We cannot allow this to happen. We shall secure the port."

"What do you want us to do?" Romulus asked.

"Stay here, for now. Eat and be refreshed. I will return soon, and we shall have more to discuss. But now I must go prepare for the invasion." Keely's face was white and her eyes were wide. "Phineas will be back soon with your lunch." Keely rose, let out a deep breath, and nodded to them, then swept from the room, leaving the travelers behind.

Several hours later, after a scrumptious lunch of chicken and vegetable soup, Keely returned. "Plans are in motion," she stated as she sat on a couch. "We shall defend this city to the last."

"Do you know how Eynali is?" Rejnik asked, worried.

"I visited the hospital on my way back here. The physician is confident he will recover. But I am afraid his injuries are the least of his worries. The elves," she added after a pause and confused faces in the room.

"Can the city be well defended?" Romulus asked.

Keely leaned forward to look Romulus in the face. Her eyes danced like she was reading. At last, she seemed satisfied and leaned back.

"It can if our enemy does not bring significantly more numbers than ours. We do not have a strong military. We are dependent on the sea protecting us, and if the sea fails, our walls are the next line of defense. And walls may fall."

"My father seems to have sent his entire armada to take the Free Isles and Balkh," Romulus said grimly. "A thousand ships."

"That may well overwhelm us. We can only pray our strength does not fail."

"What can we do to help?" Reith asked.

"I do not know," Keely said. "While you are all battle tested, what good are a few against so many?" She held up a hand to silence the protests before they could begin. "I shall think on this tonight. I do not know how we may best use you. But rest assured, we will use you for some good purpose, mark my words."

Keely instructed Phineas to situate the travelers in various rooms in her house. Vereinen and Reith were given a room together. Reith collapsed into the soft bed in the darkness.

And then a loud trumpet blasted throughout the city.

10

Reith and Vereinen leapt out of their beds and put their traveling clothes back on quickly. Reith opened the door to the hallway and discovered the others in a similar state of alarm. Keely burst from her room, still dressed for the day.

"They're here," she said. "Stay. I will send for you if I need you."

The travelers gathered again in the living room. Phineas lit several lamps and candles for them before departing.

Rejnik paced in the center of the room. "I can't stay here," he muttered.

"I agree," Romulus said. "It is a stain on our honor to stay put."

"We already skipped the fight at the Free Isles," Rejnik added. "But at least then we had something to do."

"What can we do?" Romulus asked. "Our presence at the wall would be noticed and might cause more trouble than it's worth."

"I agree," Rejnik said, looking at the elves and humans.

"But what do the elves intend? Their intention will advise our strategy."

"My father wants to see the dwarves fall," Romulus replied. "Balkh is not his ultimate aim."

"Quite right," Myon cut in. "The fall of Balkh is not his desire. He is looking farther north."

"Darren Shahr," Rejnik said. "The Dwarven capital. It's upriver a few days. But does he mean to attack Balkh at all? Or just bypass it?"

"Which would you do, if you were the elven commander?" Romulus asked.

Rejnik gave him a hard look. "If I didn't know better, it sounds like you are seeking out our weaknesses."

"Peace, Rejnik," Myon said calmly. "I believe we have proved where our loyalties lie. We need to know the weaknesses of the city so we can know where to defend."

"Very well, very well," Rejnik grumbled. "I'll tell you what I would do if I were attacking the city with Darren Shahr as my final aim. I would take the main part of my fleet and lay siege to the city, keep the defenders pinned down, shoot fire arrows, that sort of thing. And with my fastest ships, I would go around the city and enter the south of the Banu River, which flows down from the mountains where Darren Shahr is, and make great haste upriver to catch the capital city unawares."

"Would it work?" Romulus asked.

"Depends on how fast those ships can move upriver and what sort of scouts Darren Shahr has out. Right now, I assume them to be unaware. A small force could catch them unprepared and win a mighty victory while the rest lay siege to Balkh."

"I believe this may be King Koinas' strategy," Myon mused. "It's smart, it's tactical."

"So, what can we do to stop it?" Romulus asked, with a tone of desperation in his voice.

Reith, who had been listening and contemplating, piped up. "What if we blocked the river?"

"Now there's an idea," Rejnik said, leaning back in his chair.

"Can it be done?" Romulus inquired.

"Oh, certainly," Rejnik said. "The river is very shallow here by the sea. If we sunk a ship or two, we could block the way fairly easily."

"What are we waiting for, then?" Romulus declared, standing to his feet. "Let's go."

"Follow me," Rejnik said as he got to his feet.

Rejnik ushered them through the front door of Lady Keely's house and into the square. There were many dwarves running toward the sea, and no one paid them any mind.

Rejnik led them to the east, parallel to the sea. Soon they were off the square and on a main road jogging. A few dwarves were running the other way, toward the square.

They came at last to the eastern wall of the city. Rejnik led them upstairs to the top of the wall. From here they could see the moonlight illuminating the whole city. Reith saw they were at the southeast corner of the city, right at the mouth of the Banu River, which flowed silently into the ocean. Along the southern wall of the city gleamed a multitude of torches, signaling where the defenders were. Out to sea, Reith could faintly see a few ships and knew that more were hidden in the gloom.

"Come on," Rejnik said, beckoning them to the edge of the wall by the river. Reith didn't know what was happening until he was right at the edge and saw a narrow staircase was built into the side of the wall leading down to a flat sandy area beside the river. They hurried down the stairs and Reith saw that many large, flat barges were pulled up to the bank of the river and tied to wooden stakes driven into the ground.

"We need two or three of these barges to sink right here at the mouth of the river," Rejnik explained. "If we row them out into the stream and drop anchor, that will keep them from being washed out to the sea where they'd be useless to us. Once they are in place, we can light them on fire. They will sink and damage any ship that tries to pass."

"Do we have enough time?" Romulus asked.

Rejnik shrugged. "We have no other option."

"Alright, let's do it."

"Leave your weapons on the shore," Rejnik directed.

Rejnik ordered a few of his sailors, plus Reith and Romulus to hop in one barge, and assigned the others to another barge. A long oar was shoved into Reith's hands and they soon were paddling out into the river. Rejnik bore a huge iron anchor and gave another to one of the other dwarves. They rowed toward the other bank and then turned the barge to face upstream. Rejnik dropped his anchor off the back of the ship. When he felt it hit the bottom, he ordered them to stop rowing. Slowly the barge began to drift backward, then it jerked under them as the anchor caught and Reith was nearly thrown into the water. He regained his balance and now the front of the barge was drifting to their left.

"Now!" Rejnik called, and the other dwarf tossed his anchor in. Reith was ready now, so when this one caught, he kept his balance as the barge jerked below him. The barge was now in place, perpendicular to the river.

The other barge was now out in the stream, and Rejnik dove into the river and saw to it. His men hauled him up and he soon had executed the same maneuver and that barge too was in place, beside the first, so the whole width of the river was nearly blocked.

"Come on!" Rejnik called to Reith's ship, and Reith and the others made their way across from one barge to the other. Near the shore, they jumped in and waded to the beach.

"Archers, get ready." Rejnik went to the remaining barges, rummaged around for a minute, and found some old rags and a canister of oil. He tore the rags into strips and wrapped these around the arrows of the archers. Reith was assigned to shoot an arrow into the first ship. With the cloth in place, Rejnik brought the oil around and had each archer dip their rag covered arrow tips in it. Then he brought a torch. He lit Reith's first and Reith aimed and fired his arrow into the side of the first barge. The flame sputtered for a moment, and then blazed to life. Other arrows hit the first barge and it was soon ablaze.

Romulus sent a flaming arrow into the second barge, and it too was soon on fire.

"What in the fires of the underworld do you think you're doing?"

Fire and moonlight illuminated Lady Keely and made it look like her eyes were literally sparking in anger.

"We're saving the kingdom!" Rejnik protested.

"I told you to say in my house," Keely said, and Reith couldn't tell if it was the fire or her radiating anger which was giving off heat.

"Ah, well," Rejnik shrugged, lost for word. "We did what we had to."

Keely opened her mouth to speak, but another voice cut her off.

"Leave him alone, love." Eynali stepped into the fire light behind her.

"Captain!" Rejnik exclaimed.

Keely turned to look at Eynali.

"Nali! What are you doing up?"

"I'm doing much better," he said. "And I wanted to see what all the commotion was about."

Keely flung herself at the captain and they locked in a passionate embrace.

After several long seconds, Rejnik called out, "Oi!"

The couple broke apart.

"I'm still furious with you," Keely declared, giving Rejnik that sparks flying from her eyes look again.

"In coming!" Eynali called out and pointed out to sea.

Small warships were rowing swiftly toward the burning barges. Several others waited out in the harbor.

"It's going to try and break through!" Reith yelled, realizing what was happening. He strapped his sword to his hip and took up his bow once more.

"More flaming arrows!" Rejnik called out and began tearing more cloth. The ship came closer and closer and the oars were going in and out of the water at a furious rate. With an almighty crunch, it smashed between both barges. The barges lurched, held back by their anchors in the sand river bottom. The ship stuck, and fire from the barges licked at its sides.

"Let's ignite her!" Rejnik yelled, and soon a half dozen flaming arrows were buried in the side of the ship.

Realizing the cause was lost, elves began to leap from the deck into the water below. The defenders on the beach calmly picked off any elves brave enough to jump into the water on their side. The others learned their lesson and went off the other side and soon were swept out to sea to be picked up by the other ships.

"That ship is stuck fast," Rejnik said, as the elven ship sat lower and lower in the water. It appeared the barges had cut large gashes in her hull, which were now filling with water. The rigging and the mast were now aflame.

"Very good," Keely said sulkily. "You are lucky your ridiculous plan worked."

"Oh, give it a rest," Eynali said. "The plan was great. The elves can't sail upriver now. Darren Shahr is safer because of it."

"But what of my city?" Keely said. "There are hundreds of ships in the harbor."

"We must send word to Darren Shahr," Eynali said. "Either they can send reinforcements or they can defend themselves if Balkh falls."

"Yes, you're right," Keely said sadly. "I hope for our sake it's the former. Rejnik, will you go for us?"

"Of course, my lady," Rejnik answered. "I shall need a crew."

"It appears you already have one," Eynali said, eyeing the others on the beach. "You are a true captain now, no longer a first mate."

"Thank you, captain," Rejnik replied. "Will you stay here?"

"I will defend my city and my lady until I have no more breath in my lungs," Eynali declared.

"Get supplies from the huts here at the river," Keely said. "There should be dried food enough to get you to Darren Shahr. Make great haste and come back to our aid soon."

"Very well, my lady," Rejnik replied. "Alright, you heard the lady, load up!"

Rejnik claimed the barge farthest upriver and they soon began to raid the supply huts and loaded food and beer on the barge. When the barge was heavy laden, Keely and Eynali came down to say their farewells.

"Come back soon, Rejnik," Keely said, her earlier harshness gone.

"Good fortune, captain," Eynali said with a smile.

"And also with you," Rejnik replied and the two of them embraced.

"And farewell, all of you," Keely cried out to the rest of them. "Our meeting was short but may the Creator smile upon each of you."

Eynali shook hands all around with the humans and elves.

"Until we meet again," he said to Reith.

"Now go, and go swiftly," Keely called out, and she and Eynali walked back up the beach to the stairs.

"We will row in shifts," Rejnik said. "Half of you, grab an oar."

Reith again found himself with an oar and stood on the port side of the barge. Dema and Ellamora sat beside each other near him. Rejnik cut the rope holding the barge to the land and it began to drift out into the water.

"Here we go again," Dema said.

"What do you mean?" Ellamora asked.

"Once again, we are fleeing before an attacking force," Dema said with disgust. "I just want to fight."

"We'll have to fight, eventually," Ellamora said. "Maybe we'll come down this river in a few days with the dwarven host to come to Balkh's aid."

"I hope so," Dema replied. "I am tired of running from those who killed Kydar and those who killed everyone at Suthrond."

"We are making our mark on the war," Reith said as he pulled the oar through the water. "The winds have willed us this far."

The nearly full moon arched high over the world as they paddled against the gently flowing stream. Soon the lights of Balkh disappeared around a river bend. The air grew cooler. Dema and Ellamora fell asleep on the barge as Reith and the others rowed northward, to Darren Shahr.

When Reith awoke the next morning, the sun was high in the sky. To the port side, the river was lined with thick trees. To the starboard side, a flat plain stretched out for miles and miles. Reith turned and saw he was sitting near Vereinen who was standing and rowing with great effort.

"Let me take that, Vereinen," Reith said with concern.

"No, no, dear boy, it is my burden to bear."

"Nonsense," Reith said, grabbing the oar from him and gesturing for Vereinen to take a seat. Vereinen obliged with a grunt and then a long, contented sigh.

"Thank you, Reith." Vereinen said when he had settled on the floor of the barge. "I am not as young as I once was."

Reith gave him a sidelong glance as his oar cut through the water.

"Tell me a story, master," Reith said, for a moment pretending that he was back in their shared home in Coeden.

"Oh?" Vereinen replied. "Let's see, what about the Three Century War?"

"Sounds good to me."

"Well, after the fall of Erador," Vereinen began, "the three races separated from one another and consolidated their own kingdoms. At that time, Kal-Epharion was the dwarven capital city. Galismoor and Sardis were the capitals of the human kingdom and the elven kingdom respectively."

"I didn't know Kal-Epharion wasn't always a human city," Reith said.

"Oh yes, it was dwarven for a long time. The name itself comes from the old dwarven tongue. Anyway, as I was saying, the human king had his eyes set on a coast-to-coast empire. So, he mustered his troops and marched east across the desert. Ahead of him, he sent a dozen highly skilled assassins. His plan was for the assassins to kill the dwarven queen and then march right into the city with his army. It was a good plan, but he forgot one thing."

"What did he forget?" Reith asked.

"The elves. The elves had scouts all throughout the land, keeping tabs on the other races. When these scouts saw the humans leaving Galismoor to march east to Kal-Epharion, they raced back to their own land with great haste. The fastest elven messengers were dispatched to Sardis. When the king heard Galismoor was under protected, he marched his army north. They lay siege to Galismoor, but Galismoor was locked up tight. They weathered the storm."

"Meanwhile, the human king's campaign in Kal-Epharion was going well. The assassins had done their work, and the way was clear. But the people of Kal-Epharion were not as unorganized as he would have liked. They put up a fight. For a month, they held out, until the city wall was finally breached and the humans took over. It was a successful mission, but it cost the human king more than he could afford to lose."

"He disarmed the city and left a shell force in charge. Then he and what remained of his army marched back to Galismoor. The elves were on the lookout and saw them coming. They intercepted all messengers from Galismoor so the human king had no idea what he was walking back into. At the edge of the desert, the elves attacked. All day the two armies struggled, neither gaining the upper hand. When night fell, the elves fell back."

"Now the human king realized his folly. He ordered his men to march through the night and return to Galismoor. They arrived to find the city was under siege. He recklessly ordered a charge against the elves and paid dearly for his folly. He himself was slain and his army lost many men. The elves proudly displayed his body to the defenders of Galismoor, to hurt morale. But now the humans had a new leader. They had a young queen. She was but fourteen years of age. Her name was Briana."

"What happened then?" Reith asked, and he saw that he wasn't Vereinen's only listener. Anyone who didn't have an oar in hand was gathering around them to hear the tale.

"She did something incredibly brave. That night, under cover of darkness, she donned a cloak and exited the city by way of a secret tunnel known only to the kings and queens of Galismoor. She bypassed the elven army and came to the camp of her father's army, who were nursing wounds a few miles from the city. She stood among them and gave a rousing speech. Her words have been lost to history, but the impact of her words has reverberated down through the years. She rallied her troops and conducted a midnight raid of the elven camp. For a fortnight, she and that ragtag army attacked by night and retreated many miles away. This way the elves couldn't go and fight them without leaving the city. Eventually she dealt such heavy losses to the elves that they had no choice but to withdraw. Galismoor was saved."

"But that wasn't the end of the war, right?" Reith asked remembering that it was called the Three Centuries War.

"Correct," Vereinen said with a smile. "The war dragged on and on between all the races. After Briana's victory, the elves fell back to their land, but the dwarves rose and tried to retake Kal-Epharion. Kings and queens and all sides rose and desired victory for their race, but after Briana, the war was three hundred years of futility. No one gained the upper hand. Kal-Epharion remained with the humans, as it is to this day. And all the races retreated and remained separate from one another, at least until these days we see now."

"Our sages foretell of a warrior who will arise and reclaim Kal-Epharion for the dwarves," Rejnik said.

"I am afraid that Kal-Epharion has passed from the hands of men and is now a city of Shadows," Vereinen said, shaking his head in sorrow. "Solzar arose to power there. It is where he began his transformation into the monster he is today."

"All the more reason to liberate it and take it back for the dwarves," Rejnik replied. He motioned for Reith to toss him his oar, which he did. Reith gratefully sat down beside his master.

"Is there any hope?" Reith asked.

"There is always hope, Reith."

"I mean is there any hope of things going back to the way they were?"

"Once the dam is broken, you can't get the exact same water back," Vereinen said. "It has moved on. Sure, you can repair the damage and get new water, but what once was can never be again."

"Will we ever return to Coeden?" Reith asked again, a desperate longing welling up inside of him as he spoke.

"Return to what?" Vereinen asked. "Our friends and neighbors are gone, all that's left is an empty house for us."

"When all of this is over, what will become of us?"

"Me, me, I shall do what I have always done. I will write down the stories of the peoples of Terrasohnen. Maybe in the Free Isles, if there is anything left of them now. Or I could go back to Galismoor. It has been my home before, it can be my home again."

"And what about me?" Reith asked.

"Oh, we don't need to worry about you right now, Reith," Vereinen said kindly. "You have a destiny. You have a voice guiding you on. You will be alright."

"So you think we will survive this ordeal?"

"Oh no, I didn't say that. I said you would be alright. Being alright is different than being alive. Dying in the pursuit of a worthy goal is better than living in pursuit of an unworthy one."

"Your words are not comforting," Reith said as his mind wandered to what death might feel like. He brushed that thought away almost immediately.

"Reith," Vereinen began again, "there are far worse things in this world than dying."

Reith's mind went to Solzar and his dead, gray eyes. He shuddered. "I guess you're right," he said.

"If you are following the light, even if you die, you will be alright."

11

They continued to row all day. The stream was gentle, so they made tremendous progress. By late afternoon, Rejnik was so pleased that he called for a halt so that everyone could get some rest on the dry land. After some debate, it was decided that they would camp on the eastern side of the river, the side with the plains. There they would have the best vantage point to see approaching enemies. But first, they beached the barge on the western side and chopped some firewood from the trees which grew near the river. The barge now laden with wood was quickly rowed across the river to the flat and bare side.

Three fires and a guard rotation were set. Reith was pleased to find he had escaped guard duty this night but would have it the next night if they stopped. Romulus and Ellamora took the first watch and paraded around the outside of the fires while the rest bedded down between them. Reith was joined by Vereinen on one side and Dema on the other. As the sun set, snores began to ring out from the other sleepers. Reith soon heard the familiar cadence of Vereinen's breathing and knew his master was asleep.

He rolled onto his other side to try and get comfortable and found he was staring into the firelight reflecting eyes of Dema. The firelight also gleamed on her dark cheeks, and it took Reith a moment to realize she was crying.

"What's wrong?" he asked quietly.

"I miss him so much," she said as more tears fell from her eyes.

"Me too," he said. If he was honest with himself, he hadn't spent much time thinking of Kydar since they had fled from Sardis. When Kydar came to mind, a wave of grief would wash over him, but Reith had been able to tuck that grief away in a spare corner of his mind.

Better to keep that closet door shut.

"I heard you talking to Vereinen earlier," she whispered to him. "What will happen to me?"

"You'll come with me, of course," Reith said without a moment of hesitation.

"And where are you going?" she asked.

"Wherever I am led," he replied. "And you are more than welcome to come with."

"I want to kill him first," Dema whispered again, barely audible above the snores of the rest of the camp.

"Let's thwart him first, then you can kill him," Reith said with a smile. She smiled back through her sorrow. He reached forward and took her hand. He gave it a squeeze and she squeezed right back.

"Don't leave me," Dema said.

"Never," Reith answered, not knowing if she meant right this evening or on into the future, but either way, he wasn't going anywhere. "Reith and Dema, Dema and Reith, Bane of Shadows."

"I like that," she said, and squeezed his hand again.

They lay like that, hand in hand, while the stars danced above them and the moon shone its gentle light.

Eventually, Reith heard Dema's breathing slowed into the rhythmic breath of sleep too. He closed his eyes and retreated within himself, where the only real thing in the world was the hand clasped in his.

At dawn, Rejnik woke them all by banging on a metal pot. Reith realized that he and Dema were still hand in hand. They separated before anyone saw and they all retook their positions on the barge. Rejnik commanded they push the barge back in the stream, and soon they were off again.

As they were going, Myon asked, "When will we get to Darren Shahr?"

"Day after next, or maybe the one after that," Rejnik grunted as he pulled his oar through the water. "Hard to tell."

"How long can the forces at Balkh maintain their position?" Romulus asked.

"Hopefully long enough."

To their left, on the port side of the ship, the woodlands grew rougher, and occasionally a patch of rock jutted out of the ground as if some large beast from below were sticking them upward through the roof of the underworld. In the distance, Reith saw the white peaks of distant mountains.

As he rowed, Reith looked ahead at Dema who was rowing in front of him on the barge. He remembered her hand in his and wondered what she thought about it all. They hadn't spoken directly since last night, and he didn't know what to make of it.

All day, they took turns rowing their barge upriver. Whenever Reith had a break, he removed his shoes and dangled his feet in the water off the back of the barge. It was cold as steel in the winter, but very refreshing.

As dusk approached, Rejnik ordered another stop. Again, they chopped some wood from the trees on the western side of the river before crossing over to the gentler plains.

Reith remembered he had watch, so he volunteered to take the first shift. To his surprise, Ellamora volunteered to watch with him, even though she had taken the first watch the night before.

"I insist, Myon," she said when the older elf protested. "I will take your turn. Get some sleep."

And so, as the others hunkered down for bed, Reith and Ellamora paced around the camp together, keeping watch.

"Keep your eyes away from the fires," Ellamora instructed. "If you look directly at the fire, you will be night blind."

"Good point," he said, and took care to keep his back to the camp.

They paced the perimeter in silence for the next half hour. The only sounds they heard were the snores of their companions and the river gently rushing beside them.

"I saw you and Dema last night," Ellamora said simply, breaking the silence.

"Oh," Reith said lamely, not knowing what exactly to say.

"It's alright," she said. "I just didn't know you felt that way about each other."

"What way?"

"You know," she said, somewhat uncomfortably, "romantically."

"I don't know if it's quite like that," Reith protested.

"It sure seems that way to me," Ellamora said. "I kept an eye on you both today. You had eyes for only her."

"Did not," Reith protested again.

"Oh, yes you did! And she had eyes only for you."

"I didn't see that," Reith said.

"And she didn't see you," Ellamora pointed out. "There's something between you, admit it."

"I think you're overthinking this," he said.

"No, I'm not. There's something going on and has been since the battle with the sea monster."

He remembered back to that dreadful battle, how Dema had stepped in front of him and dealt the fatal blow. And then he remembered their embrace after.

"Maybe there is," he admitted.

"Maybe?" she asked. "Are all human boys so thick?"

"I'm not thick," he protested. This felt awfully like their first sparing sessions with a sword all those weeks ago. She was keeping him off guard, putting him on his heels.

Size up your opponent, he thought.

"It's okay," Ellamora said. "I think you two make a cute couple."

"Oh, we're not a couple," Reith stammered.

"Not a couple *yet*," Ellamora replied with a grin. "Someday, maybe. If you two wake up. Speaking of waking, what did you two talk about before you fell asleep last night?"

"The future," Reith answered.

"An easy subject if ever there was one."

Reith decided to push forward and put Ellamora on the defensive.

"When all this is over," he said, gesturing vaguely around them, "where will you go, what will you do?"

"You're assuming there will be a world left for us. The Shadow appears intent on burning it all down."

"He won't be able to if we stay ahead of him," Reith said with more confidence than he really felt. It unnerved him how closely behind him Solzar was since that day back in Coeden. He had followed Reith to Erador, beat him to Sardis, and now was commanding troops across the world which were dogging his steps. *That's a big if.*

"So, we beat him to Darren Shahr, and then what? There's nowhere else to run."

"Well, if you put it that way …"

"One way or another, we will stop running soon," Ellamora said. "There's no use thinking beyond that."

"No, I suppose not," Reith agreed.

"I meant for me," Ellamora said. "You have, I don't know, a destiny, or fate, guiding you on. Your quest isn't over yet, not until you find *it*."

"Fighting comes first," Reith said, remembering the constant refrain of *Save them. Serve them. Fight for them. Then find me.*

"It sure seems like you will survive the fighting though," Ellamora pointed out.

"Does it work like that?" Reith asked, unsure. "Destiny or fate, does it work like that? Don't I have a choice? What if I don't fight?"

"But would you, not fight, I mean?" Ellamora asked. "It's not like you."

"Or what if I did fight, but I ran into battle with no concern for my own safety? Would I be invincible? What if I died?"

"The God of Light holds you in his hand," Ellamora said. "Whether you live or die, it'll all work out for good in the end."

"I hope you're right," Reith replied. "I just feel helpless, out of control, like a game piece on a board."

"How do you think Briana felt?" Ellamora asked.

"How did she feel when her father was dead and she snuck out of the city to rally her troops?"

"I suppose she felt a bit helpless and out of control," Reith answered.

"And if she felt like a piece on a board, you better believe she felt that she was the most important piece on her own board. You've started down this path, you owe it to yourself to finish it. Not because of fate, or destiny, or because someone is controlling you, but because of who you are. You will not be happy unless you walk as far along the path as you can."

"Thanks, Ellamora," Reith said gratefully.

They passed the rest of their guard shift in silence. Nothing disturbed the night. After they had been replaced, Reith lay down and thought about all Ellamora had told him.

Maybe she's right about me and Dema, he mused. *But fighting and finding come first. If I come back from that, maybe.*

Then he remembered Dema's hand in his and he felt a blush come to his face. He was glad of the cover of darkness because he started grinning like an idiot at the memory.

Around noon the following day, a dwarf at the front of the barge gave a shout.

"What is it?" Rejnik asked, hurrying forward.

"A horseman, captain," the dwarf said, pointing forward and toward the land on the starboard side of the barge. All eyes turned in that direction and Reith was just able to make out a horse and rider scurrying away upriver.

"Good spot, lad," Rejnik praised. "No need to worry, all," he said, raising his voice so all could hear. "It's simply a scout from Darren Shahr. We are getting close to the city. We may have company later, though. Once he reaches the city, they will dispatch a barge or two. Still, onward!"

The news that they were close to the city gave the rowers a second wind, and Reith felt that they sped along faster now.

At midafternoon, another shout came from the front of the barge, and all turned to see another barge coming down the river toward them.

"Beach on the starboard side!" Rejnik called out, and the rowers turned toward the bank and ran the barge aground. Soon the barge was held fast and all disembarked on the land. The other barge beached fifty yards north of their position. Fifty dwarves jumped down, all armed with bows on their backs and swords at their hips and lightly armored. Rejnik walked forward to meet them, his hands held out from his body in a posture of peace. He met them far enough away that Reith could not make out anything that was said. After a few minutes, Rejnik approached with the dwarven captain.

"I am Commander Seim," the other dwarf declared. He was an inch shorter than Rejnik, and he had a long, red beard. His metal cap had a single spike sticking straight up in the air. "Rejnik has informed me of the assault on Balkh and the Free Isles. We are grateful that you have come to warn us. We are but a couple of hours from Darren Shahr. We will board our barge and my soldiers will row us back to the city. While we are on the barge, and when we reach the city, you humans and elves shall remain unarmed until the king has deemed you dwarf-friend. Is this agreeable to all?"

The humans and the elves looked toward Romulus, who gave a curt nod. Reith didn't like it, but he understood.

"It's okay," Rejnik said. "No one shall harm you."

"Let us cut this barge free," Seim said. "If the elves have made it to the river, let's put something in their path."

The spare barge was cut free, and soon all were on the dwarves' barge. The weapons of Reith and the others were locked under a hatch on deck and they sat down in the center, away from the dwarf soldiers who took up rowing positions. They set off faster than they had been traveling, on account of the extra rowers.

As the afternoon wore on, Reith became aware that there was a white noise in his ears but he couldn't remember when it had started. The barge was heading toward a bend in the river and the water was rougher here. As the barge rounded the bend, Reith and the others gasped. A huge waterfall stood in their way, cascading water down into the river.

Seim issued and order, and the dwarves rowed toward the bank near the waterfall and ran the barge up onto the sandy beach. The barge lurched, and Dema tumbled into Reith, knocking him over. They straightened themselves up and saw Ellamora laughing, but Reith couldn't make out any sound over the roaring of the water. Seim was pointing toward the bank, and his meaning was clear.

They were allowed to retrieve their weapons and soon, everyone was off the barge and deafened by the tumult of the falls. Seim and half the dwarven soldiers walked along the bank toward the waterfall. Reith and the others followed. Flecks of water pelted them and soon Reith was soaked. The dwarves kept walking and soon disappeared from Reith's view. Romulus disappeared too, then Myon, then Vereinen. At last, Reith saw that there was a path that hugged the cliff wall, creating a safe passage behind the waterfall. He edged along it and soon found himself in a large chamber. Torches on the wall illuminated the chamber and Reith saw the ceiling of the chamber was at least thirty feet high. At the back of the chamber, away from the falls, a staircase was cut into the wall which led up to a trapdoor in the ceiling.

The roar of the waterfall was too great for speech and the stone chamber caused the sound to echo. Seim beckoned for them to follow up the stairs. He led the way and opened the trapdoor. Sunlight streamed down through the hole. Reith dutifully climbed the steps behind Vereinen and soon was blinking in the sunlight again. Off to his right was the waterfall and the plains opened on one side and the mountains and forests swallowed up the view on the other side.

"Welcome to Darren Shahr," Seim called out over the sound of the falls.

Reith turned toward the city itself. It's dark gray stone wall towered dozens of feet above them and crimson banners and pennants flew above the rampart. A great wooden gate stood before them, shut fast. Seim marched to it and hammered it hard three times. Then it began to open outward with great creaks.

The opening gate slowly revealed a cobblestoned courtyard beyond. Seim's soldiers formed rank and marched into the city, and Seim waited behind to walk in with the travelers. The elves and humans instinctively drew close to one another for perceived security. Seim beckoned them in.

They walked through the gate, under the stone wall of the city. The wall was at least a half dozen paces thick. Upon entering the courtyard, Reith gasped. The city of Darren Shahr rose above them, part fortress and part cathedral. Tall stone towers jutted up before them equally formidable and beautiful. He counted at least a dozen of these spires. Above them all, a central spire rose out of the city, twice as tall as any of the rest.

There was another stone wall across the courtyard, with yet another wooden gate set into it. Seim's platoon split in two and created a tunnel of sorts between them, through which Seim and the others walked. Seim again banged on this gate, and it opened with a creak as well. As it was opening, Reith turned on the spot to look around, and saw that about twenty dwarven soldiers were on top of the wall by the first gate. Beside them were two large spokes with ropes. The dwarves were turning these and closing the outer gate. It closed with a bang.

Seim led them through the second gate. Beyond this gate was a narrow street that went left and right. He took them to the right about a hundred paces to a small door set in the wall. He opened it and led them into a large room that looked like a dining room for large companies of soldiers.

"Please, discard your weapons in the corner," Seim said, gesturing to a bare corner of the room to their right. They obeyed and soon stood unarmed in the center of the room. "Take a seat," Seim gestured. "Food shall be brought for you, while I send for King Rendar."

The travelers form Balkh took seats at a wooden table near the center of the room. Reith sat beside Dema on one side and Vereinen on the other. Romulus sat across from him and Myon beside Romulus. Within a minute of sitting, platters of round loaves of bread and wheels of yellow cheese were placed before them. Grapes on the vine surrounded the bread and cheese, and all dug into the meal. They ate in silence, and the only sounds were the sounds of knives on the cheese and bread and satisfied chewing.

When they were nearly finished, the door opposite the

one through which they entered burst open and a dwarf dressed in a fine red and yellow tunic stepped in.

"His royal highness, King Rendar of the Dwarves" the finely dressed dwarf announced.

Romulus rose to his feet and gestured for the others to do the same. Reith hastily dropped the piece of bread that was in his left hand, though he did stuff the cheese in his right into his mouth.

The herald dwarf stepped to the side and bowed toward the door as King Rendar stepped into the room. He was taller than any dwarf Reith had yet seen. His brown hair and beard had an auburn hue, and his beard was tied with a simple ribbon at its point. On his head was a golden crown in which were set several large gemstones. His robe was long and colored like rich, dark wine. Seim bowed as well to his king.

The king searched each new face before him. He held Reith's gaze for an uncomfortable second, before moving on. When he reached Romulus, he gasped.

"You!" he shouted. "Guards! Arrest this vile assassin!"

12

———

Guards armed with spears rushed into the room from behind King Rendar and circled the table, spears pointed at the newcomers.

"What is going on?" Rejnik asked as the guards closed in on Romulus. "This man is a dwarf friend!"

"Silence!" Rendar yelled. "He is no friend of dwarves, nor are any of his kin."

"I bring no treachery," Romulus said softly. "I have disavowed my father, if it's anything to you."

This took Rendar aback. He stared at Romulus as though contemplating something. Then he turned to one of the guards and said, "Bring in the high security prisoner." Then to Romulus he said, "Do you know who I hold in my dungeon?"

"I have no idea," Romulus replied, looking very confused. Reith's eyes kept going back and forth between the elven prince and the dwarf king, trying to figure out what on Terrasohnen was going on.

The door behind the king opened and two guards

walked through, each holding the arm of someone wearing a black hood over their face. The prisoner was shirtless and dirty and had scars and bruises all over his chest and arms. He either couldn't or wouldn't walk and the guards dragged him in on his knees, his feet trailing uselessly behind him. A chain connected to manacles around his wrists.

The guards dropped the prisoner to the floor and he made no effort to stop his fall, and the chains clanged on the stone floor.

"Remove the prisoner's hood," Rendar said. One of the guards bent down and pulled the hood off. His hair was long, dirty, and matted and hung in front of his face like a curtain. "Look at us, prisoner," Rendar said to him.

The prisoner shook his head and his hair parted to reveal his face. The face was bruised and dirty like the rest of him, but beneath the dirt was a face the exact double of the face of Romulus.

"Brother," the prisoner said in a low voice, gravelly from lack of use, upon seeing Romulus.

Reith and the others were completely shocked. *Romulus has a brother?*

"Remus?" Romulus asked, amazed. "But you're supposed to be dead."

"Is that what your father told you?" Rendar said sharply.

"He said there had been a hunting accident," Romulus said, still gazing in wonder at his brother.

"A hunting accident?" Rendar spat. "No, he's an assassin, sent by his father to kill me and my family."

"Why is he still alive?" Romulus asked. "He's been here two years."

"We do not execute our prisoners," Rendar said. "We do not believe it honors the Creator."

"Then have you tortured him?" Romulus asked. "Look at him, he looks like you beat him."

"I can assure you, we did not do that too him," Rendar replied. "The prince attempted a foolhardy escape last week. He made it to the top of one of the walls, and when he was cornered, he jumped."

"I am not here to assassinate you," Romulus told the king. "I am here to save you."

"Save me? From what?" the king asked.

"From my father," Romulus said. "He has been hoodwinked by a Shadow."

"A Shadow?" King Rendar said, shocked. "How do you know?"

"I have seen him, spoken to him," Romulus said. "It's kind of a long story."

"Do tell," Rendar said. He took a seat at the head of their table and gestured for all to sit down again. The guards retreated to the edge of the room, ready for anything. Remus sat slumped on the floor near the table with his guards beside him.

Romulus launched into the story of Solzar's arrival at court and then the arrival of Reith, Ellamora, Dema, and Kydar. He quickly told of Reith's story of Solzar attacking Coeden and his journey to Sardis. He left out the Erador part, however.

Romulus continued telling of their flight from Sardis to Amisos and then by ship to the Free Isles.

"We fled for Balkh, and the Free Isles fell to the elven fleet. When we were in Balkh, the fleet arrived there. They tried to make a break for it up the river, but we sank barges blocking them. Lady Keely bade us make haste to Darren Shahr to warn you. We do not know if Balkh has fallen to the elves yet or not."

"You truly have turned on your father," Rendar said in wonder. "Why?"

"Because the Shadow is falling on him, too," Romulus answered. "Dark powers are at work in the world. The God of Light bids me fight them."

"That is noble, Prince Romulus," King Rendar replied. "If there were more like you, Terrasohnen could achieve lasting and harmonious peace."

"There are more like him," Myon said. "Look before you, your highness. Humans, elves, and dwarves have come together to fight the shadow and bring peace to our world."

"Never in my days did I think such a peace would happen," Rendar said.

"But it's not achieved yet," Romulus said. "Balkh is either under siege or has fallen. Elven troops marched north out of Sardis as well."

"There is much to decide," Rendar said. "Seim, send a barge south to find out what has happened to Balkh. Light arms, for speed. If Balkh is still under siege we must go to her aid. If Balkh has fallen, we must defend our city. In the meantime, let us find comfortable rooms for these guests. If you don't mind, we will keep your weapons until we deem the time is ripe for you to have them. Stay here tonight. Breakfast will be provided shortly after dawn, and then we shall have a council. Seim's barge may have news for us then. You all are invited, and I shall bring several of my generals and commanders, as well as my queen."

"Thank you," Romulus said, giving a short bow to the king.

King Rendar gave word for the guards to take Remus away, and they dragged him off. Romulus looked after him wistfully. "Oh Remus …"

A dwarven steward entered the room as King Rendar swept from it.

"This way please," the steward called to them.

Reith was put in a bunk room with Romulus, Vereinen, and Brauron. The room was small and dim, lit by a lone torch on a bracket on the wall beside the door. It was all stone except for a large, faded rug in the center of the room. There were small beds lining the wall in the room. Reith chose one near the far corner of the room.

Romulus sat on one of the beds and leaned forward his hands dangling between his legs.

"I never knew he was an assassin," Romulus said. "Father said he had died during a hunting accident. We had no body to bury."

"Your father was determined to see King Rendar fall for years," Brauron replied. "But even I did not know about this."

"It complicates our position here in ways I could not have foreseen," Romulus said. "I don't know if I should have come here."

"All we can do is make the best decision with the information we have before us," Vereinen replied.

"I feel like a prisoner myself," Romulus said with a sigh. "No weapons, locked inside a fortress whose king is ill-inclined toward my person. Who knows how this will end?"

"I hope Balkh has not fallen," Vereinen replied. "It seems our position is more precarious if your father's soldiers are bearing down on Darren Shahr."

"Let us pray for Balkh," Romulus answered.

They slept well in their beds, their first real beds in quite some time. As the sunlight began to lighten up the room through the small window set high on the wall, the steward arrived to bring them back down to breakfast.

Platters of eggs and sausages were laid before them, and Reith heartily dove in, piling his plate high with generous helpings of both. Dema sat beside him and was more subdued in the breaking of her fast.

"Sleep well?" Reith asked her between mouthfuls.

She pushed eggs around her plate with her fork. "I slept okay," she finally replied.

"What's up?" Reith asked, putting his fork down and turning his attention fully to Dema.

"I don't know," she replied. "I just have a really bad feeling, like something bad is coming for us."

"Oh," Reith said, unsure of what else to say.

"Don't ignore that feeling," Rejnik butted in, leaning across the table to officially join the conversation. "It may be the Guardians are speaking to you."

He let the thought hang over them, and Dema's eyes widened with fear.

"Or it could be that you're just hungry," Rejnik said with a chuckle. "Eat up!"

Dema went back to pushing her food around her plate and Reith went back to his food, but his mind was still on Dema.

What if something bad is coming for us? Then he remembered where he was. *Of course something bad is coming. The elves are going to attack Darren Shahr sooner or later.*

A few minutes later, Rendar strode into the room. He was dressed plainly in a black tunic and black trousers, and no crown adorned his head. Still, there was a kingly air about him. Behind him came a female dwarf in a casual green dress. In her wake came two smaller dwarven girls, clad like the older one.

"Allow me to introduce the queen," Rendar said, gesturing to the dwarven lady. "Queen Kalis, and my two daughters, Princesses Helma and Fiara."

Now that the queen was closer, Reith saw that she bore a startling resemblance to Lady Keely of Balkh.

"That's Lady Keely's sister," Rejnik whispered, leaning across the table again.

"My lady," Romulus said, rising from his seat and then bowing to kiss the dwarven queen's ring. "I am Prince Romulus of the elven kingdom."

"I am pleased to make your acquaintance," the queen said in a graceful and soft voice. "As long as you bear us no ill will, we shall get along just fine."

"Perhaps I am alone in my family in wishing the royal dwarven family a long and prosperous reign," Romulus said with princely grace. "Peace is my desire, above all."

"And peace you shall have, oh worthy prince," Queen Kalis replied.

"When you are all done eating," King Rendar began, "we shall retire to a more comfortable side chamber for our council."

Soon they all finished eating and the steward ushered them into a large side room, with a large rectangular table in the center. Maps adorned the wall, and comfortable chairs surrounded the table. Rendar was sitting at the head of the table with Kalis to his right and three dwarf lords lined up on his left. Romulus took the seat at the other end of the table opposite the king, and Myon sat on his right.

"Reith," Romulus said, "Sit beside me please."

Reith beamed with pride and took his place to Romulus' left. Vereinen sat beside him and the rest of their party filled the empty seats at the table. Seim took a seat beside the three dwarf lords.

"You already know the Queen," Rendar replied. "These are the Lords Tabriz, Sahand, and Mengar. They are my trusted advisors and generals. Seim, you know of course. Please introduce your whole party, Prince Romulus."

"This is Myon, Reith, Vereinen, Dema, Ellamora, Brauron, Aytos, and Rejnik," he said and pointed to each in turn.

"Good, good," the King replied. "Seim, have we had word back from our scouts?"

"Not yet, Your Highness," Seim replied. "We should only have heard by now if the elves were very near the city indeed."

"That is good," Rendar answered. "But it leaves us in a bit of a precarious position. We do not know if Balkh has fallen, so we don't yet know whether to leave Darren Shahr to the aid of Balkh or hunker down and wait for the siege to come."

"Can we not meet them in open battle?" Romulus asked. "If Balkh has fallen that is, can we not pick a place for open combat?"

The dwarf lords muttered at that suggestion.

"It is not advisable," Rendar said, with a sideways glance at his advisors. "Here in the city, we are so well defended. To engage in open battle would make our losses considerably greater and leave our city open to attack if their force beats ours or has significantly more numbers."

"So, we face the choice between saving ourselves or saving Balkh?" Myon asked.

"Hardly," the king replied, shaking his head. "If we knew for sure which way the battle was going in Balkh, it would make our decision for us. But until we know, we cannot simply abandon them to the elven fleet."

"What do you suggest, sire?" the dwarf lord named Tabriz asked.

"I do not presuppose to suggest anything," Rendar answered. "That is why we are having this council."

"So, what we need," Queen Kalis interjected, "is a plan that looks after our interests in Darren Shahr but also the interests of Balkh and the brave soldiers fighting for her survival."

Reith's mind began to spin.

"Easier said than done," Mengar replied sarcastically. After a pause, he added, "my Lady."

Rendar glared at him, but Kalis appeared to pay him no mind.

"If Balkh has indeed fallen," Sahand began, "Are we assured that the elves will immediately head upriver toward us?" He looked sidelong at Romulus and Myon.

"We do not know their full strategy, but that is what my assumption is," Romulus answered carefully. "It's a war my father wants to win, not just a battle."

"What if," Reith began, and every eye turned to him. All except the dwarf lords looked at him expectantly, while they looked at him with haughty disdain. "What if, we were able to stretch out our hand in such a way that we could pull it back if needed."

"Go on," Rendar urged.

"If the elves win Balkh, they will immediately head upriver," Reith continued. "So, if we sail down river, one of two things will happen. Either we will run into the elven fleet coming upriver, or we will reach Balkh with no issue. If we reach Balkh, we can join in the defense of that city and sink our barge like we sunk the barges at the river mouth in Balkh to prevent elves from breaking up stream."

"If they managed to get through into the river and we meet them somewhere between here and there, we anchor the barge in the center of the river and light it on fire to block their way again. I think it plays to our advantage to drive them to the shore. Their supplies are on the ship, so they will have to stop and unload and carry their things. In the meantime, we send a lightly armored force on horseback that accompanies our barges and those riders could pepper the elves with arrows and perhaps burn their ships in the river before their supplies could be unloaded."

"We would be on horseback and could easily retreat to the waterfall before they could arrive here. Even our barge soldiers could march back here in time if the elves are slowed enough. We would inflict heavy casualties, particularly to their supplies, which will be especially important if they aim to lay siege to the city."

He ended his strategy there and saw everyone seemed to be pondering his suggestion carefully, even the dwarf lords.

"It seems we have a young general in our midst," King Rendar said with a smile.

Vereinen beamed at Reith.

"And what of Balkh?" Queen Kalis asked.

"If our barges arrive in Balkh, those soldiers will be let into the city to reinforce the defense," Reith answered. "Perhaps we send our forces in waves. A few barges at a time laden with soldiers ready to fight or help Balkh with horsemen as cover for them."

"The boy speaks well," Rendar noted. Reith bristled at the "boy" comment. Vereinen noticed and placed a calming hand on Reith's arm. "What say you?" Rendar asked the dwarf lords.

"It seems to be an adequate plan," Mengar replied begrudgingly. Rejnik snorted at this reply.

"I find no fault with it," said Sahand, looking very much like he was quite disappointed to not find any fault with it.

"There are worse courses of action we could explore," Tabriz answered.

"Ringing endorsements, all around," Queen Kalis said as she rolled her eyes.

"Well then, it is decided," Rendar declared, clapping his hands. "Seim, organize three rounds of three barges, to leave eight hours apart, fifty dwarves in light armor on each. Lord Tabriz, arrange for 300 horsemen, sending 100 with each set of barges."

Seim and Tabriz rose, bowed, and departed.

"What of us?" Romulus asked the king. "We want to fight; we want to help."

"Absolutely," Dema chimed in. Reith nodded his agreement.

"Well," the king mused, looking at Sahand and Mengar. "I suppose it wouldn't hurt to send you with the horsemen. Which of you want to go?"

Romulus, Reith, Dema, Ellamora, Brauron, Aytos, and Rejnik all stood to their feet. Myon and Vereinen remained seated and exchanged a rueful smile.

"All good riders? Good with a bow?"

"Yes, your majesty," Romulus replied. "All tested in battle as well. We are yours to command."

"Very well," Rendar replied. "You will go with the first round of horsemen. I will permit you your weapons. Sahand, please go and inform Tabriz of his new charges. And you all," he said, looking at the humans and elves and Rejnik, "do try not to let me down."

The steward led them from the chamber into the dining hall. He unlocked a closet and there they found all their weapons. Reith embraced his sword and bow as an old friend.

"Farewell, friends," Myon declared to them. "We older ones will await your return."

"Goodbye, Vereinen," Reith said, giving his master a small hug.

"Be safe, Reith," Vereinen whispered. "I don't want to lose you again."

"Nor I, you," Reith replied.

"Come, add to your arms as you require," the steward said, leading the way through a door off the hall. Reith and Vereinen broke apart and Reith waved to his master and friend as they walked through the dining hall. They entered a large warehouse like room with weapons hanging on the walls and stacked on shelves. Reith's jaw dropped.

Everywhere he looked, he saw a new type of weapon. There were swords of all shapes and sizes, some large and requiring two hands and some small enough to be daggers. He saw bows of various lengths and curvature. Axes with either one or two sharp sides and some that had two sharp axe blades and a spear point between them. There were large, spiked metal balls attached to chains, clubs with and without spikes, and a variety of war hammers. Near the bows, he found stacks and stacks of arrows, which he took to replenish his quiver.

Dema got herself a small sword with a thin blade. She even grabbed a handful of throwing daggers.

"Just another tool to add to the arsenal," she said to Reith's raised eyebrow.

Ellamora took two small swords from the armory. She whirled them around with great ease and skill and smiled with pleasure.

Like Reith, Romulus added arrows to his quiver, but did not take anything to supplement his own sword. Rejnik took a large war hammer and tucked it into his belt. He also selected a short bow and a new quiver of arrows.

"This way," the steward called when all had selected what they needed. They followed him through the fortress, a different way than they had come. After many twists and turns, they came to an outer wall of the fortress. The gate stood open and a hundred horses and horsemen milled around, preparing for action. Dwarves saddled horses and strapped armor on themselves and adjusted their weapons.

One of the dwarves noted their arrival and stepped forward.

"Greetings," he said. "I am Captain Khito, I am the leader of this battalion, and your leader on this mission."

"Prince Romulus," Romulus replied, extending a hand to the dwarven captain, who looked remarkably younger than other dwarves Reith had seen, younger than King Rendar by a few years.

Romulus introduced the rest of them in short order.

"I am very pleased to have you in my charge," Khito said to them all. "To be honest, I was not the first choice to lead this group. One of the older commanders had the command, but he refused when told there would be elves and humans. Some of the soldiers went with him. I jumped at the opportunity. Know that every soldier here appreciates your presence, so there is no need to worry about any of them. Come, let me show you to your steeds."

Reith hadn't even thought that the dwarven soldiers would be less than pleased to fight alongside them. He took it as a given that their willingness to fight would be appreciated. The feeling that some were not so welcoming gave him flashbacks of Crain and Gwandoeth's head falling from a bag.

The group followed Khito around the crowd of

dwarves and horses away from the fortress city. To their left, the river flowed beside the city. Before them, the plains stretched out below them, endless and rolling. He turned on the spot and saw the mountains rising above the fortress.

There were horses for each of them loosely tied to a stake in the ground. They were already saddled and bore full saddle bags. Romulus took a large black war horse. Reith found he was beside a smaller chestnut horse. It neighed when he drew close. He reached out a hand gently and stroked the mane.

"We will mount up on my trumpet blast," Khito said. "Feel free to ride at the end of the train. We will ride hard through the day until we see the elven fleet or night falls, whichever comes first. If we need to camp, we will."

Reith swung into the saddle, happy to again find himself on a horse. The others similarly mounted and they all waited for Khito's trumpet.

Reith took in the wide vistas around Darren Shahr. Mountains, plains, rivers, all of it so beautiful and so foreign only a short while before. Now he was mounted up in a dwarven cavalry, a sword at his hip, and dwarven arrows in his quiver. Vereinen was safe in the walls of Darren Shahr for now, but once again Reith was going to put himself in harm's way.

Fight for them.

"I will," he whispered. Then Khito's trumpet blasted and they were off.

13

The pack of horses set off up the hill away from the city along the bank of the river. After several minutes of riding, the river curved away to their left and they continued along on the plateau on which the city was built. Khito then turned to the right so they were traveling sideways down the slope to the open plain below. After several tense minutes of descent, they reached the open plain and Khito urged them into a gallop.

Darren Shahr loomed above them and Reith was invigorated by the wind in his face as they galloped on. Soon the roar of the waterfall began to assert itself over their horse hooves. They could see the churning waters of the river as they galloped south along its eastern bank. A few hundred yards ahead of them were three barges packed with dwarven soldiers. They were hardly rowing, but the current was taking them fairly swiftly as they drew even with the barges, Khito slowed them down to an easy trot to keep pace.

Reith took this lull to take stock of his saddle bags which had been packed for him. He reached down to the right bag and unclasped it and flipped it open. He stuck his hand in and found that this one was filled with food. Bread and dried meat he was able to identify by touch alone. There were some other things in there that were not immediately recognizable by touch, but he thought they were fruits or vegetables. He withdrew his hand and closed the bag again. He switched hands on the reins and reached to the bag on his left, unclasping it and plunging his hand in. He found it contained a flint and steel, a knife with its blade in a leather sheath, and small cooking pan, and a few small items and bags he couldn't identify.

"Anything good?" Dema asked. She had trotted alongside him on her silver mare.

"Food and camping supplies," he replied. "And some other stuff I couldn't identify by touch. We'll see later."

"I am so glad to be off a ship," Dema said, changing the subject. "I much prefer a horse."

"I don't mind ships," Reith said, "but I definitely like horses better."

"Can you believe King Rendar allowed us to go on this expedition?" Dema asked.

"Hardly," Reith answered. "We always seem to be at the cusp of the action, though."

"Always the cusp, but never in the thick of it," Dema replied.

"Well not since Sardis, at least," Reith said. "There and before we were in the middle of everything going on."

"But the Free Isles, Balkh," Dema protested. "We left before the action."

"Well, we might be catching back up to it."

The rest of the morning went by with a series of gallops, walks, and trots. Trotting seemed inefficient, even if it kept them alongside the barges. Khito would order a gallop ahead to the next bend and then a long walk while the barges caught up. They ate the noon meal in the saddle, and Reith took some of the bread and dried meat out, though he didn't eat nearly as much as he would have liked.

"We don't know how long this will need to last us," Khito had warned all of them.

At late afternoon, Khito ordered a full stop after finishing a gallop a mile ahead of the barges.

"We will camp here tonight," he declared. He selected half a dozen riders and commanded them to go another couple of miles downriver to act as advance scouts for the night. If they saw any ship, their orders were to gallop back to the camp as fast as possible.

The barges beached on the sandy shore of the river and the 150 dwarven soldiers made camp beside the horsemen. Reith discovered that a soft bedroll was tied to the back of his horse, and he very much looked forward to lying on that instead of the usual hard ground.

Reith, Dema, Ellamora, Romulus, Brauron, Aytos, and Rejnik set up their own small camp between the horsemen camp and the barge camp. Reith started a small fire with his flint and tinder, and they all laid their bedrolls around the fire. Reith and Dema found themselves beside each other.

As the sky darkened and stars appeared one by one, they lay beside the fire, willing sleep to come upon them. Reith was hyper aware of Dema beside him. She was mere feet from him, and if he wanted, he could roll over, extend a hand, and touch her.

Just take her hand, he told himself, but for whatever reason, he was paralyzed.

What if she doesn't want that? said another part of his mind. *What if she doesn't feel like that?*

The battle raged on as more and more stars exploded

into the night sky. The fire crackled and popped. Crickets chirped and the soft sounds of the river drifted by in the night.

Just do it. One … Two … Three.

He compelled his arm to reach across the wide chasm between him and Dema while the other part of this brain screamed, *No!*

In the darkness, his hand found her arm and snaked down to her hand, which he squeezed. She turned her hand and intertwined their fingers and squeezed back. Neither of them said a thing, but it felt as though a great weight had lifted off Reith. *Whatever this is, I like it.*

He let his mind drift and sleep gradually came for him. But before he was able to fall asleep, Dema dropped his hand.

Startled, he pulled his hand away.

But then he saw her shift by the light of the fire. She scooted her bed roll toward him, so they were side by side. She turned onto her side and faced away from him, but offered an arm to him, beckoning him closer. He obliged and embraced her. His hand found hers again and they cuddled in the darkness. Dema soon fell asleep, but Reith's mind raced.

At dawn, Khito gave a blast of his trumpet and they broke camp. The barges pushed out into the river and the horsemen gathered around Khito for last minute instructions.

"We will push forward today, ahead of the barges as much as we can," he declared to his gathered battalion. "Hopefully, we can camp again tonight with no sign of an attacking force. Then tomorrow, we join the defense of Balkh."

The soldiers gave a battle cry and Khito turned his horse south and urged it to a gallop. They all fell into place behind him. They quickly overtook the barges and a gap opened between the land-based part of the team and the river-based part. Khito always kept the barges in sight, but when there was a bend, he sent a half dozen horsemen forward to scout the way. After the barges rounded the bend, he ordered another gallop to increase the distance.

The morning went by in this constant flurry of activity. As they rode, Reith's mind strayed back to the night before with Dema. He remembered the feel of her skin, the warmth of her body as they lay together in the darkness. They had hardly moved, until Khito's horn had pierced the still morning air.

"Good morning," Dema had said to him in a soft voice, while a smile graced her lips.

"Good morning to you, too," Reith had replied, mirroring her smile. They broke apart and packed their things for the day's ride. As he rolled up his bed roll, he caught Ellamora smirking at him and his face had turned bright red. She had laughed but did not say anything further.

Now, on the road, Reith blushed again at the memory, but no one was looking at him now. Dema was riding in front of him, graceful as ever in the saddle. He knew Ellamora was somewhere behind him, but he refrained from looking around.

All of a sudden, he felt his horse slowing beneath him and saw that everyone was stopping. Six horsemen were galloping toward them and Khito had called for a halt. The dwarves galloping toward them were shouting something, but Reith couldn't hear what because he was near the back of the party. The horses came to a stop in front of Khito and the riders spoke to him. Then Khito urged his horse toward the middle of the pack, and riders nudged their horses to the side to let him pass.

"A dozen or more elven ships have broken through at Balkh and are a mere mile from this point," Khito cried out. Everyone instinctively turned their head downriver, but a bend in the river kept the elves from view.

"I will instruct the barges to anchor just on this side of the bend, so the elven fleet has little warning that a trap has been set for them. Once the barges are anchored, those men will swim and wade to our side of the river. We will cover them with volleys of arrows high into the air descending on the elven decks. Let us keep them pinned down and unable to retrieve many supplies. We will light the barges on fire and force them to turn back."

Khito appointed three to ride swiftly north and inform the barges of the plan, and then he gathered the rest into position. They trotted a quarter mile downstream to the bend, and Khito ordered a dismount. They formed ranks and each archer put an arrow on their string.

"Remember, volleys together, high into the air. There will be plenty of time to pick off individuals later."

The barges drew near and their captains ordered them to row backward to maintain position. One by one, anchors dropped, much like Rejnik had done at Balkh. The barges turned sideways and formed an impenetrable barricade. All the soldiers jumped into the water and swam and then waded to the bank, where they dried off. Each captain readied their fire, and Khito raised a hand in signal. As soon as the prow of an elven ship came into sight around the bend, he dropped his hand and the barges were lit. The captains came at last to the land.

There was a commotion on deck of the first elven ship,

and Reith saw several more come into view behind it. The oars stopped rowing and the ship gradually came to a halt, a few yards short of the barges.

"Fire!" Khito commanded, and Reith sent his arrow high into the sky to rain down on the first ship. The elves on board ducked for cover, and some raised shields above their heads. Most of the arrows fell harmlessly. Reith realized there was an opportunity on the next volley and soon had an arrow on the string.

"Fire!" Khito yelled again, and this time Reith paused and did not fire with the others. When the other arrows reached their apex, he saw an elf near the front of the ship raise a shielded hand to the sky and then Reith let go of his string. The arrow sped forward and took the elf square in the chest as the rest of the arrows fell. Reith put another arrow on his string and looked for another target.

"Fire!" Khito called out a third time, and this time Reith caught sight of the captain of the first elven ship at the ship's wheel. He smiled grimly and took aim. The captain held up a shield with his left hand and held the wheel with his right. Reith sent an arrow just under the captain's shield arm into his heart and the captain fell over, still clutching the wheel. The wheel turned violently and the ship began to turn sideways. This caused the elves on board to scatter in confusion. Rather than pointing upriver, the elven ship was pointing directly toward the shore where Reith and the others were standing.

The ship continued turning, and with no one to steer it and no one rowing, it soon pointed downriver, right at the next elven ship. The current slowly but surely made it pick up speed. With a loud thunk of wood on wood, it struck the other ship. Wood splintered and the elves on deck of both ships lurked. Some even fell into the water.

"Fire at will!" Khito called out, and Reith fired at one

of the bobbing heads in the river. His arrow hit home and that elf never made it to shore. Reith chose another target on the deck of the first ship and sent arrow after arrow toward elven soldiers.

The elves were in disarray. The first two ships were locked in a tight embrace and were going nowhere. Arrows continually fell like snow and they panicked. The flaming barges and the two crippled ships blocked the way forward. A few ships toward the rear of the procession tried to turn around, but they got stuck on the bank or drew too near another ship for their oars to row. All the while Reith and the others kept picking off targets.

Some elves in the water crossed to the other side of the river. They tried to take cover among the trees, but even there they were not fully safe. Reith took out several as they retreated or if they poked their necks out too far.

Elves from one of the ships caught on the near bank tree down a gangway disembarked. They retreated out of bow shot down river but huddled together forming a plan. Soon other ships joined them and a great throng was forming on the defenders' side of the river. It dawned on everyone at the same time that the elves on land had more numbers, so they began to advance toward Khito's force, shields held out in front of them.

"Form rank!" Khito yelled. "Cavalry charge followed by foot soldiers." He drew his sword. "Romulus, take your people and swing out onto the plain and pepper them with arrows from the side. If they engage, make all haste back to Darren Shahr with news for King Rendar. I hope we will be on your heels."

"Come on," Romulus called, and the seven of them urged their horses out on the plain to shoot arrows at the advancing elves.

They set up fifty yards away from the elves and began

to shoot from the saddle. Khito's soldiers continued a barage from the front, so the elves didn't dare turn their shields to the side, so Reith and the others were able to take out a good number before Khito's cavalry slammed into the front of the elven horde.

Khito was a magnificent figure, towering over the elves on his horse. He had led the charge and had penetrated deeper into the elven ranks than anyone else. His sword gleamed in the sunlight as it flashed down on his foes. He turned his horse and cut a path back to his cavalry, and no elf could stand before him.

And yet, the dwarves were horribly outnumbered. Reith guessed that each elven ship contained a hundred elves, meaning the elves numbered at least a thousand. Khito's force was a fraction of that, though his horses gave him an advantage.

After the initial thrust into the elven ranks, the elves reasserted their numbers. Reith and the others continued to pepper them with arrows, but seven archers against so many made little difference. One of the elven captains took his men and turned toward them and charged. A hundred elves were coming at them.

"Retreat!" Romulus called, and they stopped shooting to gallop clear of their attackers. The elves charging them turned and attacked Khito's force from the side.

Khito realized the battle was lost. He rode clear of the fighting and blasted his trumpet.

"Retreat!" he bellowed.

The dwarves turned to flee from the wrath of the elves. Khito dropped his trumpet and went on the offensive, cutting a path through to give some space between his men and the elves. The soldiers who had been on the barges were horribly exposed. The horsemen could have gotten away easily, but the dwarves on foot were miles from safety.

How will they all get away? Reith thought. But then he remembered that another force was coming down river a few hours behind them.

"Romulus!" he called. "There's another force of barges and horses coming down a few hours from us."

"By the light, you're right, Reith!" Romulus said.

"We must break free and hurry toward them. The dwarves on foot can ride barges to Darren Shahr."

"Let's go!"

The seven of them pressed into a gallop and rode ahead of the slowly retreating dwarves. When the horses needed a break, they slowed to a trot, but kept going swiftly. They alternated like this for an hour before stopping to allow the horses to drink in the river. But then they were right back at it.

The dwarves and elves had long faded into the distance, and even the sounds of battle were lost in the air. The sun blazed down on them, and the horses slowed their relentless pace, tired from the journey.

At last, they saw two riders coming toward them. They broke into one last gallop and the distance between them closed quickly.

"Greetings," one of the dwarves said, concern etched on his face.

"Khito and the rest are engaged in battle," Romulus said quickly. "They are retreating, but a thousand or more elves are hot in pursuit. The horsemen are attempting to keep the elves away from the soldiers on foot, but they will never all make it back to Darren Shahr. We need help."

"We will take word back to our captain," the dwarf who greeted them replied. "How far away are they?"

"Many miles. We left them three hours ago at a fast pace to bring word to you."

"Wait here, rest your horses," the second dwarf said.

"We are a twenty-minute ride from our forces. We will urge them to come swiftly."

The two dwarves turned and rode back upriver, and Reith and the others dismounted. They led their horse down to the river to drink, which they did eagerly.

"I hope we're not too late," Ellamora said quietly.

"I hate waiting," Dema said. "Can't we head back?"

"Our horses need a rest," Romulus said. "At least until the dwarves catch up. And what could we do?"

"We could at least do something," Dema said. "Rather than sitting around here."

"There's nothing to be done at the moment," Romulus said sadly. "Khito and the others need to get along by themselves. And don't forget," he added, "we are following Khito's orders."

Dema moodily kicked a rock into the river but said nothing. They waited in silence until they saw the horsemen round the bend upstream. Romulus mounted his horse, and the others followed suit.

"My men have told me everything," the dwarf captain Farrin said after introducing himself. "I have urged the barges to increase their pace. Let us hurry to the aid of our comrades."

Reith and the others fell into place in their new company and they steadily rode again southward, galloping and trotting as they had on the way upstream. The barges maintained their pace and managed to keep within sight of the horsemen at all times.

After about two hours, they sighted the harassed dwarven retreat. The horsemen were weaving in and out, keeping the advancing elves off the heels of the retreating dwarves on foot.

Farrin ordered the barges to beach near them.

"We will defend against the elves so our soldiers can

board the barges," he declared. "Use arrows to keep them at bay, and if needed, we can swoop in with swords to give them the time they need to get on board safely. Now fan out."

The horsemen spread out in a long arching line away from the river. Reith pulled his bow and readied an arrow.

The retreating dwarves doubled their pace, knowing safety was near. This created some space between the elves and dwarves, and Khito's horsemen filled in the gap.

Khito still rode, but he was badly wounded. He had blood all down his left side, so much so that Reith could not tell where the wound was or if he simply was wounded along his whole side. His left arm hung limply at his side, useless.

Reith and the others began firing arrows at the advancing elves, and this slowed them down even more. The dwarves rapidly approached the beached barges and began to swarm onto them, collapsing on deck from exhaustion.

Urged on by their leaders, the elves made one last frantic charge. Among the horses, they were able to cut down some riders. They reached the dwarves on the banks and arrows became useless. Dwarves and elves screamed in rage and agony. The fighting was fierce and so intermingled that the riders couldn't sweep into the battle.

"Push out!" Farrin urged the three barges, even though not all the dwarves on foot had boarded. One by one, the barges pulled away from the bank and floated out to the middle of the river, given a reprieve from the fighting. Dwarves on foot plunged into the river and waded out to the barges to be pulled on board. However, most left behind had to turn and fight lest they be cut down.

Khito jumped down from his horse and began swinging his sword recklessly at the elves. He managed to beat a few back, allowing several dwarves to enter the water and head to safety.

"To me, to me!" Khito roared in a hoarse voice. Blood dripped freely from his left side as he held his sword aloft. The remaining dwarves on foot rallied to their commander and formed a tight pack and faced the advancing elves.

The dwarven cavalry reformed and charged toward the side of the elves, and for a moment, the fighters on foot broke apart. Dwarves jumped into the water to get onto barges, and soon there were only twenty or so left with Khito on the bank. The cavalry circled but were so overwhelmed by the numbers of the elves. They surged forward again toward Khito and the remaining dwarves.

"Go!" he bellowed as his sword met the sword of an attacking elf. The remaining dwarves fled to safety. The other dwarf captain on horseback urged his men forward to Khito's aid, but Khito was undone by his useless left arm. An elven sword struck him on his left and he fell, dead.

"Retreat!" Farrin yelled. By now all the dwarves on foot had been pulled onto barges. Oars went into the water and pulled the barges forward upriver. The horsemen galloped away, leaving a bloody bank of corpses from many fallen elves and dwarves.

The elves stopped their pursuit, knowing they could not catch the barges or the horsemen. As Reith looked back, he saw the bloody body of Khito lying in the sand and tears came to his eyes.

14

———————

When the barges were safely away, Captain Farrin called for a halt.

"Those elves aren't going anywhere," he said, pointing back down river where the elves were still on the bank near their ships. "They outnumber us, but we do have an advantage on horseback. We must decide what to do."

"Another set of barges and riders should near us by nightfall," Romulus spoke up. "Might we attack with more?"

"Perhaps," Farrin replied. "But it depends on what the elves do between now and then. They may try to take to the water again and continue up the river. Or they could travel on foot to Darren Shahr. With us on this bank, they may opt to cross the river and take their chances in the forest and hills."

"What of Balkh?" Rejnik asked. "Could the elves have reinforcements coming from there?"

"There have to be more coming," Romulus replied. "This was but an expeditionary force."

"We can't empty Darren Shahr to meet the elves in

battle," Farrin said. "So, what remains is to decide how we are to proceed. I am open to any suggestions."

"With us on horseback, we have the advantage," Reith said. "Maybe not in pitched battle, as we just saw on the bank. But it allows us to come and go as we will without fear of reprisal. Let us keep our distance and be a pain in their butts as long as we can before falling back into the city. We can set up archers at a distance and keep them pinned down. If they make for their ships, we shoot at them from the shore. If they travel upriver on foot, we pinch them between us and the river with archers and brief cavalry charges."

"So, no matter what they do, we are there, making life miserable and eating into their numbers," Romulus summed up.

"That seems like the best course of action," Farrin said. "What if they cross the river?"

"We pick off as many as we can as they cross and are vulnerable," Reith replied, "then we keep an eye on them from our side of the river."

"This seems like the best course of action," Farrin said. "What are the elves doing now?" All turned to look down river. The elves were very close to where the battle had occurred by the smoldering remains of the barges. Some elves were entering the water."

"I think they're trying to clear the river!" one of the dwarf soldiers declared.

"Well, we can't have that," Farrin said. "Bows at the ready, and we ride!"

And so they went back toward battle. As they drew near, Reith saw that the elves were extinguishing the fires on the barges and were cutting the anchors to let the barges float downriver. As the horsemen approached, the elves fell into a defensive position with shields facing the dwarves. Fifty yards from the elves, Farrin gave the command to stop.

"Fire at will!" he called.

Reith looked at the elves with their shields and decided not to waste any arrows there. He saw a couple of elves staggering up the bank from the water, and he sent two arrows in quick succession, felling both elves. He smiled with grim satisfaction.

The third ship in the elven line had oars in the water and was attempting to circumvent the two crippled elven ships and the smoldering barges. Reith turned to his companions.

"Come on, let's go toward the water and shoot at that ship."

Reith dug his heels into his horse, and the horse jolted forward. He turned and saw Ellamora and Dema following him.

As they arrived at the riverbank, an arrow whizzed over their heads.

"Duck!" Ellamora shouted. Another few arrows flew by them. A couple of elves were crouched behind their company and were shooting at the three of them. Reith hunched over in the saddle and retreated out of bow range upriver.

Now they were too far away from the elven ship, which was slowly making its way past the barges now. The elves that had been shooting at them turned their attention to the main dwarven force on horseback and began returning fire. Farrin ordered the dwarves back from the arrows, and they retreated out toward the plains, out of range. With all enemies out of range, the elves turned and ran down river. Reith saw a ship was near the shore waiting for them.

"Come on!" he called to Dema and Ellamora. "They are going to board that ship!"

The three raced forward and kept their bows in hand. As they drew close enough, they launched arrows at the backs of the elves, and managed to hit a few.

"Watch out!" Dema yelled. Reith turned to look at her, and she was turning her horse sharply left, away from the river. And then he felt a sharp pain in his right calf. An elven arrow was protruding from his leg.

"Ah!" he yelled in pain, instinctively reaching down to hold his leg. He managed to turn his horse to follow Dema as his leg burned like fire. Blood began to seep from the wound and soon drenched his pants and shoe.

"What happened?" Ellamora asked, looking at him with concern. Then she paled as she saw the arrow shaft in his leg and the pain etched on his face.

"Come on!" Dema said, noticing the arrow too. "We need to get to safety before we do anything."

The horses galloped away from the river toward the dwarves marshaled out on the plain. With each step the horse took, pain shot through his leg. Tears came to his eyes and all he wanted to do was yank the arrow out right then and there, but his years of hunting knew that was the worst thing he could do at the moment. So he tried to keep his leg as still as he could.

"He's hurt," Dema declared to Farrin and the others as they approached. "Hit by an arrow."

"By the light," Romulus exclaimed, "are you okay, Reith?"

Reith couldn't answer through his gritted teeth.

"Help him down," Farrin ordered several soldiers. Strong hands grabbed Reith and lowered him to the soft grass below. They tried to be gentle, but each movement caused Reith even more agony. He lay there groaning, unaware of anything other than his arrow pierced leg.

"Here you go, lad," a dwarf said after several minutes.

He was raised to a seated position by several strong hands and a small bottle was pressed to his lips. Its smoky liquid burned his mouth on the way down, causing him to sputter.

"It'll help the pain," the dwarf said. "Take another gulp, there you go." Reith obediently took another sip. It burned again but not as much. He was lowered back to the ground and opened his eyes to look down. The arrow was still protruding from his leg and his pants had been cut off at the knee. He noticed the crimson-stained fabric lying next to his leg. Two dwarves were kneeling by his leg inspecting the damage.

"The arrow has to come out," the first dwarf said. "It'll hurt like fire, but we have to get it out."

"Hold him down," the other dwarf said. Other dwarfs stepped close and pinned his arms and legs to the ground.

"Don't move, if you can help it," the first dwarf said to Reith, kindly.

Reith nodded and gulped.

"Bite down on this," the second dwarf said, pushing a piece of cloth between Reith's teeth. Reith did as he was told.

The same flask that Reith had drank out of was poured over the wound and Reith nearly passed out from the pain as the liquid stung his wound. He struggled against the dwarves holding him down and screamed through the cloth, but they held him fast.

"Close your eyes," the first dwarf said. "You don't want to watch."

Reith closed his eyes and braced himself for the next wave of agony. He felt a hand on his leg and then a sharp pain right beside his arrow wound. He tried to thrash as it felt like they were trying to cut his leg off. The pain was so intense that he lost all his other senses. There was only the pain.

And then his arms and legs were released. He cracked one eye open and saw that the arrow was gone and the dwarves were wrapping a bandage around his wounded leg.

"All done," the second dwarf said. "Should heal just fine after a week or two."

"I hate to be the one to be the bearer of bad news," Farrin said, standing over Reith and the two dwarves, "But the elves are all on their ships and are making their way upriver again. We must get back to the city, and soon."

"Help him up," the first dwarf said. "Don't put any pressure on that leg, lad."

Two dwarves stooped and wrapped their hands around Reith's arms and back and lifted him up. He kept his right knee bent so the foot wouldn't touch the ground.

"Help me up to my horse, please," Reith said. They lifted him and placed him on top of the horse, and he gingerly lowered his right leg down to the stirrup. Every slight movement caused the wound to throb, but he was soon seated on the horse.

"That bandage will need changing every few hours for a few days," the second dwarf said, inspecting Reith's bandage with concern. "As long as we are on the road, I will do it. Once we are back in the city, you can stay with the healers. Don't walk on it for at least a few days."

"Thank you," Reith said with a grimace.

"Let's ride," Farrin said. "We need to warn the next round of barges with plenty of time for them to turn and head back to the city." He mounted his own horse and led the way upriver. Already several elven ships were ahead of them on the river, but on horseback, the group managed to pass them rapidly. They stayed far out on the plains as long as they were near the elves to avoid any arrows that might come from the ships.

"Are you okay?" Dema asked, riding up next to Reith, looking at his leg with concern.

"I'll live," Reith said through gritted teeth. The riding was jolting his leg every step the horse took.

"I'm so sorry," Dema apologized. "I tried to warn you."

"You were brilliant," Reith replied. "We weren't expecting the arrows from the ships."

"All the same," Dema answered, "I feel bad."

"Don't," Reith said shortly. "I'll be fine soon."

"I will take good care of you," Dema declared.

"And me too!" Ellamora added. "We did a good job when you were attacked by a bear."

"Yes you did," Reith said, remembering when he had been injured so much worse than now. He had lost several days to unconsciousness as his body fought to heal from that nearly fatal attack on the way to Sardis.

"Stop getting hurt," Dema demanded.

"I'll see what I can do," Reith said, and even managed a small smile.

They kept up a steady pace throughout the rest of the day. Farrin left scouts to keep pace with the ships while the group pressed forward. Twice, Reith's bandage was changed. Each time, the bandage was soaked with blood, and the wound appeared to still be bleeding. Cold water from the river was poured over the wound to wash dried blood away before the new bandage was applied.

At sunset, Farrin ordered a stop, but he was unsure about camping or continuing. They had not yet encountered the next wave of barges and horsemen nor caught up to their barges they had sent back upriver earlier.

"It all depends on the elves," he said to Romulus. "If they keep going, we have to keep going to stay ahead of them."

Reith was helped down by several dwarves and his bed roll was laid out for him. He lay down and his bandage was changed by the kind dwarf, whose name was Harth.

"Rest for a while until the captain decides what to do," Harth instructed.

Soon though, two of his scouts returned with news.

"We have good news and bad news," one of the dwarves said. "The good news is the elves have dropped anchor. I assume they're warn out from the day."

"What's the bad news?" Farrin asked.

"Three dozen more ships have caught up to the ten we were tracking."

Farrin swore.

"Should we push on through the night?" one of the dwarves asked. "We could reach Darren Shahr by dawn, if we hurry."

"No," Farrin replied. "Let us rest for a while. But I want to be back in the saddle before dawn." Farrin set a watch schedule and sent more scouts down river to keep an eye on the elven fleet. Reith was grateful he did not have to get up from his bed roll.

Dema and Ellamora set up on either side of him.

"Good night," Ellamora said.

"G'night," Reith mumbled.

"Night, Ellamora," Dema answered.

In the darkness, Reith felt Dema's hand on his arm. He managed to roll over onto his left side, and through the gathering darkness he could just make out her face.

"I meant what I said earlier," Dema began. "Stop getting hurt. I … I need you."

"I'll be here for you," Reith answered. "It would take a thousand arrows to stop me."

"I don't know what I would do if something happened to you," Dema said. "Something changed today. I've felt it coming, but seeing you hurt like that, it made me think."

"What do you mean?" Reith asked.

"You and me," Dema said. "I want it to be you and me. For real. I love you, Reith."

Reith was momentarily stunned by the declaration but managed to come to his senses enough to reply, "I love you too, Dema."

She scooted slightly closer to him. The starlight glinted off her eyes as he looked deeply into them. He squeezed her hand. And then she was leaning in and he closed his eyes. Their lips met in the darkness, and Reith felt a warmth spread from his lips to his whole body. Her lips drove all thought of his wound from his mind, and it was as if she were the only real thing in the world.

After several long seconds, their lips broke apart, but they nuzzled close in a tight embrace.

"I love you," he said again.

"I love you, too," she replied.

They were woken before dawn by Farrin calling the company to move out. The sky was just beginning to lighten to the east. Dema packed her saddle bags quickly and then moved to help Reith. Harth came by to change his bandage. Soon, he was once again helped back into the saddle. His leg was incredibly stiff today, and the skin around his wound was sore to the touch. He grimaced as he took his place in the saddle, and Dema looked up at him with concern.

"I'm fine," he answered her unasked question.

"Company, ride!" Farrin called. The horses fell into the practiced procession and the miles began to slip away under their hooves. The eastern horizon glowed first purple, then red, orange, yellow, and then the sun blazed over the horizon, lighting the world. The horses and riders cast long shadows that stretched into the river.

Within an hour, they caught up to their barges, and another hour after that they met the next batch of barges and horsemen. At their meeting while Farrin spoke to the cavalry and barge captains, Harth took the bandage off Reith's leg and inspected it.

"Good news," he declared. "It appears the bleeding has mostly stopped." He wrapped a new bandage around the leg. "Don't put any weight on it today, and perhaps tomorrow as well," he warned.

"I won't. I promise," Reith swore.

"Even if there is an interesting battle to be joined, stay off it," Harth warned again.

"Fine," Reith answered. "I'll just let the elves finish me off then."

Ellamora snorted with laughter, but Dema did not look amused.

The barges turned around and began rowing upstream. The new company of horsemen also turned to travel north with them.

At noon, all of Farrin's scouts returned to the main party.

"The elves are making good progress up the river," the lead scout declared to Farrin and the others around him. "They will be at Darren Shahr tonight or early in the morning if they decide to drop anchor again."

"But what is their end goal?" Farrin asked. "Will they make their way to the waterfall? Or will they leave the river before then?"

"They will not attack Darren Shahr at the waterfall," one of the dwarves declared. "That is an impenetrable barrier. No, they will go either left or right, out onto the plains to attack from that side, or around to the hills and forest to attack from there."

"Let us keep watching them," Farrin said. "And we must make great haste to get back today."

More scouts were selected from Farrin's company and from the new company and they were sent down river. The remaining force continued along at a brisk pace.

Romulus rode his horse alongside Reith. "How are you feeling today?"

"Much better," Reith said, glancing down at his leg reflexively. "Should be right as rain in a few days."

"You've been strong on this stretch, since you got hurt," Romulus replied. "I'm proud of you."

"Thanks, Romulus." There was a question he had been wanting to ask for a few days now, since they had arrived at Darren Shahr, and now he blurted it out. "What are you going to do about your brother?"

Romulus' face darkened. "My brother, my brother," he began. "My brother was dead and is now alive again. I don't know what to do with him. I don't know what I can do for him."

"Tell me about him," Reith invited.

"We're twins, Remus and I. Twins born on the full moon. I came first, and then he came a bit later. So it's not as if his resurrection changes anything in elven politics. But growing up, we were inseparable for the first few years. We did everything together. We studied under tutors together, learned swordsmanship together, learned to ride horses together, and in our free time away from the responsibilities of court, we played together. And then mother died."

Romulus paused here for several long seconds. Reith said nothing, not wanting to break the flow of the story.

"When she died, everything changed. It was like some sort of wedge was driven between us. It seemed like he changed. All of a sudden, it was like he was starving for attention. He would do anything to get approval or praise from our father. He tried to beat me in everything, in studies, archery, fencing, riding, you name it. We stopped seeing each other much outside of official court duties. We saw each other around the palace, but we didn't seek out each other's company."

"When my father came to tell me Remus had died during a hunting accident, I hadn't even known he was out. That's how disconnected we were. And I'm ashamed to admit it, but I did not feel anything when he was gone. But now, he's alive. Alive and imprisoned. I supposed I must get him out, but at what cost?"

"Did your father send him?"

"Absolutely," Romulus replied. "I have been mulling that over in my mind since we found Remus. He was so eager to please our father he might have even suggested it himself."

"Why did he care so much?" Reith asked.

"Why do any of us do anything?" Romulus asked. "Our mother's death caused a special kind of wound in him. Maybe it had something to do with him being second born. He knew he was behind me in line for the throne. But whatever triggered it, he craved my father's approval like water."

"Did your father know he died?"

"I've been thinking about that too," Romulus

answered. "I really don't know. He grieved as if my brother were dead, but my father can be a good actor. But what really gets me wondering is whether or not my father recently found out my brother was still alive. Perhaps this is the reason for the invasion attempt. Maybe he's trying to kill two birds with one stone: conquer the dwarves and rescue Remus. Who knows?"

"Could Solzar have brought news?" Reith asked. "He's a Shadow, and maybe he had access to that information somehow."

"That is very possible. It could explain how my father trusted Solzar so readily."

"I wish I had answers to tell you," Reith said. "About everything."

"Answers may come, or they may not. But all we can do is act upon the knowledge we have in front of us. And that means thwarting my father and rescuing Remus if possible."

"Maybe King Rendar would let you visit Remus," Reith proposed.

"Perhaps, perhaps," Romulus said thoughtfully. "But I'd rather not push my luck. We are treading a dangerous path. Disaster lies around every corner. May the God of Light illuminate our path."

"May it be," Reith replied with the traditional elven prayer ending.

At dusk, Reith first heard and then saw the waterfall. Farrin led them out onto the plain and then up the steep slope to the back of the city. When they arrived at the stables, Farrin ordered a stretcher to be brought. Reith was lowered down onto it and unceremoniously carried into the fortress city. Dema, Ellamora, Romulus, Brauron, Aytos, and Rejnik followed behind the four dwarves supporting him.

After a few twists and turns, they arrived at a large wooden building. There was a garden in front of it with a variety of herbs and flowers, many of which Reith did not recognize. He didn't get a long look at them before he was taken into the building. Dwarf women in long white robes walked to and fro. One of them instructed the dwarves carrying Reith to take him to a small room on the second floor of the building. It had a bed, which Reith was placed on, a small bedside table, and across from the bed was a wooden dresser with three drawers. Next to the chest was a wooden chair.

"Thank you," Reith mumbled to the dwarves as they left the room. His friends crowded around his bed in the small room. A dwarf nurse came in.

"Out, all of you," she said in a firm voice. "The patient needs his rest."

"Can we visit?" Dema asked as she deposited Reith's possessions on the chair.

"Visiting hours begin at midmorning," the nurse replied. "Now please, I need to check his wound."

"We'll see you tomorrow, Reith," Ellamora said.

"Heal up," Romulus said.

Dema surprisingly gave him a quick kiss on the lips in front of everyone. They all gawked as he grinned sheepishly.

"See you in the morning," Dema said, and she too swept toward the door.

"So it's happened then?" Ellamora asked, a sly grin on her face.

Dema said nothing, but instead turned and blew a kiss to Reith. Then she walked out and the rest followed.

"Now let's look at that leg," the nurse said.

His leg soon had a fresh bandage after some sort of ointment was smeared on the wound. A simple meat stew was brought to him for dinner, which he devoured eagerly.

"You need some rest," the nurse said. "I will leave you for the night. If you need anything, ring this." She placed a small silver bell on the bedside table. "That includes anything that involves getting out of bed. You are not to put any weight on your leg today. Perhaps tomorrow you can walk, but not until we give you the all clear."

"Thank you," Reith said gratefully. "And what is your name?"

"My name is Rose," she replied, and she turned and left the room, softly closing the door behind her.

Not a minute later the door opened again.

"Vereinen!" Reith exclaimed.

"Reith, how are you?" Vereinen asked with infinite worry on his face. "I only just heard from Romulus what had happened."

"I'm fine," Reith replied. "Or I will be."

"You need to stop getting hurt," Vereinen said. "I couldn't bear it if something happened to you."

"I'm fine, Vereinen," Reith protested. "Just a small wound, that's all."

"All the same," Vereinen replied. "I would rather you had no wounds."

"So what did you do while we were gone?" Reith asked, changing the subject.

"I went to the library of course."

"Of course, you did. Did you find out anything interesting?"

"Not much, I am afraid, in my short perusing," Vereinen replied. "I shall require weeks and weeks here someday."

"Hopefully that research can begin soon."

"The elves are coming, Reith," Vereinen said. "I look into the future and all I see is war, war, miserable war."

"It will end someday," Reith pointed out. "Wars always end. You taught me that."

"Some wars stretch on for generations."

"Not this one."

"How do you know?" Vereinen asked. For once, the Master was asking questions like a student, and Reith found that funny.

"Because there is one Shadow and many, many more of us," Reith replied simply.

"Sometimes I wish I had your faith," Vereinen said, somewhat sadly.

They chatted for a few more minutes about nothing much in particular before Vereinen excused himself so Reith could get some rest. As he left the room, Vereinen blew out the candle on the dresser. When he was gone, Reith realized how tired he was. He had scarcely closed his eyes when he fell into a deep sleep.

Hours later, he was startled awake by yelling outside and the sounds of people running. He sat up in his bed and tried to look out the window, but all he could see from the bed were roof tops and the city wall in the distance.

Then his door burst open and Rose stepped in. "The siege of Darren Shahr has begun."

15

———————

Reith did not fall back asleep that night. Unfortunately, his leg kept him down in his bed, and Rose kept checking on him to make sure he wasn't going anywhere.

Outside his window, the sounds of battle came to his ears. Shouts from the defenders on the walls pierced the night air. Soldiers ran through the city to reach the walls.

After about thirty minutes of agonized listening, there was a knock at his door and Dema and Ellamora entered.

"How are you?" Dema asked.

"My leg is the least of my worries at the moment," Reith replied. "What's happening? Tell me everything. I hate being stuck here."

"Well," Ellamora began, "about an hour ago, we were woken by the steward informing us that the elves had arrived at Darren Shahr. He also told us the others, Romulus, Brauron, Aytos, Myon, and Vereinen were summoned to help with the defense effort."

"We offered to help," Dema chimed in. "But the Steward would have none of it."

"So what did you do?" Reith asked.

"Went to the wall to help, of course," Ellamora said and flashed a grin at him.

"Naturally," Reith said with a smile.

"We went to the storeroom first and got more arrows," Dema said. "Then we went to the wall. Got a few shots off at elves. They were coming toward the wall with tall ladders."

"So why are you here now?" Reith asked.

"Vereinen saw us and sent us," Ellamora answered. "He knew you would be worried sick stuck here in your bed."

"He wasn't wrong," Reith replied.

"He wanted us to come keep you company," Dema said. "He said it would be more helpful in the long run."

"And we agreed with him," Ellamora said. "So here we are."

"What did he mean by, 'in the long run?'" Reith asked.

"This battle is going to last awhile," Dema answered. "It's a full-on siege."

"What do you know of the battle?" Reith asked.

"The elves have surrounded the city," Ellamora explained. "They seem intent on breaching the walls, but they have cut off supply lines, so they might be content with trying to starve us out."

"That's a cheery thought."

"Quite," Ellamora agreed.

"So, when you're healed, you'll have plenty of time to shoot that bow of yours," Dema said.

"Was Vereinen going to fight?" Reith asked with concern.

"No, and neither was Myon," Ellamora answered. "They made themselves available to King Rendar for consultation and advising."

"Good," Reith replied. "I'm glad he won't fight."

"Let's hope it stays that way," Ellamora said.

"So how do we win this fight?" Reith asked. "How do you assess the situation, our defenses, and the elves strategy?"

"Time is on their side," Ellamora said. "If nothing changes, eventually we will not have enough food to keep fighting. We'll either starve or surrender. We need to change the game to win."

"Like Briana," Reith said, thinking back to the history lesson Vereinen gave.

"Exactly," Ellamora said.

"Easier said than done, though," Dema replied.

"Well, let's think on it. We can come up with something that will work," Reith said.

Dema and Ellamora stayed by his side all day, though occasionally one would leave to go and get news of how the battle was progressing. Reith in particular enjoyed the quiet moments alone with Dema. They did not say much, but simply enjoyed one another's company.

Every few hours, a nurse would come check Reith's bandages. It was often Rose. In the late afternoon, he was permitted to walk across the room and sit in the wooden chair. He winced with every step of his right leg, but he gritted his teeth and made his way across the room before plopping down in the chair.

At dinner, Vereinen and Myon came into his room. Vereinen was delighted to see Reith sitting in the chair. After the pleasantries were over, Reith asked what was on his mind.

"How is the battle going?"

"Neither well, nor poorly," Myon responded. "It's hard to say for sure. We are looking at only the first few hours of a siege that shall last weeks or months."

"Well, at least it's not going poorly," Reith answered.

"From what we can tell," Vereinen began, "more and more elven ships have been making their way up from Balkh, strengthening their numbers."

"The walls should keep them out," Ellamora pointed out.

"Well, I don't think we have to worry about them breaking into the city," Myon said. "They've cut off supply lines. Balkh has fallen and it seems the rest of the kingdom is unaware of our plight."

"Is there no hope?" Reith asked, and the words *fight for them* echoed in his mind.

"There is always hope," Vereinen said. "While there is breath in our lungs and beauty and goodness in the world, there is hope."

Later that afternoon, Rose gave Reith a glimmer of hope.

"If all goes well, you should be able to leave tomorrow," she said. "You'll be right as rain. Just don't take it too hard for a few days."

"You mean I can't immediately start fighting?" Reith asked disappointed.

"There will be plenty of time for that when you're fully healed," she scolded.

At sunset, Dema and Ellamora bid him farewell and departed. Dema planted a kiss on his lips which he thoroughly enjoyed.

Ellamora rolled her eyes at them.

The sounds of battle still rung out in the distance, but it seemed to be less than the commotion of the previous night. He settled down for sleep, and all he could think of was the long, bloody fight before them.

After breakfast, Rose deemed him fit for leaving.

"Just as I suspected," she said, inspecting his leg, "you are healed enough to leave. You won't want to run or jump or anything like that for a few days, or else you might end up right back here, and then what use will you be to anyone?"

"Thank you, Rose," Reith said gratefully.

He collected his things from the chair. His quiver only had a couple of arrows left, so he made a mental note to visit the armory as soon as possible. He strapped his sword on, and instinctively grasped the handle as if readying to unsheathe it for battle. The metal felt warm and familiar in his hand. It was now an extension of himself and lying-in bed without it for so long felt wrong.

As he was readying to leave, Dema and Ellamora returned.

"You're wanted in the strategy room by King Rendar and Romulus," Dema said. "We all are."

"What do they want?" Reith asked.

"What else but the war?" Ellamora replied.

The three of them departed, and Reith gave a final wave to Rose.

"Thanks again," he said. "I hope to not see you here again."

"That's my wish too," she said, giving him a smile.

Dema and Ellamora flanked Reith on either side as they walked through the city. He had no idea where he was going, so they provided the directions. His calf was stiff from the bruising and lack of use, so they walked slowly. But the pain was nearly non-existent.

"How is it feeling?" Dema asked after they had walked for several minutes.

"Better than I thought it would feel," Reith answered.

"That's good," Dema said. "If we need to slow down or take a break, just let us know."

"Thanks, but I think I'm okay right now."

As they walked, the streets of Darren Shahr were desolate, which surprised Reith.

"Where is everyone?" Reith asked.

"Every able-bodied fighter is at the walls or resting from a shift at the walls," Dema explained. "Everyone is on half day shifts. Everyone else is lying low. There's nothing to do anymore. They're all waiting to see what's going to happen."

"Strange," replied Reith. "I would have thought the streets would have been crowded today."

"It was more so yesterday," Ellamora said. "People were going out and buying supplies. I wouldn't be surprised if all the shops and street vendors had sold out of their goods that people wanted to stock up on."

"Do we have any idea how much food is stored up in the city?" Reith asked.

"No idea," Dema answered. "Though we may find out soon."

They entered the military center of the city where the barracks, dining hall, armory, and strategy room were. Armed guards saluted as they passed.

"That was interesting," Reith noted.

"We're important," Ellamora said with a smile.

A guard opened the door to the strategy room as they approached and Dema took the lead, followed by Ellamora, then Reith. Rendar was seated at one end of the table with his advisors and Queen Kalis, much like they had been seated the other day. Romulus was on the other end, flanked by Myon and Vereinen. Rejnik, Brauron, and Aytos sat farther down the table on the other side from the door. Dema took a seat, leaving a space between herself and Vereinen, and Reith eased himself down, grateful to take the weight off his leg which was now protesting at the amount of work required of it.

"Reith," Rendar said warmly, "how is your leg?"

"It's fine," Reith said as he gently massaged the place where the arrow had struck him.

"I am pleased to see you up and about," the king said. "Thank you for joining us. Now, onto the grim business at hand. Tabriz, would you catch everyone up on where we stand?"

"Yes sire," Tabriz replied. "The elven force has steadily grown larger as more and more ships approach Darren Shahr from the south. We have no real knowledge of the size of their force, but we've estimated them to have a force of somewhere between 5,000 and 15,000 soldiers. All the while, their number continues to grow. By how much, we do not know. Our standing army in Darren Shahr is only 3,000 soldiers, but we have conscripted 7,000 more, putting our numbers right at an even 10,000. In the event that things grow worse, we can call on an additional 10,000 older men and younger boys, but we would like to avoid that at all costs."

"Thank you, Tabriz," Rendar said. "Now, Mengar, can you tell us what the elves' strategy is at the moment?"

Mengar nodded, then spoke. "The elves have sent their soldiers all around the city. They have stationed roughly a quarter of their force at each of our four main gates. This effectively blocks us in and prevents us from accessing the river, as Darren Shahr was constructed in such a way to prevent enemy ships from sailing right into the city itself. It makes us more secure from attack but prevents us from sending out any messengers or any ships to break through the elven lines. We are stuck here. For the most part, the elves have stayed away from the walls of the city themselves. They have archers shooting arrows at our defenders, but it's mainly to be a nuisance to us than an actual strategy of war. Still, we have lost a couple of dozen soldiers to their arrows by my count. The bulk of their forces are working in the forest, building siege machines. We have seen trees felled. They haven't shown their hand, but we can assume they are making battering rams, towers to roll up to the walls, and long ladders. They may even be making catapults to fling rocks and such at us. When they have enough side machines, we assume they will attack with full force."

"Thank you, Mengar," Rendar said when the dwarf general had finished. "And lastly, Sahand, will you give us the state of the city itself."

"Our biggest concern now is food," Sahand said. "We have plenty of water. By an estimation, if we consume food as we have been, with no change in our supply lines, all our food would be gone in three or four weeks. With heavy rationing, we can stretch that out to two months. In short, we must seek an end to the fighting and drive the elves off before then or …" and he trailed off, leaving the grim reality unspoken.

"That gives us some time to devise a strategy," King Rendar said. "We do not have to win today or this week, but we will have to get rid of them soon."

"What can we do to get rid of them?" Romulus asked. "Surely at some point, an attack is warranted."

"We can hold them at bay for an indefinite period of time," Mengar replied. "Their attempts to breach the wall will be futile. But I agree with you that we need to plan an attack at some point."

"An attack will require opening our gates," Sahand answered. "They out number our fighting force and can prevent us from even riding out. They may swarm into the city as we try to attack them."

"Yes, that is quite risky," King Rendar said. "I would prefer to not take that course of action if we can help it."

"We need to make sure we do not wait too long to take whatever course of action we decide," Reith piped up. "If we are going to attack, we need to do it while our fighters are strong, and not in two months when their stomachs are empty and their strength is gone."

"Good point, Reith," Rendar praised. "There is something to be said about haste in our actions. They are busy with their construction right now, so maybe we could catch them unaware, strike a quick blow, then retreat into the city."

"I don't like it," Sahand replied. "Any opening of our gates could very well prove disastrous."

"Is it not better to die fighting for our freedom than dying by famine?" Romulus asked.

The question hung over the table like a fog.

"What we need," said Kalis, breaking the silence and speaking for the first time, "is to determine what exactly would drive them away from the city. How many men could they stand to lose and continue fighting? What motivates their commanders and their soldiers? If Romulus is right about his father's motivations, this is his father's war, this is the Shadow's war. The average elf soldier may not care a lick about dwarves or besieging Darren Shahr."

"How can we determine that information though?" Tabriz replied with a scoff. All eyes turned to Romulus.

"Queen Kalis is right," Romulus began. "The average soldier doesn't care about this war. They simply want to survive and go home. That would play into our favor if it came to a direct confrontation. The general and commanders in charge could not go home in retreat, but the average soldier would, I think."

"So how do we use that to our advantage?" Rendar asked. "Will they faint in battle?"

"No, they're too well trained for that," Romulus replied. "But perhaps if we somehow managed to take out their general and commanders, that could cause them all to go home."

"How do we do that?" Rendar asked. "Do we know who the general is? Or how many commanders they have? We don't even know the full size of their army."

"There will be one general," Romulus replied. "And most likely there are three lesser generals under him. And each ship has a captain."

"Can we tell them apart from the average soldier?" Rejnik asked.

"The general will almost certainly never show his face to the walls," answered Romulus. "He will be camped in the forest somewhere directing the troops. I don't even know who that general is. The three lower generals will be wearing silver leaf pins on the collars of their shirts. Captains are wearing the same, but in bronze. The general's pin is gold if anyone were to see him."

"So if the general is in the forest, are the lower generals commanding the forces on the other three sides of the city?" Reith asked.

"Good question, Reith," Romulus replied. "That would make sense to me."

"Could a lone assassin make his way into the camp by

night and murder the general?" Rendar asked. "And perhaps three other assassins take out the other three?"

"That would be an interesting strategy," Romulus said, thinking it through. "Any assassin would have to know they are on a suicide mission. I assumed we would lower them down from the walls on a cloudy or moonlit night. If captured, we can provide no help. If successful, they will not be able to return to the city. We can't open the gates for them. They would be in disarray at that point. But would it be enough to force them to leave? I don't know the answer to that."

"I think it's worth thinking about more," Rendar said. "We have time, so we don't need to decide on that today. But for the meantime, I will make an announcement in the city square this afternoon that everyone needs to cut back on their food intake and that each person should help their neighbor in need. Let us meet again tomorrow morning. Each of you think on our problem and try to come up with a strategy to get us out of this mess."

With that, the meeting adjourned.

"Let's go to the armory," Reith suggested. "I need more arrows."

Dema accompanied Reith, but Ellamora said she was going with Romulus and the others.

They entered the chamber with all the weapons, and Reith went to the stock of arrows, which was greatly diminished from the last time he had entered. He stuffed as many as would fit comfortably in his quiver and looked around. He spotted Dema whirling a battle staff around her head with such tremendous speed and skill that it caused him to stop in his tracks.

"Wow!" he exclaimed. "That's amazing?"

"Oh, this?" Dema replied with feigned disinterest. "Mere child's play." She stopped the staff and beat the end on the ground, and it echoed off the stone with a loud boom.

"How did you learn to do that?" Reith asked, thinking about how useful such a skill would be in battle.

"I've been twirling sticks and staffs for as long as I can remember. I've always just picked them up and given them a whirl."

"You never cease to surprise me," Reith said.

"I hope I never do."

Dema dropped the staff and stepped toward Reith with ferocity in her eyes. Before he knew what was happening, she was kissing him as she had never kissed him before, and he surrendered to the kiss and her touch.

16

The following week went by slowly with each day closely resembling the previous. Each morning, the war council met to discuss the ongoing siege and strategies for winning. Nothing concrete had yet been decided, but with each passing day, the tension in the room heightened. Everyone knew the clock was ticking, and no one wanted to wait until they were forced to act in a desperate way.

After the council meetings, Reith explored the city, often with only Dema by his side, but sometimes Ellamora and Romulus. Vereinen and Myon spent their days in the libraries and record halls of Darren Shahr, and the two of them were becoming fast friends.

Most of all, Reith enjoyed the time he was able to spend alone with Dema. He was swept along in the passion of their romance, and if there weren't a war going on, it would have been the happiest time of his life. Even so, she frequently drove the siege from his mind.

Amid all of this, he still managed to take to the walls a couple times a day and shoot arrows at elves who strayed too close to the walls. In the distance, trees continued to fall, and with each passing day, it seemed that the elves were about to mount their all-out offensive. But the waiting continued.

On the morning of the seventh day after they had returned to Darren Shahr, Rejnik asked at the council whether it would be a good idea to send out a raiding party to try and damage the siege works the elves were building.

"Waiting allows them to grow strong and us weak," Rejnik pointed out after outlining his idea. "They are nowhere near the walls, for the most part. A small raiding party on horseback could ride out with flaming arrows and attempt to do some damage."

"It's a worthy idea," King Rendar replied, and his hand stroked his chin as he pondered.

"We don't know their exact position or what sort of siege work they are building," Tabriz pointed out. "Our riders would be riding swiftly toward Creator knows what. The odds of even a handful of that group surviving are too small to be considered seriously."

"Well put," Rendar replied. "But that leaves us in the situation Rejnik just described. While we wait, they grow strong and we grow weak. We must act."

"At what point is the risk worth it?" Rejnik asked. "When we are starving and the elves are beating down our gate?"

"Would you lead this charge?" Rendar asked pointedly.

"It would be my honor," Rejnik answered, puffing his chest out in pride.

The answer caught Rendar off guard for a moment, but he quickly shook it off.

"Very well, Rejnik," Rendar said. "You are very brave, or very foolish. Your desire is granted. How many men do you require?"

"As many as my king is willing to spare," he responded dutifully.

"Your force must be small," King Rendar replied. "I will not risk the lives of many men on this errand. Beside yourself, I will give you five other riders. That should be enough to ride in, wreak some havoc, and perhaps escape, if you catch them by surprise and do not linger."

"So, your plan is to charge out of the gate, set some things on fire, and then what?" Romulus asked.

"And then get back to the city," Rejnik answered. "Or escape to the mountains."

"And you are sure you want to do this?" Rendar asked.

"With my whole heart," Rejnik said. "If this gives our city a chance, I will do whatever it takes."

"And you'll permit this, Rendar?" Romulus asked with a ferocity he had yet to show at Darren Shahr.

"Easy, Prince Romulus," replied Rendar, even remembering his court manners. "What choice do we have? As this council has stated repeatedly, we must do something to achieve the upper hand before it is too late."

"But sacrificing this man's life, and the lives of five others?" Romulus asked. "Can there be no other way?"

"I don't think we are necessarily sacrificing our lives," Rejnik said quietly. "I have no intention of dying. We have horses, they have none. If we are heavily armored, we can escape."

"And what would you do, Rejnik," Rendar asked slowly, "out in the forest, you and five men?"

"Survive, and help," Rejnik replied. "We can more easily raid them from outside the gates than we can from inside."

"It's like Princess Briana," Reith said. "She was more powerful outside the city than inside."

"Exactly, Reith," Vereinen said proudly.

"Then why limit Rejnik's raid to six?" Reith asked. "Why not a hundred? Two hundred? Unencumbered by the walls, they could do quite a bit of damage in short raids, then ride away into the forest. The elves wouldn't pursue them away from the walls. For one, they couldn't run with horses. And it would allow us to swarm out from the city and overwhelm them."

"I find this line of thinking stirring my heart," King Rendar replied. "What about five hundred men charging from the city, immediately into the wilderness, and then raids at various times for the next few weeks?"

"Whatever my king commands," said Rejnik.

"Do any of you have objections of this course of action?" Rendar asked the council.

"One," Tabriz interjected. "When these five hundred horses and riders leave the city, how will we prevent the elves from rushing in?"

"Oh, I think that's relatively easy to arrange," Rendar replied. "On either side of the gate, we station a thousand men. The riders will gallop through the center, and once clear of the gate, they are on their own. On the wall above the gate, we have as many archers as possible, covering them as they depart. When the last horse is clear of the gate, our force pushes together with spears out to the wilderness while the gate is lowered. We can have boiling oil on top of the wall, just in case. If they attack, they will not win entrance, and their effort will deal them heavy losses."

"Then I am satisfied," Tabriz replied.

"All in favor of this course of action?" Rendar asked the room, and "Ayes" chimed all around. "Very good. It is settled. At dawn, we shall open the gate."

"May we be part of the company of five hundred?" Romulus asked.

"No, Prince Romulus. I need your bows on the walls and your brains in this room. It's a long struggle ahead."

The rest of the day, preparations were made throughout the city. Rejnik chose his company and they saddled their horses and packed supplies for weeks in the forest. Reith and the others found a chance to practice archery at a practice range.

While they were shooting arrows into the targets, Queen Kalis arrived.

"As you were," she said with a smile as Reith and the others stopped what they were doing to acknowledge the queen's presence. "I'm here to shoot, same as you."

Queen Kalis proved to be quite the remarkable shot. Arrow after arrow struck the center of the target at the other end of the room.

"You're amazing!" Romulus exclaimed.

"I ought to be after twenty years of shooting," she replied with a smile. "I am much better than my husband."

"Will you be on the wall tomorrow?" Romulus asked.

"Of course," she answered. "Rendar will be too. Kings and queens must fight for their people."

"Your bravery is admirable, your majesty," Romulus replied.

"You know, you are nothing like your brother," Kalis observed.

Romulus stiffened.

"Oh, I mean that as a compliment. You are nothing like I would have thought."

"I will take that as a compliment," Romulus replied. "I mean you no ill will."

"Nor I, you," she answered. "But we must find a way to end this tension between our people."

"When I ascend the throne, there will be peace. We

will send ambassadors to you and hope that you do the same."

"Good," replied the queen. "Let peace and your ascension come swiftly then."

———

Before dawn, Reith was awoken by the steward's knock on the door. He dressed quickly, belted his sword to his hip, and retrieved his bow and quiver from the empty bed he had laid it on the night before. He and Romulus met Brauron and Aytos in the hall. In the dining hall, he saw Dema and Ellamora, each dressed for action with bows and quivers.

"Good morning," Reith said with a yawn. He gave Dema a quick hug before he sat.

"Good morning," she and Ellamora replied.

Breakfast was a simple toast and jam, which Reith devoured eagerly. When they were done eating, they departed for the walls.

It was colder than Reith had expected, and the wind made it all the chillier. He shivered in the predawn air. By the light of a torch, he could see his breath. He saw Dema shivering too, so he put his arm around her waist and pulled her closer. She buried her head in his chest, and he smiled despite the cold.

Below them, the sound of horses snorting and stamping and the jingle of saddles rose to them. The entire exercise was supposed to be silent, but Reith feared they were making too much noise.

Outside the city, all was quiet.

That's odd. You'd think they'd be attacking the city, at least with a few soldiers.

He stared into the darkness, but the torchlight

prevented him from seeing much beyond the walls. Behind him, the sky began to lighten ever so slightly in the east.

The click of a wheel and chains began and Reith realized the portcullis was being lifted. When it was up, the gates slowly creaked outward. Horses began galloping out of the city and he put an arrow on the string, ready for anything.

Then a horn blasted from the direction of the elven camp.

As horses and riders streamed from the city, the sun broke over the horizon and cast a pale light on the morning. From out of the trees, thousands of elves stepped from the shadows and pointed spears at the advancing cavalry.

Reith spotted Rejnik in the lead, and he hesitated, slowing his horse just a hair. Then he reeled back as if punched, and he fell from his saddle. Reith lost sight of him as the rest of the horses galloped past him. Without their commander, the next dwarves were unsure of what to do and arrows soon took them from their saddles too.

The cavalry was in complete disarray. Riderless horses aimlessly ambled about, causing the horses with riders to stop in their tracks.

"Fire!" a general called on the wall and Reith sent arrow after arrow at the elves, but they had shields up as they advanced. No arrow slowed them.

Now riders were attempting to go back to the city, but the gates were already shutting behind them.

"Flee! Flee you fools!" King Rendar bellowed from the top of the wall as he sent arrows toward the elves.

The remaining horsemen galloped both left and right, escaping in either direction, but not as a cohesive whole. The whole operation was a mess.

The elves ignored the fleeing riders and continued to

advance on the gate. Just then, tree branches parted and two rows of elves stepped from the forest carrying something large between them. It was the trunk of a large tree, and they had fitted metal to one end and handles along its length. It was a battering ram.

"All arrows on the battering ram!" Rendar yelled to the archers. Reith took aim at the lead elf, and let fly an arrow, but it glanced harmlessly off its shield in its other hand. The elves carrying the ram were armored head to toe, with the shield in front of them providing even more protection. Reith looked for a hole, something to aim for. He saw two small weaknesses.

"Shoot for their eyes and their hands!" he called out. The eye slits of their helmets were small, but an accurate arrow might have a chance. He noticed their gloved hands holding the ram were simple leather.

He aimed at the first hand, and his arrow missed by the narrowest of margins and glanced off the battering ram. Other arrows focused on that area and eventually one hit the mark and the first elf let go. Another took his place.

Reith aimed at the eyes of this one, and his arrow missed the tiny mark, and simply dinged off the metal helmet. He tried again with similar results. He shot at the hand again and was rewarded with a strike. And yet another elf took that one's place.

The ram was now a mere ten yards from the wall, and Reith and the other archers were shooting nearly straight down. Eye slots were out of the question now, their only hope was the hands.

Above the gate, dwarves swarmed with a large black kettle, full of boiling oil. As the elves approached, they pulled ropes and cascaded the hot liquid down on the advancing ram.

The oil splattered down on them and the elves

shrieked, throwing themselves down in agony. The front of the ram fell as the first ten or so elves let go.

"Fire arrows!" Rendar shouted, and Reith wrapped a cloth around his arrow tip and dipped it in a torch. He shot at the ram itself now, and his arrow impeded in the wood and ignited on the oil. The battering ram was soon engulfed in flames and even more elves let go. The oil on the ground caught fire and consumed the fallen elves in flame as well. Their shrieks and screams and writhing on the ground gradually died away as the fire took their lives.

"Oh my," Dema said, a look of disgust on her face. "That's awful."

The remaining elves retreated, and soon the only thing left before the wall was the fallen ram and the bodies of elves and dwarves who had fallen in the battle. A few riderless horses ambled around, unsure of what to do or where to go. Reith thought he could make out Rejnik's body, broken and battered by hooves, but he was not sure.

"What a waste," Rendar said, throwing down his helmet and kicking it with his boot. The helmet clanged against the stone wall, and bounced down the stairs, making a loud metallic clunk with every step. It finally came to a rest in the courtyard.

"At least we stopped the ram," Reith said quietly to Dema.

"But at what cost?" she replied. "And what a monstrous tactic."

Reith had nothing to say to that.

Later, when the flames had extinguished, the elves returned and carried off what was left of the ram. Then they soon returned with another, and there was no oil to pour on them this time. Reith and other archers managed to make small dents in their numbers by shooting at hands, but the ram continued moving forward, step by step. Finally, they were at the wall, and the elves picked up their pace and flung the ram forward into the gate with a loud crash. The gate held, but the main siege had officially begun.

The defenders realized arrows were nearly useless, so the command came to drop bricks and rocks on the heads of the ram wielders. This proved to be a more effective strategy, as the falling rocks did quite a bit of damage to the heads of the elves below, even with heavy helmets protecting them. Furthermore, the fallen rocks littering the ground proved treacherous to not an insignificant number of elven ankles.

Ram hits came few and far between as a result of these tactics, and Reith was cheered by the minor victory. The gate was holding firm before the few hits that did come, and the courtyard behind the gate was crowded with soldiers in the event of a breach.

"It's going well!" he triumphantly declared to Ellamora, who was beside him chucking bricks down on the heads below.

"Why on Terrasohnen would you say a thing like that?" she asked angrily.

Reith shrugged. "Well, it's true."

"I know it's true," Ellamora scolded. "But you don't declare it!"

"Why not?" he asked.

"Bad luck! Things could change in an instant. You're tempting fate."

"You believe in that?" he asked.

"You don't? You who hear voices calling you toward a destiny, you don't?"

"Well, if you put it that way …"

"Better to leave it alone. If things are going well, don't go blabbing about it."

Ellamora proved prophetic, though Reith was unsure about the fate or luck aspect of it. About an hour after his comment, more elves poured from the woods, pushing giant towers on wheels toward the walls of Darren Shahr. The towers were enclosed, with small spaces for elves to shoot arrows from. As far as Reith could tell, they were empty while being pushed, but once they were against the walls, elves would swarm up them.

"Every available man to the battlement!" King Rendar roared. There was a flurry of activity on the wall. The defenders threw down their bricks and stones and took up their arrows instead and began to pepper the oncoming tower pushers with arrows if anyone showed themselves. But these elves too were heavily armored, and most arrows bounced off.

Slowly, ever so slowly, the towers crept toward the walls.

"Fire, fire!" Rendar bellowed. "Set the blasted things on fire!"

Torches and oil were brought to the battlements with great haste, and soon flaming arrows were fired toward the towers. But one by one, the arrows sputtered out on the towers. The flames could find no hold on the wood.

"Why won't they light?" Dema asked.

"They probably drenched the wood with water just before rolling them out of the woods," Reith replied grimly. "It's what I would have done. It's smart."

"Archers, away from the towers," Rendar called to the defenders. "Keep shooting! Let's burn these things. Everyone else, spears and swords at hand. We fight for our freedom!"

"Go with the archers," Reith pleaded with Dema and Ellamora.

"Not on your life," Dema replied, returning her bow to her back and unsheathing a sword.

"We're in this until the end," Ellamora added.

"But you'll be safer with the archers!" Reith protested.

"So would you," Dema retorted. "But I see that you're planning on staying here and fighting," she said, pointing to the sword in his hands.

"Is it because were *girls*?" Ellamora asked.

"What? No!" Reith replied. "I just want you to be safe."

"Safe?" Dema asked. "When have we ever been safe since you met us?"

The towers rolled ever closer and Reith saw through the cracks in the wood that elves were climbing up inside it while it rolled. They were a mere twenty yards from the walls now.

"Fine, stay," Reith said. "But promise me you'll be safe."

"It's a battle, Reith," Dema answered. "We can't promise anything." And then she stood on tiptoes and planted a kiss on his lips, which surprised him at first, but then he surrendered to it. The battle and all else faded away until—

"Hey!" Ellamora shouted at them. "There's a battle going on if you hadn't noticed."

Reith and Dema broke apart and gripped their weapons and gritted their teeth for battle.

It was now clear that the nearest tower wasn't coming right at them, but rather at a spot on the wall about ten yards to their left. Dwarves lined up with spears, ready for action.

At ten yards, Reith could spot hinges on the front

wooden panel of the tower. Behind it crouched many elven soldiers. As the tower continued rolling slowly toward the wall, the front panel swung forward and crashed down on the top of the wall. Elves pounced forward with spears pointed at the defenders. With an almighty crash, the tower came to a stop against the wall. Dwarves lunged forward with their own spears, but the first few fell to the fury of the elves attack. Reith, Ellamora, and Dema could only watch helplessly as the elves gained the upper hand and several reached the very wall itself. More and more elves streamed from the tower and more were climbing to take their place.

Looking down, Reith saw there was a thick line of elves leading to the tower, each ready to climb up and attempt to take the city. He quickly turned on the spot and saw that four of the towers were now engaged with the wall at various points and the dwarves had their hands full keeping the elves at bay.

The elves nearest Reith managed to cut their way all the way to the inside edge of the wall. Then, they turned each way, with half pushing toward Reith, Dema, and Ellamora and half going the other way.

"Let's go!" called to Dema and Ellamora, and the three of them leapt forward into the fray.

The first elf Reith met was surprised at his sudden attack and swiftly fell beneath Reith's blade. Another quickly took his place, but Reith was able to knock him off balance and finish him off with a quick backhand stroke followed by a forehand swipe at his neck. The third elf matched up well with him. With his spear, the elf was able to block Reith's attacks, and Reith was able to dodge the elf's stabs. Reith worried that he wouldn't overcome this one, but then the elf fell. Reith looked around and saw that Ellamora had stabbed him in the side with a dropped spear. He gave her a quick smile but was immediately engaged with another elf attacker.

Foe after foe presented themselves to Reith, but he won victory after victory. For his troubles, he received many small cuts and bruises, but nothing substantial. Just when he thought he would collapse from exhaustion, several dwarves pushed past him and entered the melee. He appreciated the break, fell back and rested against the wall away from the fighting.

He gasped for breath and took inventory of his wounds. He was covered with blood, but he was pretty sure it wasn't all his. With space to breathe and recover, he began to think of a way out of the situation.

He leaned out over the wall and saw elves were still using the battering ram on the gate. Four towers were still up against the front wall of the city, and at each point the elves and dwarves seemed evenly matched.

We need to light those things on fire or topple them, he thought to himself.

With so many elves on top, he reasoned that the towers were pretty top heavy. But they couldn't be pushed away from the city wall, because of the elves attempting to attack from the tower.

But what if they could be pushed to the side?

His mind raced at the possibility.

"Dema! Ellamora!" he called, and soon they were by his side, disentangled from the fighting. Each looked like him, covered in blood and panting and sweating.

"We need to push the towers over," he explained. "But sideways. We need something long and sturdy to push with. Help me find something."

"I know just the thing," Ellamora replied, and she raced down the stairs near them to the courtyard below. She returned with three long poles.

"What are they?" Reith asked.

"I think they are flag poles," she said. "I saw them earlier. They were piled up against a wall down below. There's no need for flags when the city is at war." She handed one to each of them.

"We have to be quick," Reith said. "I don't know how long we will have. I also don't know if this is even possible. But we must try."

With the flagpole in hand, he pushed closer to the tower and to the fighting. There was at least a couple of dwarves between him and the nearest elf soldier. He inspected the side of the tower quickly and noticed a board near the top that stuck out a bit. He reached out with the pole and stuck it under the board. He began to push. Dema stepped in next to him and placed her pole on the tower as well, then Ellamora.

The tower did not budge with his push, nor with Dema's. When Ellamora began pushing, nothing happened for an agonizingly long second.

"Keep pushing," Reith grunted.

And then, the tower began to slowly move away from them. He stepped into his push again and the tower began to move faster. The front wooden part that was laying over the wall was wrenched free with a crack, and then the tower was falling. With a huge crash, it hit the tower next to it, which began to topple over, too. Elves were sprawled out on the ground from the fall, some stirring feebly, and some not moving at all. The defenders cheered and quickly dispatched the remaining few elves unlucky enough to be on the walls with no backup.

The two remaining towers were on the other side of the gate, so Reith rushed forward, holding the pole above his head. Dema and Ellamora followed him.

They soon reached the first tower and saw King

Rendar engaged in the battle. His massive battle axe swung left and right, felling all who stood in its way.

"We need to push the tower over," Reith yelled to the nearby dwarves. "Cover us!"

The dwarves jumped into action and formed a wall between the elves and Reith, Dema, and Ellamora. Like with the other tower, they pushed their poles up against the wood and strained to push it over. This tower would not budge.

Reith grunted and strained, trying to increase his purchase on the stone wall and will the tower over, but nothing happened.

But then some of the dwarves noticed and began to add their weight to the poles. Soon half a dozen had joined them, all pushing with as much force as they could muster.

Then, ever so slowly, the tower rocked away from them slightly. The pushers redoubled their efforts and pushed with increased determination. An elf jumped from the tower onto the wall and that provided just enough weight shift that the tower began to topple. Reith and the others fell forward into the side of the wall as their poles disengaged from the tower. It crashed to the ground and spilled elves everywhere. This one did not fall into the next tower. As Reith got to his feet, he saw there was still one tower to go.

As he moved to go push that one over, there was a commotion near him. Dwarves crowded in, and he couldn't see what was going on. But then, through the throng, he caught a glimpse of King Rendar, slain and lying in a pool of blood.

17

The following morning, the strategy room was quiet and somber. Reith and the others awaited Queen Kalis to arrive.

The previous day had ended with a flurry of activity that temporarily repelled the elves from the walls. After Rendar was slain, dwarves had managed to topple the remaining tower and eliminate all elves remaining on the wall. With the towers down, the defenders were able to focus their attention on the battering ram, and soon the ram and its carriers were retreating to the cover of the forest.

With the immediate threat of attack dispelled, the defenders took care of their wounded. Rose and the other nurses and physicians were kept busy with a stream of injured dwarves. Dead bodies of elves were thrown from the wall down onto the bodies lying before the wall. Bodies of dwarves were removed to be honored.

Rendar's body was retrieved and placed on a table in the throne room. All who were able gathered and mourned over their fallen king. Kalis and her children stood beside the body. The children wept freely, and tears came to Kalis' eyes at regular intervals until there were none left to shed. Dressed in black, she was the embodiment of sorrow.

That evening, when the sun set, all who could be spared from the defense of the city gathered in the city center. Body after body was engulfed in flames, as the dwarves sang a mournful funeral ballad in an ancient tongue.

Reith struggled with how to feel. He had barely known Rendar, and he was sad at his passing, but tears did not come to his eyes as quickly as they had come with other deaths he had experienced. He felt that his mourning should not approach the level of grief that the dwarves felt.

Last of all, Rendar's body was to be burned. Kalis herself lit the funeral pyre and stepped back as flames licked her husband's frame. The firelight danced on her face, and fresh tears again fell from her eyes. She still wore black, but now she wore her ornate golden crown. Its jewels and metal reflected the light and sparkled in the night.

When the flames finished their work, a chant rose from the dwarves.

"Hail, Queen Kalis! Hail, Queen Kalis!"

Over and over, the chant rose, growing louder and louder. Then, just as soon as it began, it died away to nothing. Kalis stepped forward from her children and addressed the crowd. A hush fell over them all. Then she spoke.

"My people, today is a sorrowful day. My soul is burdened unto death at the loss of my husband, and the rest of the warriors who have fallen this day. As your queen, I will lead us out of this dark time and into the light of a new day. We will win the war and punish those responsible for our grief."

She stepped back between her children and the crowd roared their approval at her words.

And now, in the light of the new day, the strategic minds of the defense waited for their queen. At last, she entered the room. And took her usual place, leaving Rendar's former spot empty at the head of the table. His absence was made even more obvious.

"Good morning," Kalis began, addressing the room.

"On behalf of all of us, your majesty," Tabriz began, "we would like to extend our deepest condolences to you and your family."

"Thank you," she replied shortly.

"King Rendar will be sorely missed," added Sahand.

"Let us not forget brave Rejnik," Kalis stated, addressing the other empty chair in the room.

"Indeed," Romulus said. "He will be missed. A lot has happened since we last met."

"We have much to discuss," Kalis replied. "We must move forward, no matter what has happened. Let's discuss Rejnik's foolhardy errand first."

"I do not necessarily think the mission itself was foolhardy," Myon said. "But the result of the mission left a lot to be desired. Who could have known he would have charged right into the bulk of the elven force?"

"Of his five hundred, many fell," Tabriz stated. "And the rest are scattered and unorganized."

"Can we count on them completing their mission?" Kalis asked. "Can we count on them raiding the elves?"

"That is hard to say," Mengar replied. "Perhaps they will come back together. I assume there are at least three hundred left of them. But I think it would be unwise to assume that they will come together. Any contribution from them should be seen as a bonus, not an expectation."

"A sore blow indeed," Kalis said regretfully.

"I still think it was the right idea," Romulus said. "The result wasn't what we wanted, but we needed to do something to change the course of the war, and we tried a very good option."

There were murmurs of assent around the table.

"On a more positive note," Kalis replied, "we were able to repel the elves from the walls. I think the thanks for that goes to Reith, Ellamora, and Dema."

"We only did what was necessary," Reith replied, embarrassed that everyone was looking at him now.

"Well, you saved many lives," Kalis said. "If those towers remained standing, there's no telling how many would have died. The elves may have even taken the whole city. But for now, we get a reprieve. Even the battering ram has retreated."

"The situation remains dire," Tabriz pointed out. "We are still rapidly running out of food, and our first foray from the city was a disaster."

"Yes, our aim is the same as it has always been," Kalis replied. "We must find a way to repel the elves, permanently."

There was silence around the table.

"Very well. Generals, keep me posted on the war effort. Everyone else, we meet here in the morning. Keep thinking about what we can do to turn the tables and get things working in our favor."

With that, the meeting dismissed.

Reith and his companions sat down at an empty table in the dining hall.

"It seems like we are caught in between a rock and a hard place," Romulus said.

"Romulus, do the elves know you're here?" Reith asked, curious.

"No, I don't think so. It's possible they recognized me when we fought at the river, though."

"What about Remus, do they know he's here?"

"I doubt it. I didn't even know he was alive."

"What will we do about poor Remus?" Myon asked.

"I want to try and talk to him," Romulus replied. "I don't know what good that will do, but I want to try."

"Would Kalis let you?" Reith asked.

"I think so, but I need to pick an opportune time. It seems too close to Rendar's death."

"That doesn't leave you a lot of time," Vereinen pointed out. "Sooner or later, we will run out of food."

"True, true," Romulus replied.

They sat in silence for several minutes, each pondering aspects of their present difficulty. The problem of Remus and the problem of the rapidly depleting food and the war they seemed destined to lose went through Reith's head like rabbits running through an open field. Gradually, an idea began to unfold in his mind.

"Romulus," Reith began, "how do you think the elven general would react if you simply walked into the camp?"

"Depends on who the general is," Romulus replied. "Most would be utterly surprised, and I have no idea how they would behave. What do you have in mind?"

"I was just wondering; would it be possible for you to take control of the elven force by virtue of being the crown prince? These elves could hardly know that you are at odds with your father."

"That's an interesting possibility," Romulus mused. He looked toward Myon, who sat with an elbow on the table and hands closed in front of his face.

"It would be highly risky," Myon said at last. "Either

you would take control of the army or they would expect you to fight against us. And you would need a story about why you are here."

Reith looked around to make sure no dwarves were nearby, then whispered, "What if you and Remus walked into the camp together? You could say you were here on a rescue mission, and their attack was just cover for you to enter the city."

"Now that is an interesting strategy," Romulus replied in a low voice. "That may just work. If we could only get Remus."

"Would Remus even go along with such a plan?" Myon asked. "We don't know where his heart lies."

"It doesn't matter what he thinks if he's in a prison cell," replied Romulus.

"Would Kalis allow him to be released?" Reith asked.

"There's no saying," Vereinen replied. "But I think before we get to that point, there is wisdom in speaking with Remus. How Kalis reacts to such a request would enlighten our designs to free him."

"If we ask for his release and she says no, our plan is completely ruined," Romulus said. "So let us keep this plan a secret for now. I will request to speak with him, alone. If she acquiesces, which I have no doubt she will for this small request, then I will meet with him and get to the bottom of where his loyalties lie, without divulging our plan to any listening ears, of which I am sure there will be some nearby. After, I will relay all that I have learned to you."

There were nods of assent around the table. Romulus pushed his chair back and stood.

"I will go to Queen Kalis now," he replied. "Wish me fair fortune."

He departed, leaving the rest of them silently at the table.

"Well, I suppose we should go up to the wall and see how we may be of use," Reith declared.

Reith, Dema, and Ellamora rose and left Myon, Vereinen, Brauron, and Aytos. They stopped by the armory to restock their arrows and a few minutes later, found themselves on the wall. It was a chilly day and Reith shivered when an icy wind from the mountains ruffled his clothes.

The battering ram was continuing its assault on the gate and dwarf soldiers had piled up rocks and debris in front of the gate in the event the elves broke through. On top of the wall, Reith, Dema, and Ellamora pulled out their bows and began aiming at battering ram carriers. To Reith, it seemed like a waste of arrows. The elves were heavily armored and no weakness presented itself to them. After a few fruitless arrows, Reith lowered his bow.

"It's no use," he said as the battering ram boomed against the portcullis again.

"I agree," Ellamora replied, also lowering her bow.

"What can we do?" Dema asked. "We can't just let them keep banging away at the gate."

"The only thing we can do is end the battle once and for all," Reith said. "Hopefully we can do that soon."

That evening, after dinner, the humans and elves remained at their table while dwarves slowly dispersed to their beds or to the wall. When most of the dwarves had gone, Romulus began his story.

"I was able to meet with Remus," he said. "Kalis agreed to my request to meet with him straightaway."

"How was her temperament?" Myon asked. "Do we have a clue as to what she would say if we asked for his release?"

"There was nothing in her action toward me this morning that gives me a clue one way or another," Romulus replied.

"So, what happened with Remus?" Ellamora asked.

"I was led by two guards down into the dungeons," Romulus said. Reith shuddered at the memory of his stay in the dungeons of Sardis.

"The guards remained by the door, took my weapons from me, and opened the door for me to go in and see my brother. It wasn't a cell like you would think of as a dungeon. It was just a small room with a bed, a small table, and a few books. They are taking care of him."

"Well, that's good," Myon replied.

"Remus was reading on his bed when I entered, so I sat at the table. I asked him to tell me everything, about how he ended up here, about what our father told him, everything. I won't tell the whole tale, that's his to tell, but here is the gist."

"Growing up in Sardis, he constantly felt under appreciated. He was acutely aware of his position in relation to me and the throne. He felt he needed to do things for our father to earn his love. He tried always to be the best at everything, at his studies, at swordsmanship, at riding, at everything. But he never felt it was enough. So one day, he snapped. He went to our father and told him he would do anything for him. My father, cruel man that he is, saw the opportunity, and sent Remus and two others to assassinate the king of the dwarves. So Remus loaded up and rode through the wilderness and came down on Darren Shahr from the north. They traversed the mountains and great mountain lakes and came quietly to the city. In the evening, they stealthily climbed the wall and entered the city. Well, you know the city now. They had no knowledge of it, no idea of where they were going. And they became cornered by guards. The guards shot Remus' two companions, and at that point he surrendered. He has spent two years here."

"How is his thinking now?" Myon asked. "How does he feel about the dwarves, about your father?"

"He has had many long days and nights to think," Romulus replied. "He is still confused about our father. Something deep down in him wants to earn our father's approval. But I told him about the Shadow and he seemed to come around. But there is still much bitterness in his soul. Time and the God of Light alone can heal his soul."

"So where does that leave us?" Reith asked. "Are we any closer to ending this war?"

"Alas," Romulus sighed, "we may not know the answer to that question unless we test out this plan of ours. But in doing so, we stretch out our hand beyond the point of safely bringing it back. If we seek Remus' release, with the queen's blessing or without, our fate is intertwined with that course of action, for good or for ill."

"The future is but a mystery," Myon replied. "All that is left to us is to make the best decision with the information that we have before us."

"And if we're wrong?" Ellamora asked. Her question hung ominously over the table.

"Then the God of Light will receive us into is everlasting light soon, whether slain by famine, elf, or dwarf," Romulus answered.

"There's our answer," Reith said. "We will die from famine if we do nothing. We will die at the hands of the elves if they breach the walls or if they are unresponsive to Romulus and Remus. We will die by the dwarves if they are unwilling to part with Remus. The only hope we have of escaping death is the risky path before us."

"Well said, Reith," Vereinen answered.

"Are we all in agreement, at least on this: that we attempt to take command of the elven force with myself and Remus at the head of it?" Romulus asked.

Every head nodded in agreement.

"That still leaves us with many other questions to decide," Myon replied. "Shall we commit to our plan without the blessing of the queen? Or shall we seek her blessing, knowing our plan has failed if she refuses, but knowing our resources will be greater if she acquiesces?"

No one answered. Reith's eyes flicked from face to face. Each was a mixture of fear and determination in various quantities.

God of Light, help us.

Finally, Myon broke the silence.

"If Rendar were still alive, I would consider it foolish to seek his blessing on this. With him gone, the decision is far from certain."

"I am in agreement on that score," said Romulus. "Our decision would have been easy in that circumstance."

"What if we tried to see things from the queen's perspective?" Ellamora asked. "What would influence her in either direction?"

"Letting Remus go would certainly be an unpopular decision, especially in the wake of Rendar's death and so early in her reign," Romulus answered.

"Yes, the dwarf lords would hardly be supportive of such a measure," Vereinen replied.

"Yet a good leader makes the right decision, even if it is unpopular," Myon pointed out.

"What would incline her to our cause?" Romulus

asked. "We must present it in such a way that emphasizes the goodness, the rightness of our plan."

"It's a gamble, that's for sure," Dema said. "But I don't think it's too lopsided. If successful, it means an end to the siege. If we fail, what does she lose? A political prisoner she had no desire to execute, nor use as a bargaining chip. It's less mouths to feed."

"The downside for her is purely emotional," Myon agreed. "Logically, it makes sense to go with our plan."

"The heart is not so easily swayed," Vereinen replied. "But can hers be?"

"That's the question," said Romulus.

They sat in silence for several minutes. Reith pondered the conundrum before them. If they asked Queen Kalis to release Remus and she said no, they would almost surely have no chance of breaking him out of prison. The number of guards would surely increase to prevent them doing just that. Even now, the prospect of breaking Remus out of the dungeon and sneaking him and the rest of them out of the city seemed farfetched.

"I recommend we throw ourselves upon the mercy of the Queen," Reith said, breaking the silence. "If we broke Remus out, all of us would have to go to the elven camp, we couldn't stay here. And who knows if the plan would succeed if humans accompanied you, Romulus. No, the better thing would be to ask the Queen and hope she sides with us. Then Romulus, Remus, Myon, Brauron, and Aytos could go. And maybe Ellamora too," he added, looking at her. He didn't want her to go.

"And if she says no?" Romulus asked.

"Then so be it," Reith replied. "We can try to come up with another way. But I feel in my bones that she will say yes. The God of Light has brought us this far, I do not think this is where our story ends."

"I am convinced," Romulus said, banging his fist on the table to punctuate his agreement. "Does anyone object?"

No one spoke.

"Then all that's left is to decide when to present this plan."

"Tomorrow morning, in the strategy room," Myon suggested.

"With the dwarf lords there?" Romulus asked. "That seems risky."

"Better that we are there to refute them at every turn, rather than allow them to speak of our plan away from our ears," Vereinen pointed out.

"Very well, that makes sense," Romulus agreed. "I will present our plan and we will hope for the best."

"No, my prince," Myon replied. Romulus lifted a confused eyebrow toward him. "If you presented the plan, it may lead her to view it unfavorably. She may think you are wearing your heart on your sleeve and putting your blood above any other consideration. I think Reith should present it. After all, he seems to be the one coming up with all these ideas."

"He's right, Romulus," Ellamora agreed. "You're too close to the situation."

"Well, if you all are sure," Romulus began, his tone betraying that he was not at all sure about this change in tactics.

"It's for the best," Myon said, and he patted the prince on the shoulder.

The next morning, they gathered around the table in the strategy room waiting for the queen to arrive. The dwarf lords were silent and generally ignored the humans and elves at the other side of the room.

Reith yawned. He had been awoken early in the morning by Myon and Romulus who went over and over his presentation of their idea for the salvation of Darren Shahr. At long last, they were satisfied that Reith would give a good account of their plan, but Reith was emotionally and physically tired from the unexpected ordeal.

When the queen arrived and opened the meeting, Reith spoke up.

"Your majesty," he began, "I have an idea for a plan that might save the city from ruin."

The queen peered across the table in surprise.

"Really?" she asked.

"Yes, your majesty," Reith replied. "I will warn you before I begin that it is a strange plan. But I think it might just work."

Reith launched into his well-rehearsed plan. He told them how Romulus, as crown prince, might have the authority to persuade the commander to give control of the army over to him. To give Romulus a cover for being in Darren Shahr, Remus would need to be released so that Romulus could say he was on a secret rescue mission. At the mention of releasing Remus, the dwarf lords grew angry, but Kalis held up a hand to silence them. Reith continued outlining his plan, and Kalis let him finish, all the while keeping her hand up to the indignant dwarves.

"As you are well aware, there is opposition to this plan," Kalis said finally after a long pause following the conclusion of Reith's presentation. "And I myself am not totally sold on the merits of it either. Romulus, you think this may work?"

"Yes, your majesty," he replied. "My father sending an

army to attack a city as a cover for a secret rescue seems like something he might do. I think I can persuade the commander of this fact."

"And he will give you control over the army, just like that?" she asked.

"That is my hope."

"And if you fail?"

"I will not fail."

"Humor me, Romulus," the queen replied, slightly exasperated.

"If the commander is determined to continue the attack, I believe assassination may be in order."

"You would assassinate the commander of your own army?"

"If that's what it took to end this foolish battle, I would. Enough blood has been spilled."

"Hmmm," Queen Kalis said thoughtfully.

"May I speak, my queen?" Tabriz interjected.

"You have held your tongue long enough," the queen replied. "Go ahead."

"This plan is utter folly," Tabriz began. "I can see plainly what this has all been about. Prince Romulus is here on a rescue mission for his brother, and wants to discover our weaknesses. If we let him and Prince Remus leave, they would betray all our secrets to the elves. They would indeed go and command that army, but why should they leave? The city would be in their hands. This plan reeks of deception and treachery."

"I would like to add my agreement to Lord Tabriz's points," Sahand replied. Mengar nodded vigorously.

"Noted," the queen replied coolly. "And I have similar concerns. What assurance do you give that you will not betray us?"

No one answered.

"It makes no sense to let a prisoner whose life is forfeit go for the vague hope of salvation," she said. "Not unless we make arrangements beforehand. So here is what I propose, Prince Romulus. You and your brother alone will be released from this city. We can lower you from the wall by night. But the rest," she said, gesturing to Reith, Dema, Ellamora, Myon, Vereinen, Brauron, and Aytos, "will be kept as collateral. For every dawn that breaks with the elves still at our gates, we will kill one of them." Reith looked at the others in horror.

If Romulus is unsuccessful, we will all perish.

"Furthermore," she continued, "I want you to swear by the God of Light that you are true to your word. If you break your word, you will live a cursed life now and in the hereafter. So, do we have a deal?"

"By the God of Light, I will not betray you. My words are true and my heart is pure. May disaster and darkness fall upon my head if not. We have a deal."

"Very well," Queen Kalis replied. "We must send for Prince Remus at once."

18

A short time later, Remus entered the strategy room. His bruising was mostly faded and he looked much better than he did a few short weeks ago. He walked stiffly from being stuck in a cell for two years. His eyes swept the room, avoiding eye contact with the dwarves. He saw his brother and sat beside him.

"Remus," Queen Kalis began, "for the crime of attempted assassination, your life is forfeit to my people. You have been paying your life debt in prison, but now it is time for you to make payment in another way. Romulus, if you would explain the plan."

Romulus briefly explained how they would go and take command of the elven force. He finished with the note that the rest of his companions would be held for ransom, and if their effort failed, it would mean their lives.

"Do you also agree to these conditions and swear by the God of Light?" Kalis asked Remus.

Remus looked at Romulus, who gave a small nod.

"What choice do I have?" he asked.

"There is always a choice, my prince," Myon said quietly.

"Then I swear by the God of Light that I will attempt this errand."

"If you are successful," Kalis said, "then I will commute your sentence. In saving the lives of everyone in this city, your debt will be paid. If you are unsuccessful, if ever you come into dwarf lands again, your life is once again forfeit, as are the lives of all of these." She gestured to Reith and the others.

"We will do it tonight," Kalis declared. "Romulus and Remus, you will be lowered by rope to the ground below the wall. After that, you are on your own. If you are successful, give three trumpet blasts. When we hear those blasts, your friends will be free to move around the city as before. If we don't hear them by dawn, well, it will be a messy business. Because of the nature of this endeavor, I do not want any elves or humans carrying weapons within the city today. Romulus and Remus, your weapons will be returned to you when we lower you down tonight. The rest of you, yours will be returned when the trumpet sounds, as I hope it will."

Guards came and took their weapons from them. Reith regretted losing his sword but hoped to be reunited with it soon.

The rest of the day dragged on slowly. With no weapons, going to the wall to help in the defense was impossible. Kalis seemed to still have suspicion, or the dwarf lords did, for it seemed there were dwarf guards in closer proximity to the elves and humans than usual.

Dinner that night was a subdued affair, and only partially because of the measly ration of half a potato and the smallest bit of meat the city could spare. The threat of imminent death hung over them like a cloud and conversation was limited.

Toward the end of the meal, Ellamora spoke up. "What will we do if Romulus and Remus are successful?"

It was a fair question and one they hadn't really considered in light of the immediate challenges facing them.

"You could come with us," Romulus proposed. "But it will be dangerous. Who knows how my father will react at our coming with the army and his mission unaccomplished? We may have to remove him from the throne."

"Whatever happens, I don't want to go back to Crain," Ellamora declared. "I have no desire to see my stepfather."

"I don't blame you," Reith said, shuddering as the image of Gwandoeth's head falling from a bag came unbidden to his mind.

"Maybe I will go with you," she said to Romulus.

"I want to go home," Dema answered. "Back to Suthrond. Or what's left of it, anyway. I want to see Heth and Trigg and the rest of them."

Reith pondered what he would do. He looked around the table at each face. Myon, Brauron, and Aytos would surely go back with the princes, Ellamora with them. Dema would go to Suthrond. And Vereinen?

"Where will you go, Vereinen?" Reith asked.

"I have no where left to go," Vereinen replied with weariness. "Perhaps Galismoor. What about you?"

Fight for them. Then find me. The words came to his head again. Would it be time for fighting or finding?

"I think I must travel north," Reith replied after a pause. "Remember what Onias said? I think it will be time to find the Temple of Ice."

"I hope we are successful," Romulus said softly, leaning

in so only those at the table could hear. "But you need to be realistic. If the trumpet doesn't blow by dawn, you need to find a way to escape the city. Tonight, if you can. I don't want any of you to die if we are unable to complete this task."

"We will wait on the walls," Myon replied. "All night if we have to. If the sky begins to lighten, we will fight our way out. Better to die in an escape attempt than one by one."

"With what weapons?" Romulus asked. "I don't think you'll be able to fight your way out. You might need to go over the side of the wall."

"While we wait on the wall, we can look for rope or anything that can help us," Reith said quietly. "There will be plenty of time to figure out a plan. But the trumpet will blow."

At dusk, they were summoned to the main city gate.

"This will need to be a quick escape," Kalis explained. "Any elves who see you must be convinced that you are running for your lives. To that end, you'll need to sprint across the courtyard. There are grappling hooks on top of the wall by those stairs," she said, pointing, "and you'll need to quickly make your way down. I have a squad of men waiting to *pursue* you."

"Thank you, Queen Kalis," Romulus said.

"Your majesty," Remus began, "I am very sorry that I came here with such hate in my heart."

"All will be forgiven if your debt is paid this night," Kalis replied. "Now, say your farewells."

Each member of the company hugged Romulus and shook hands with Remus.

"Be safe," Ellamora said when it was her turn.

"May the God of Light illuminate your path," Reith said.

"We will see you again," Romulus said. "When we are successful, those coming with us should come down from the walls. The rest of you, may good fortune follow you until we meet again."

Romulus and Remus were taken to the far end of the courtyard, and the *escape* was on. They began running, and dwarven guards began shouting and chasing them. They reached the stairs and raced to the top, where they found grappling hooks. They threw the ropes over the wall and climbed to the top. Dwarven soldiers approached them from either side. Romulus gave them a little wave and then dropped below the wall, with Remus right beside him. The dwarves on the wall shouted and some even pulled their bows to shoot arrows past them. Shouts from the elves reached their ears.

"And now we wait," Vereinen said in the darkness.

Waiting was agony. The humans and elves were permitted freedom of movement during the night, but there were always guards nearby in case they tried to escape or get weapons.

Reith carefully watched the grappling hooks that had been used by Romulus and Remus. He saw that they were simply wrapped up and left on the wall.

That might be our way out if the trumpet does not blow.

Night continued on, and the air grew chilly. The stars drifted lazily across the black sky. A fire was lit in the courtyard, and Reith and the others huddled around it for warmth. Blankets were even brought for them, and he was grateful. Reith and Dema shared a blanket, and he put his arm around her and pulled him close to himself.

"I love you," she whispered to him.

"I love you, too," he replied.

A short while later, while looking across the fire, Reith saw that there were tears in Ellamora's eyes. He prodded

Dema's arm and when she looked at him with a question in her eyes, he nodded toward Ellamora. Without speaking, Reith and Dema rose and sat on either side of Ellamora.

"What's wrong?" Dema asked.

"I didn't realize how much I would miss him," Ellamora replied.

"He'll be okay," Reith replied. "And we will see him again soon. You can even go to Sardis with him."

"I don't feel peace about that decision at the moment," Ellamora said. "Something in my heart says that was goodbye for a longtime."

"You're always welcome with us," Dema replied. "Come to Suthrond, or wherever we go from there."

They sat in silence for several minutes, but then Reith remembered the grappling hooks. He leaned in and whispered to the other two about them.

"That may be our best chance of escape," he finished.

"Good eyes," Dema replied. "I don't think there's a better option if-if the trumpet doesn't sound." Reith was sure she was about to say, "if Romulus and Remus fail" but she caught herself just in time.

They continued to sit and wait by the fire all night long. Using the change of the guard, Reith guessed that they were now in the last watch of the night, just a couple of hours from dawn. And still, no trumpet had blown.

Dread slowly began to well up in Reith.

Why hasn't the trumpet blown yet? What went wrong?

He turned his attention from what was happening beyond the walls to what was happening within them. In a few hours, if the situation hadn't changed, one of them would be killed. He stood and went to sit between Vereinen and Myon. They leaned in and he whispered to them about the grappling hooks. They arranged for Reith to lead the way when the first light of dawn gleamed on the horizon. Myon agreed to pass the information onto Brauron and Aytos.

Reith returned to his place beside the fire and waited. The minutes slowly dragged on. The night continued growing colder, and he began rubbing his legs under his blanket to get some more warmth in them before he fled for his life. All the while, he still hoped and prayed for a trumpet blast to sound and save them from their fate.

In the darkest, coldest part of the night, despair filled his soul. All hope was gone and the Shadow had finally fallen on them all. Ice pierced his heart and he felt all joy leave him. He felt like part of himself was now lost, as if he were somehow an incomplete person. Melancholy and sorrow mixed a bitter drink of regret.

"Help us," he whispered skyward. It was all he could muster, a trace of faith in the night.

Almost at once, the night seemed less bleak, as if the stars somehow shone brighter than a minute before. He felt himself strangely warmed and he knew, though he didn't know how, he knew in his heart that things would turn out alright in the end.

He took a deep breath and exhaled slowly, watching his breath dance in the cold air and the firelight like he was a dragon. He was warm like a dragon, brave like a dragon.

To the east, the sky turned from black to midnight blue. It was almost time. Reith looked around the nearly empty courtyard to strategize their escape. There were three armed guards near them, but they were hardly paying attention. If they ran, they would take them by surprise and be far enough from them. There were a few soldiers on the walls, but not many. The elves hadn't attacked at all in the night, so all was quiet up there. He had no idea if all of them would manage an escape, but they faced no choice.

The dark navy sky continued to grow gradually lighter, and Reith began to look around the circle and making eye contact with the others. When he caught an eye, he would nod, and received a nod back. After a few minutes, he had finally reached everyone and they were all awaiting his signal to go. He closed his eyes, breathed out one more prayer, and began to countdown from five in his head.

Five.

Blood coursed through his body and he felt energy flowing through him.

Four.

Long shadows began to fall across the courtyard from the sun rising in the east.

Three.

He squeezed Dema's hand, hoping that this would not be the last time he would get a chance to do that.

Two.

He looked across the fire at Vereinen and love flooded his heart for his master.

One.

A loud trumpet blast cut through the air like a knife. Reith was so stunned he nearly jumped out of his own skin. In a flash, he was on his feet, and the others were too. A second blast followed shortly after the first. And then a third blast rang through the air. This one held on longer than the other notes and Reith let out a yell of excitement. They were saved, Darren Shahr was saved, Romulus and Remus had done it!

He and Dema embraced and kissed in jubilation. They broke apart and there were hugs all around the circle.

Queen Kalis rushed out of a nearby building with a fur coat wrapped around her shoulders.

"They did it!" she cried. "I began to worry they wouldn't."

Just then, there was a commotion on top of the wall. Dwarf soldiers were rushing together.

"What is it?" Kalis called out.

"A messenger with a white flag, your majesty," one of the dwarf captains called down. "He wants to speak to you, the humans, and the elves."

Kalis led the way up the stairs and Reith and the others followed her. On top of the wall, dwarf soldiers bowed to their queen and moved out of the way to let her see.

When Reith reached the wall, he looked down to see Romulus standing in the open land between the forest and the walls. He was bearing a white flag high on a stick.

When he saw the queen and them, he called out, "Can you pull me up? I have urgent news to share."

Kalis gave orders for a rope to be thrown down, and Romulus dropped the stick and began to climb while dwarves heaved him up.

"What happened?" Kalis asked when he was safely up on the wall again.

"It took longer than we had hoped, but we were successful," Romulus replied. "Just like we planned, our escape did not go unnoticed by the elves. They brought us straight to General Praekin. He, Remus, and I spoke for many long hours. He wanted to know how we had ended up here, which took a long time to explain. He bought the story that I was here on a rescue mission. We ran into issues though. He wanted to see through the mission here, for he rightly guessed that the city would shortly fall. His orders you see, were to take down the city, destroy it, and leave no survivors, then march north and west to meet another elven force marching toward the humans. They were to meet at Palander. Well, Remus and I want to take this force back to Sardis and deal with our father, so we were at an impasse. In the heat of the argument, Remus struck down the general with a knife."

"Oh my!" Kalis exclaimed.

"The attack was so sudden the general hadn't called out, so we were given a few minutes to decide how we wanted to proceed. We decided to call the commanders together and tell them General Praekin had disobeyed a direct order from the crown prince, which is true enough. We explained to them about the rescue mission and all of that, and they quickly agreed with us to recall our troops and make the trip back to Sardis."

"Did you find out anything about the Free Isles or Balkh?" Reith asked.

"Aye," Romulus said sadly. "Both fell to the elves, with few or no survivors."

Kalis gasped and began to sob. Reith had suspected that had been the case for both, but he was sad for all the people they had met and left behind in those places. Dema and Ellamora also began to cry, and he placed arms around them to comfort them.

"Oh, Keely," Kalis wailed and it was several minutes before she was ready to resume the conversation.

"Remus and I will take this force south by the river and back to Sardis," Romulus said. "But I think the dwarves should muster a force to send to the aid of the humans."

"That is not something I am willing to do at the moment," Kalis replied. "My people are worn out from defending the city. Our food supplies our low. One of our cities has been destroyed. No, I think we will stay here."

"But the humans may fall, doesn't that matter to you?" Romulus protested.

"It does matter to me," Kalis said. "I am not a cold-blooded tyrant. I am simply realistic about my kingdom's situation."

"We'll go," Reith spoke up. "We'll go and support the humans. There may be only a few of us, but the elves will be expecting thousands of their own as backup. We will be an unpleasant surprise and carry tidings of Darren Shahr and Sardis to the king of the humans."

"The most I can do for you," Queen Kalis began, "Is send with you a small company. You will ride on horseback through the mountains and you will need guides and supplies. I will give these to you. Those guides can be my ambassadors to the humans."

"Thank you, your majesty," Reith replied. "That is more than generous."

"Then I will take my leave," Romulus declared. "I hope to remove my father and the Shadow, Solzar, from power upon my return to the city. If I am successful, the dwarves have the hand of friendship from my people. If I am unsuccessful, there will be more war in the future."

"Very well," Kalis replied. "Who in your company will travel with you to Sardis and who will go to the humans?"

Myon, Brauron, and Aytos stepped forward, but Ellamora looked torn.

"Where will you go, Ellamora?" Romulus asked kindly.

She looked long and hard at Romulus with a look of longing, but finally she shook her head.

"I must go with Reith, Dema, and Vereinen," she said. "I feel called to the north."

"Then we part in sweet sorrow, for the moment," Romulus declared, and he stepped forward and embraced Ellamora with a hug of great ferocity, which she returned in kind.

When they broke apart, he spoke again. "You always have a place in my court, my lady. But go now and be my ambassador to the humans. You may speak with my voice and my authority. Farewell, Lady Ellamora."

They all now said their farewells, with a note of finality in them. Kalis left them to make preparations for the small company to go north and had all their weapons returned to them.

Rather than taking a rope down the wall, the city gate was opened so a single person could walk out. Myon in particular was grateful for that.

"I am too old to make that descent," he said with relief.

Finally, it was time for Romulus and the others to leave. Reith had grown fond of the elf prince who had saved their lives in Sardis so many weeks before. He was sad to see him go, but he was not nearly as sad as Ellamora. She came back to Romulus for one more hug. When they separated, Romulus led Myon, Brauron, and Aytos through the gate, which was swiftly shut behind them with a final crash.

19

Shortly after, they were summoned to the courtyard, where twenty dwarves were gathered around Queen Kalis.

"This is Captain Reza," Kalis said, indicating a tall dwarf. He was surprisingly young and had red in his brown beard. "He will lead your company. Right now, I have supplies being loaded onto horses for you and you will depart as soon as possible."

"Greetings," Reza said. "I am thrilled to accompany you on this adventure." Reza had a good natured and likable personality, as Reith could see, and he liked him right away.

Reith, Dema, Ellamora, and Vereinen all introduced themselves.

"I am glad you are getting along nicely," Queen Kalis said. "And now I must bid you farewell. I am exhausted from last night's ordeal and must go to bed."

"It was a pleasure serving you and the city, your majesty," Vereinen replied.

"If any of you ever return to Darren Shahr, you will be

welcomed as friends," Kalis declared. "May this war end swiftly and your hearts find peace."

With that, she turned and departed. A few minutes later, a stable groom came to them and led them to another gate in the city wall, on the northern side of the city. Twenty-four horses saddled and packed were waiting for them. Reith was led to a fine chestnut horse named Ronan.

"He is a fine beast, sir," the chief stable master declared. "He won't lead you astray and he is fearless in battle. As good as a dwarf in a fight, with those hooves."

"He is fine indeed," Reith agreed, stroking the horse's nose affectionately.

In no time at all, it was time to ride. They mounted up and Reza led the company through the gate and toward the mountains beyond.

Ronan was an excellent horse, as the stable master had said. He followed obediently behind Reza's horse.

The same could not be said for Ellamora's horse. She was riding a stubborn white mare named Mina. Mina seemed none too pleased at having an elf on her back.

"This horse will be the death of me," Ellamora declared as she pulled the reins to get Mina back in line for the fifth time. Mina kept wanting to go sideways to snack on some grass.

The forest loomed over them and the mountains loomed over the trees. They followed the course of the river, traveling north. Occasionally, Reza would call for a halt for the horses to drink. At these short breaks, Reith would dismount and stretch his legs.

His exhaustion was catching up with him. He had not slept at all that previous night while they anxiously waited by the fire and had been woken early the morning before.

As the day wore on, it took all his concentration to not fall asleep in the saddle.

At noon, they stopped for a longer break, and a quick lunch. Reith ate ravenously of the food placed before him, but like his meals in the city, it was not nearly enough. As they sat and ate, Reza filled them in on the plan.

"We will travel for two days and reach Lake Banu, a lake high up in the mountains and the source of this river," Reza explained. "We will traverse around the river and then descend to the plains, following the Rammis River which flows east to west. At some point, we will need to leave that river and travel north, but once we are out of the mountains, my knowledge of the world is lacking. I do not know where this battle may take place. Does anyone know?"

"Romulus said it's at Palander," Reith said. "It's a small human town northwest of Suthrond."

"We can go through Suthrond!" Dema said excitedly. "Oh, that will be so good!"

"Maybe we will see Laneras and Pallin!" Ellamora said, and a smile graced her face for the first time since leaving Romulus.

"We can't stay there for long," Reith replied. "We have business to attend to."

"We'll need a place to get more supplies and maybe even sleep in a bed," Vereinen pointed out.

They continued to climb higher and higher into the mountains. Snow covered the peaks above them and the air grew cold the higher they went. Their breath and the breath of their horses drifted up like smoke in the wind.

The river beside them grew rougher with the

occasional rapids flecking the water with white. The river cut a valley through the mountains and occasionally the path grew rough and treacherous. Reza expertly maneuvered them through, and toward nightfall, they came to a wide flat plateau overlooking the river. They stopped for the evening, and several large fires were soon crackling merrily, giving light and warmth to the travelers. Reith and Dema cuddled near one and were joined by Ellamora and Vereinen.

"The mountains are beautiful," Dema said, looking up at the peaks towering above them.

"And dangerous," Vereinen replied. "If the legends are even half true, there are many things which could kill us here."

"Thank you for the cheery thought right before bed," Reith replied, rolling his eyes.

"I just want us to be aware," Vereinen said with a shrug.

"Have you ever spent time in the mountains?" Ellamora asked him.

"Me? Goodness, no," Vereinen replied. "I have lived my life on the plains of Galismoor and in the forest of Coeden. Though I did see the Northern Mountains way off in the distance as I traveled to and from Kal-Epharion."

"What creatures do the legends speak of?" Dema asked.

"Oh, all sorts of nasty things," Vereinen replied. "Wolves and bears are the tamest of them. They also speak of other things, like ghost leopards, giant cats that move silently so you never hear them until you're already dead. There are ice snakes, which are furry snakes that are huge and venomous. The stories also speak of yetis, giant ape like creatures who walk on two legs like a person, who are devilishly smart and deadly. And worst of all, they say there are giant white spiders who spin giant webs in the high mountain passes." He shuddered at the thought.

"I hope the legends were exaggerating," Ellamora replied. "I shouldn't like to meet any of those creatures."

"Nor should I," Vereinen replied. "If we stick to the river, Reza will guide us right."

As the sun sank behind the mountains, they sprawled out for bed, keeping as close to the fire as they could tolerate, as the temperature dropped steadily. Reza, knowing they had spent the whole previous night awake, did not require any of them to be on guard duty, for which Reith was grateful.

His dreams that night were of unseen and unnamed monsters chasing him through the snowy mountains. He kept slipping on the snow and ice and falling while howls and screeches closed in on him from behind. Each time he fell he leapt back up and kept going. He eventually found a narrow valley with towering cliffs on either side, and slipped in, hoping the monsters wouldn't see or couldn't follow. He ran and ran, and just when he felt he couldn't run any more, the valley opened to a wide space, and in the center glittered a large cathedral carved of ice. Just then, a loud screech behind him alerted him to the presence of the monsters. He raced toward the cathedral, but found the door looked. He looked around for a key, but there was none. He reached for his sword, but it was gone too. And then a shadowy creature pounced on him and he awoke with a start.

He sat up, breathing heavily. Dema lay beside him, and he saw firelight dancing on Vereinen and Ellamora. He lay back down, but it took him a long time to go back to sleep.

The next day, they rode off in the frigid dawn air bundled in as many furs as they had in their bags.

"We should reach the eastern shore of the lake tonight," Reza declared.

They rode single file along the bank of the river which was surging below them. They were about thirty feet higher than the river, with a steep, rocky bank going down to the water. Every so often, Reza would turn away from the river and lead them inland a short distance along an easier path for the horses to tread.

Around noon, as they navigated a particularly dangerous stretch of river, one of the horses slipped and tumbled down sideways toward the river. The horse and rider slid down nearly to the river itself before coming to a halt in a shower of rocks and dust. The horse was on its side and pinned the dwarf's legs. Reza and another dwarf dismounted and slid down the slope to help their comrade. They managed to free the dwarf while the rest looked on in horror. The horse's leg was clearly broken.

"Look away," Reza called up to them, and he drew his sword. The horse's squeals of agony were soon silenced. Reza and the two other dwarfs removed what they could from the horse's bags and scrambled back up to the path. Other than the horse, no one else was hurt. The dwarf's possessions were distributed to several of the other dwarfs and he himself took a seat behind Reza for the next leg of the journey. Every so often, he would switch horses and share with a different rider. The horses that had two riders needed more breaks which slowed the whole party down.

Needless to say, they did not reach the lake that evening. They camped below a cliff which jutted out over them, acting as a shelter. This was good as it began to snow that evening. Their campsite was spared from most of the snow, and the fires they lit melted the rest near them. Even so, it was a bitterly cold night, and Reith and Dema cuddled close for warmth.

Reith, Dema, and Ellamora were given guard duty in the last watch of the night. They sat with their backs to the fire, looking outward at the snowy mountain world. The firelight reflected on millions of snowflakes and made the world shimmer with light, so that even in the darkest part of the night, it wasn't as dark as usual. After an hour of guard duty, Reith thought he heard sounds from out in the darkness, toward the river. The sounds of the river muffled all others. He peered intently into the gloom, and once or twice thought his eyes were playing tricks on him, for he thought he saw movement.

"Do you see or hear anything over there?" he whispered to the other two while pointing toward the river.

For a minute, they all strained their ears and eyes. The only sounds Reith heard was the occasional crackle of the fire and the rushing river, and he did not see anything.

"I don't see or hear anything," Dema whispered.

"Me neither," Ellamora replied. "Did you?"

"I thought I did," Reith said, now certain that his mind was playing tricks on him.

The rest of their guard shift passed uneventfully, and when the sun rose, they woke the others. Reith stepped away from the camp to relieve himself and noticed tracks the snow made by some extremely large animal. The paw print shapes resembled a cat's but were about a foot long. Reith pointed them out to Reza and Vereinen, and they both shuddered.

"We had a close call last night," Reza said. "It looks like a ghost leopard came very close to us. If it had the mind to attack, we'd all be dead."

They mounted up and all were more aware of their surroundings than the previous day, particularly going around curves or when near overhanging cliffs. After a couple of hours of riding, the world opened before them. A great lake glittered in the sun, and they could not see the other side. Much of the surface of the lake that they could see was covered in a great sheet of ice.

"Behold," Reza declared, "Lake Banu. We will go around the north side and then descend to the plains below."

They left the river behind and stuck to the shoreline of the lake. It was much easier terrain to navigate, as the mountains gently sloped down into the lake, leaving a fairly wide and flat area along the edge of the lake to walk. Instead of single file, the group morphed into a looser formation that allowed several horses to walk abreast, leading to greater and more conversation.

Reith soon found himself riding four across with Ellamora on the far left beside the lake, then Dema, then himself, and Vereinen beside him. The sun shone down on them and it felt as though they were on top of the world, with everything except the highest mountain tops below them.

"It's very nice up here," Reith said with a sigh, surveying the mountains, the lake, the snow, and the sunshine.

"A bit cold for my liking, but quite beautiful," Vereinen agreed.

They continued in silence for a few more minutes. The sunlight reflecting on the surface of the lake and the snow as dazzling to Reith's eyes, and he had to keep turning away, but as soon as he could, his eyes were drawn to the majestic beauty all around him.

"I wish we didn't have somewhere to go," Reith said finally. "I wish we could remain up here as long as we'd like."

"Me too, Reith, me too," Vereinen replied with a sigh. "But perhaps not for the same reason you do."

"What reason is that?"

"Up here," Vereinen said, gesturing around, "everything is so clear. But down on the plain, everything becomes so muddled. Here, I feel and see everything clearly. Down there, it's all shadow."

"I still don't know what you mean," Reith replied.

"It's Solzar," Vereinen bemoaned. "His presence is a Shadow on the world, but also a Shadow on my heart. For some reason, here in the mountains, I feel like a burden has lifted. I feel light. I feel the light. Does that make sense?"

"A little bit," Reith replied, though it still didn't make much sense to him.

"Maybe it's just an old man and his cowardice," Vereinen continued. "Maybe I am afraid to face him again."

"What do you have to be afraid of?" Reith asked. "You've already seen him again. You already know what he has become."

"Seen him in a foreign land, yes," Vereinen said. "But soon we will be in Suthrond, a place decimated by him. We will see him in our own homeland. It's different, somehow."

"And you feel responsible?" Reith asked.

"To an extent, yes. But what will be my welcome from others?"

"Are you afraid of how King Calmon will receive you?" Reith asked. "Are you afraid he'll hold you responsible for Solzar?"

"I suppose that's it," Vereinen agreed. "I do now know Calmon personally. I knew his father and grandfather, but I am sure he knows about Solzar, and even about me."

"If he is a man of any sense, he will receive you warmly, with open arms after all you have done these past few months."

"One can only hope," Vereinen replied. "Speaking of open arms however," he said and leaned in toward Reith and whispered, "things seem to be getting along nicely for you and Dema."

Reith blushed. "Yeah, it's going well," he whispered back, with a quick glance toward Dema, who appeared to have not heard the question.

"I never married, myself," Vereinen said. "But she seems like quite the extraordinary young woman."

"She is, indeed," Reith replied, smiling.

"I hope you two are good to each other," Vereinen continued. "There is so much darkness in the world and love is the only spark of light."

They rode in silence for another minute before Vereinen spoke again. "I'm proud of the man you are becoming."

Reith smiled and emotion welled up inside him, rendering him temporarily speechless.

Their pace was greatly increased by the relatively flat land beside the lake. By the time they stopped for the night, the river was out of sight. The lake stretched out to the horizon. In the distance, Reith saw indistinct white shapes, but he was not sure if they were clouds or the distant peaks of mountains across the lake. Inland, the mountains loomed over them like cliffs, so even if they had wanted to climb them, they would have been unable. Reith had seen enough maps to know that if the mountains were able to be traversed, that the desert and Kal-Epharion lay beyond them.

They lit a large fire on the beach and settled in for the night around it. One of the dwarves pulled a wooden flute from his pack and began to play a lively tune. The other dwarves joined in and sang.

Banu was a lonely giant, tall as he was wide
He likes to roam the mountains and, in their shadows, hide
For when the sun was high and the heat was very great
He would lie down and sleep and wait, and wait, and wait

But one day the sun was scorching hotter than before
And so, Banu began to sweat upon the Valley floor
It was so hot that poor Banu, well, he began to bake
And all that was left of him was a wide and deep lake

Reith, Dema, Ellamora, and Vereinen clapped heartily at the conclusion of *The Ballad of Banu.*

"Well done," Vereinen praised.

"It seemed appropriate, given the surroundings," the dwarf with the flute replied, gesturing to the lake.

It was the first of many songs the dwarves would sing for them that evening beside Lake Banu. Reith and the others quite enjoyed the display, and even joined in to sing a few that they caught onto quick. Eventually, though, it was time to go to sleep. The darkness had settled in and the temperature was dropping. Reith snuggled in beside Dema, and was soon asleep, with *The Ballad of Banu* still going through his head.

20

After a quick breakfast, they rode off swiftly beside the lake.

"We should reach the end of the lake tomorrow," Reza declared. "Then we will follow the river down to the plains."

They kept up a steady pace all through the day, even with having to shuffle an extra rider between them. In the afternoon, the sun was staring them straight in the face, so it was hard to look forward. Reith kept his head slightly turned away from the sun and toward the mountains on their right. And it was lucky he was.

High up on the nearest slope, he saw a disturbance in the snow, as if powder had been kicked up into the air like a cloud. He looked closely, hoping to see what had caused the disturbance. He brought his left hand to his face to block the sunlight more to help his vision. Out of the cloud, he saw something moving swiftly down the slope.

It was as if a great ball of snow was coming down at them, picking up speed and growing as it rolled ever faster toward them.

"Look!" he called to the others. "Up on the slope!"

All eyes turned to spy the snowball that was hurtling down toward them.

"Defensive formation!" Reza shouted. "Line up, quick!"

"What is it?" Reith asked.

"A nightmare," Reza called back. "A giant snow spider!"

It did not look like a spider to Reith, who still saw just a white ball of snow plummeting toward them, but he pulled his horse alongside Dema's and Vereinen's.

"Judging by its path, it will come to a halt a couple hundred yards ahead of us," Reza called out to the group. "It is a good thing we saw it so we'd be prepared. Imagine if we kept riding and that thing bowled into us."

Reith did imagine and shuddered at the thought.

"How do you know it's a giant snow spider?" Vereinen asked. "Couldn't it be a regular old avalanche?"

"If only," Reza answered. "Snow and ice, we can deal with that. A giant spider is another matter. Now, when it comes to a stop, it will be slightly confused as to where we are. Stay silent and still. Perhaps it will go away on its own. Under no circumstances are any of you to engage it with arrows until I give the order. There is no sense in inviting an attack if it doesn't realize where we are."

The ball of snow was coming ever nearer, and it now was slowing down as it hit the flatter slope of the lower mountain. Just when Reith thought it would roll right into the lake, the ball jumped up into the air and plopped to the ground on the beach several hundred yards away. The snow dropped away and a cloud of powder hid what was inside from view. But then a hairy white leg stepped out of the cloud and into the light of the afternoon sun.

Reith clutched his bow tight. It truly was something

from a nightmare. As the cloud of snow blew away, a monster was revealed. Eight terrible white legs led up to a great white body. Sunlight glinted off sharp black fangs, and even from this distance, Reith saw that the beast stood taller than any of them on horseback. A rider could go right under the beast and not hit his head.

The horses tensed at the new arrival. Reith heard several soft calming words from the dwarves. If a horse bolted, they'd be seen for sure.

The spider was tapping around in the snow it had recently discarded from its body, hoping that something had been caught by its surprise attack. When it found nothing, it turned and looked away from them, then turned and seemed to look directly at them. Dema gasped beside him.

"Not a word, not a movement," Reza whispered loudly to them. "It doesn't see well."

The spider took a few tentative steps toward them, and then stopped. The afternoon sunlight was directly in their eyes, and Reith had a hard time keeping from looking away.

And then the spider began to charge. Quicker than even the fastest horse, the spider advanced on them, closing the gap between them in an astonishingly short amount of time.

"Shoot, shoot!" Reza declared.

Bows were drawn back and arrows were flung at the beast. Most of the first volley shot over the spider's white head, as it was much quicker than they had anticipated. Several on the second volley did hit their mark, but the beast continued unabated.

"Swords!" Reza called, and all drew their swords. The spider did not slow down but went straight at the middle of their line. It towered over them, and Reith saw that its legs on one side were coming right at him. He drew back his sword to strike. His blow nearly wrenched his sword from his hand. The spider gave an almighty screech and passed by them. A dwarf screamed, and Reith turned to see a dwarf had been plucked clean from his saddle and sent flying to the ground twenty feet behind them.

They turned their horses around to face their foe, and the spider turned back toward them.

"Surround it!" Reza called. The riders on the end of their line rushed forward and made a large circle around the great hairy beast. The spider crouched lower to the ground, like a cornered cat.

"Force it to retreat!" Reza yelled.

One of the dwarves behind the spider coaxed his horse closer and swiped at the spider's leg. The blow bounced off and the spider whirled around to face the threat. Reith was now looking at the side of the spider, and urged his horse forward, then aimed a heavy blow at the joint in the spider's leg. His stroke was sound and the spider's leg broke. It was not severed, simply damaged, but the spider couldn't put any weight on that leg.

Before Reith had a chance to congratulate himself, he was staring into eight dark eyes. The spider advanced at him on seven legs, and he held up his sword ready to stab it in the face. But then the spider shrieked again and spun around.

Reith saw his chance. With the spider facing away from him, he prodded his horse forward, between the spider's horrible hairy legs. He soon found himself directly under the spider's large, engorged belly. He urged his horse into its back legs and swung his sword up at the same time. With the force of Reith's arm and the horse rearing back, the blade pierced the spider's soft underbelly. The spider shrieked again and its legs seemed to close in together, and for a second, Reith thought he would be trapped. But the spider tried to put weight on its injured leg and began to topple in that direction. As it fell, Reith rode clear and several dwarves lunged forward to stab the beast again and again in its belly. Soon, the spider was dead.

Reza dismounted and checked on the dwarf who had been thrown. Miraculously, he was fine, just winded. Everyone else was unhurt.

"Let's get away from this thing," Reza declared, and they rode hard until they were out of sight from the spider's dead body. It was only then that they were able to relax and smiles came to their lips.

"How dare you!" Dema scolded Reith with a mixture of horror and awe on her face. "That was a stupid thing to do. You could have been killed!"

"It was brilliant!" Reza declared, shaking Reith's hand and clapping him on the back. "Nerves of steel, and courage to spare. How daring! Good job, Reith!"

Reith simply smiled and soaked in the praise.

Reza decided it was too dangerous to camp, so they continued into the gathering twilight.

"Sleep in your saddles," was his instruction. It was easier said than done.

All eyes were to the mountains when they journeyed on. Soon the shadows obscured the slopes so they had no idea if something was coming down at them from above.

"That's good though," Ellamora pointed out. "It means nothing up there can see us."

Still, the dread of a surprise spider attack kept everyone on edge and made sleeping in the saddle immensely difficult. Reith managed a couple of hours in the dead of night, but it wasn't enough. By the time the sun rose, he was groggy and aching from being in the saddle all night.

By the light of the sun behind them, they could see the western shore of the lake. They had made it nearly around Lake Banu. Reza kept them pressing on and soon they found where the river began. The river cut its way through the mountains, forming a splendid valley. The mountains diminished in size farther down the valley. Beside the beginning of the river, Reza finally called for a halt.

Reith jumped down from his saddle, stumbled over his surprisingly numb feet, and crashed to the ground.

"Smooth," Dema said, grinning down at him. She gracefully dismounted, and then reached down a hand to help him up. Once back on his feet, he dusted himself off.

"We're almost there," Dema said, looking down the valley. "Home is not that far away. We've been gone so long."

"Yes, we have," Reith said, following her gaze.

After their short rest, they mounted up and left the lake behind. The elevation changed rapidly as they followed along the path of the river. Sometimes they had to leave the river and pick a course around to bypass a waterfall or a rapid where the horses couldn't traverse the rocky terrain.

After several hours of slow going, they suddenly found that the river flattened out and flowed gently for a long stretch. The mountains were now thoroughly behind them, and hills formed the barrier to the valley now. Grass now overwhelmed the rock and the horses neighed appreciatively. For the first time all day, Reza encouraged them to gallop and the miles flew past them. When the horses had enough, they stopped for water and grass, and lunch for the riders.

Here, the Rammis River was wide and gentle, and the horses waded in to get a drink. Reith knelt at the edge and drank some of its frigid, refreshing water. As he straightened, with water dripping down his face, he saw a buck in the undergrowth across the river. Instinctively, he slowly reached behind him and gripped his bow which was still slung on his back. He pulled it down and pulled an arrow from his quiver. He sighted along the shaft, took a deep breath, and let it fly. It whizzed through the air across the river and struck the buck right in the neck. It staggered around for a few seconds before falling dead.

A short while later, a fire was roaring and chunks of meat were roasting on a flat rock beside the fire. Everyone was glad of a longer break from the saddle and the prospect of fresh meat. It was exactly what they needed after their ordeal with the spider the day before.

With their bellies full and their horses rested, they pushed on hard until nightfall. The river remained gentle and the ground soft and smooth for their horses. By the time the sun was dropping in front of them, the mountains were distant memories on the horizon behind them.

Out from under the shadow of the mountains, with soft grass below them, the company slept soundly. The horses whinnied contentedly nearby and watched the stars dance across the sky as he took guard duty with Dema and Ellamora. They did not talk much this night, but Reith felt a sense of connection and contentment between them, even in the silence. Firelight danced on their faces and the stars shone in their eyes. He had traveled across the whole world with these two, just to end up in nearly the same place they had started.

A few feet away, Vereinen snored softly. Here they were, on the cusp of the human's land. They hadn't been together in their homeland since that dreadful morning when Solzar had come. Solzar, the Shadow, who had started this whole affair. Solzar, who had sent armies across Terrasohnen to seize power for himself. It all came back to Solzar.

And in a few short days, Reith and the others would face his forces again on the field of battle. Would he be with them? Or was he hiding in Sardis, biding his time?

A wave of weariness washed over Reith. He had spent so much time running, so much time fighting. When would he be able to rest again, a proper rest with a proper home?

His mind went back to Solzar and the trouble he had caused. How many would have to die for the Shadow?

***

Around midafternoon the next day, they came across the waterfall and the crossing point where Reith had led the Suthronders across the Rammis River into elven territory.

"We're almost to Suthrond!" Dema exclaimed.

It was true. Due to the waterfall, they had to go farther away from the river to find more easily traversable ground for the horses. When they had successfully navigated the waterfall, they returned to the river and swiftly rode the short distance down to the sandy beach where the Suthronders had camped. Evidence of their being there remained, even all these weeks later. Remnants of old campfires remained and the sand was still disturbed from the footprints.

"Come on!" Dema urged them on, and she prodded her horse into a gallop and took the lead. They pressed on through the forest, and at any moment Reith expected they would burst from it into the light of the plains behind it, but that moment never came. Dema pulled her horse to a stop and Reith wondered what was wrong. He brought his horse alongside Dema's.

"What's wrong?" he asked and was startled to see tears in her eyes.

"Look!" she said and pointed.

He followed her gaze and her finger and did not see anything except trees. But then he looked closer. All around them were trees that most assuredly had not been there when Reith had come through Suthrond. He understood.

Peaches three times bigger than his fist hung on the branches all around them. Some were near enough to reach up and pluck from the saddle, which Dema and then Reith did with pure joy. Heth had planted peach groves from the fruit of Erador that Reith had given her.

"Ah, this must be some of that magic fruit," Vereinen noted, plucking a peach and sniffing it before taking a bite. Soon the whole party was enjoying peaches.

Dema dismounted and led her horse forward at a walk. She picked her way through the trees until at last they came to a clearing where several small wooden shelters had been constructed. Sitting in a chair beside the door of one of the shelters, eating a peach, was none other than Heth. She nearly dropped her peach in surprise. She stood up and looked at Dema like she was dreaming. But then she and Dema both ran to each other and embraced.

"Dema! How good to see you, child!" Heth said.

They hugged for a long time, and tears streamed down each of their faces. Because of the noise, several Suthronders walked out of the trees, some carrying baskets full of peaches. When Dema and Heth broke apart, Heth's eyes fell on Reith and she beckoned him into a long hug as well. After this hug, Reith saw that nearly all the Suthronders had surrounded them. The Suthronders eyed the dwarves with suspicion, and kept their distance.

Reith saw Titus and Tara, and their mother Lara. He rushed over to embrace them. He went from familiar face to familiar face, shaking hands and giving hugs and soft words of "good to see you." But there was one face that was missing.

"Where is Trigg?" he asked Heth, and her eyes immediately filled with tears. Dema stepped closer, concern etched on her face.

"He's gone," Heth said finally. "That old man died of a heart attack not long after we got back."

Heth broke down crying, and Dema joined her. The two women, one old and one young, held each other and wept.

"Show us where he's buried," Reith requested when the crying had subsided.

Heth led them away from the peach trees to the old town cemetery, which had been spared by Solzar and his men from any damage. Simple gravestones lined the field, and Heth led them to a spot of freshly dug earth. Already new grass had overtaken the mound and a few lilies had sprung up and around it. There was a small circular stone laying above Trigg's head, and "Trigg" had been roughly cut into the rock. Heth patted Dema's shoulder and stepped back, and Reith and Dema stepped forward to pay their respects at the grave of their friend.

For Reith, Trigg's death was a great shock. The gruff old man seemed to have so much life in himself, that Reith had a hard time picturing him dead. He couldn't imagine what Dema was feeling, for she had known him her whole life.

They stood in silence for a long time. Dema's left hand

was in Reith's right and she rested her head on his shoulder while she softly cried. They stared down at the new life creeping up from the remains of an old one. Grass and flowers bloomed while Trigg's light had faded.

After several minutes, Dema wiped her face with her sleeve and turned from the grave. She walked over to Ellamora who embraced her in a hug.

This was not how Reith had envisioned his and Dema's return to Suthrond would be.

21

That evening, Dema told the story of all that had happened to them since they left Crain. There was much to tell, and her story lasted well into the night. The fire had burned low by the time she finished.

When she was done, Heth told their tale.

"After you left, we departed. Pallin and Laneras and their men escorted us as far as the river. We crossed and took inventory of our supplies and our situation. We set to work immediately. We chopped down trees for lumber to make new shelters and homes. Reith, your peaches helped us out greatly. We planted the pits and now have this whole grove, thanks to you. Three days after we got back here, Trigg passed away. And ever since, we have worked the soil and built new homes. It has been a quiet life, and we are grateful."

"Did you ever see an elven force cross the river?" Reith asked.

"No, we haven't," Heth replied, "But we did hear about it. Pallin and Laneras keep us informed on the goings on in the world to our south. They sent us word a week ago that a force had been massing on their side of the river and would be crossing soon. Luckily, they crossed the river some ten miles west of here, so we did not see them."

"Did they say if Solzar, the Gray Man, I mean, was with that force?" Reith asked.

"They didn't say one way or another," Heth said.

It was decided that Reith and the others would depart at dawn and ride along the road to Palander to join whatever battle may be raging. Of all the Suthronders, Titus was the only one to volunteer to come with them, the rest being too old, too infirm, or unwilling to fight. Two additional horses were procured, one for Titus, and one to replace the horse that had died in the mountains.

After a splendid night of sleep in one of the new shelters, the party rose and departed at dawn.

"We'll be back," Dema called to Heth.

"I hope so," Heth replied. "I hope so."

Their packs were laden with peaches and they rode north out of Suthrond. They rode two by two along the road going north toward Palander. Reith rode beside Vereinen and Dema and Ellamora rode in front of them. They rode hard, hoping to make it to Palander by nightfall.

"Will you fight?" Reith asked Vereinen as they trotted along the road.

"No, I am not much for fighting."

"Then why didn't you stay behind in Suthrond?"

"Because I feel that I have some part to play in this whole affair. Solzar is who he is because of me. I want to see the battle, whether it go for good or for ill."

There was little talking the rest of the day. Everyone knew battle would be joined, and perhaps joined that very evening. Reith felt a sense of finality as they rode. He hoped that this at last would be the end of his journeying.

In the late afternoon, Reith found himself riding beside

Dema. He found himself staring at her as they rode. He was struck anew how beautiful she was. She glowed in the afternoon sunlight.

"Whatever happens," he said, "know that I love you."

"I love you, too, Reith," she replied, smiling at him.

As they pressed on to the north, it gradually grew darker, and it took Reith awhile to notice it wasn't the sun setting, it was great gray clouds rolling in from the west. The temperature began to drop and the large droplets of rain began to pelt them from above. Every head bowed before the rainstorm. Lightning flashed in the air and distant thunder rumbled. The horses grew uneasy. The road, which was hard packed dirt, became muddy. The horses sloshed through the mud as best they could, but they were slowed down.

They all agreed to wait it out for a bit to see if the rain would let up. They departed the road and sought a dry place to wait amid the trees. The branches blocked most of the rain, but some of it still managed to find them. Between the rain, the wind, and the cold, they were all quite miserable.

"It's no use," Reza declared. "The rain is not letting up. Let us camp here for the night and begin again first thing in the morning."

They all agreed, and soon the horses were unpacked. Each person looked for the driest piece of grass they could find and then burrowed down into blankets and extra shirts.

It was a cold and miserable night. Reith hardly slept at all. Water constantly dripped on him all night long and he could never get properly warm. It was so wet they were unable to light any fires. Add in the anxiety of the approaching battle, and it was a recipe for a sleepless night.

At first light, the sentries woke them. Looking around,

Reith saw that he wasn't alone in his sleepless night. Every person looked weary and unrested.

Just how you want to be before battle, he thought sarcastically.

The rain had stopped, and they were all soon back on the road. No one spoke.

They heard the battle before they saw it. Clangs of metal on metal and shouts of men and elves began to reach their ear. They continued forward cautiously.

The road curved and all of a sudden, Palander stretched out before them. It was a town much like Coeden, or at least how Coeden was before Solzar had sacked it. Small wooden huts and buildings lined streets. No one was in sight, but the sounds of battle drifted to them from the other side of the town.

Reza called for a halt at the edge of town.

"It sounds like the battle is on the other side of town," he pointed out. "Does anyone know what we are likely to find there?"

"If I had to guess," Vereinen began, "I assume the battle is taking place in the plain just north of the city. The forest does not go much farther north than Palander. I assume the elves will have their backs to us, and the humans will be engaging them from the north, from the direction of Galismoor."

"If that's the case, what is our course of action?" Reza asked.

"We are few in number," Reith pointed out. "Let us send a scout team with no horses to the other side of the town to see what they may see. They can hide behind buildings. Then we can know what we're facing and how we can help."

It was quickly decided that Reza would accompany Reith and Vereinen. Reza and Reith because of their strategic thinking, and Vereinen because of his general knowledge.

Reith handed his reins to Dema, and the three of them walked quietly along the edge of the street, as close to the buildings and houses as possible.

"Where is everyone?" Reith whispered to the other two.

"Might have fled," Vereinen replied. "Or they could be hiding in their homes, scared for their lives."

"It's eerie, that's for sure," Reza replied.

They continued on, pausing at each street to peer around the corners to make sure they wouldn't run into any elves or Solzar's men. Each time, the streets were empty.

They came at last to the final house on the road. It blocked their view of the plains beyond, but it also blocked them from sight, for which they were grateful. Reza led them to the left of the building, and they crept along the side toward the back. The sounds of battle were louder now.

They reached the corner. The midmorning sun cast the shadow of the house over them, keeping them from easily being spotted. From there, in the shadows, they watched.

The elven camp was in front of them. There was a city of tents stretching out before them, with supply wagons and carts interspersed throughout the camp. Beyond the camp, the battle was raging. The elves' backs were to them, and their line stretched a mile long as they engaged human soldiers all along it. Ranks of elven soldiers waited behind the front line for their chance to fight. Nearly all were holding spears, and Reith saw they also had swords and bows.

Beyond the elves, Reith couldn't see much of the

humans. Occasionally one on horseback would loom large over the elves, but not for very long. It appeared the humans were all mostly on foot, as Reith couldn't see them.

"What do you think?" Reza whispered.

"It's hard to say from this angle," Reith whispered back. "We can't even see the human army. I wish we could get higher."

"I have an idea," Reza said, and he went back toward the town, leaving Reith and Vereinen bewildered. A minute later, Reza returned.

"Come on," he whispered, and beckoned them with his hand.

Reith and Vereinen looked at each other and shrugged, then followed the dwarf. They found him at the front of the house. A ladder was propped up against it.

"We can get on the roof," he pointed out.

The roof was nearly flat, with just a slight slant down from the back to the front. Vereinen declined the chance to climb the ladder, but Reith and Reza ascended it in short order. They crawled on their bellies from the front of the house to the back, taking great care to keep their heads down to avoid catching any unwanted attention.

From their perch about a dozen feet from the ground, they had a much better view of the battle. The battle line stretched out a mile. Sunlight glinted off the elven host, and from here, Reith saw that there were some humans among them, likely Solzar's men. Across from them, the human army was spread out like a colony of ants swarming over the ground. Their numbers were slightly greater than those of the elves by Reith's estimation.

Though the battle line was long, the vast majority of fighters on each side stood unengaged, waiting for their chance to fight, as those in front of them did the dirty work.

Reith's eyes swept back and forth, looking for some sort of weakness they could exploit.

"We are so few, we can't turn the tide of this battle," Reza declared.

Reith had to give him that. There were scarcely more than a score of them. That many in a battle of thousands was just a drop of water in the ocean.

"We can still be useful," Reith said. "We could shoot at the elves from this side and force them to contend with us. If they think we are more than we are, they may split their force too much and give the human army an advantage."

"If only we had more people," Reza sighed.

They descended the ladder and when they reached the ground, Reith looked everywhere for Vereinen, but he was nowhere to be seen.

"Vereinen!" Reith whispered as loudly as he could. "Vereinen!"

But the streets were empty and silent. The chronicler had vanished.

"Where did he go?" Reza asked, looking around.

"Maybe he went back," Reith replied, turning to look up the street. "But we weren't up there that long. He couldn't have gone far."

"I don't want to speak of doom, but couldn't it be that there are elves in the town?"

Reith and Reza both drew their swords nervously.

"Let's go back to the others," Reith decided. "Hopefully that's where he went."

They had hardly taken a dozen steps when there was a squeaking sound behind them. Reith and Reza leapt around with swords at the ready to face the danger.

"Vereinen!" Reith exclaimed, as Vereinen stepped out

of the house they had just been on top of. "What are you doing?"

"Making friends," the chronicler replied amicably. "Come and see." He held out a hand of invitation to the two of them. Reith sheathed his sword and followed Vereinen into the house, with Reza right behind.

The house was dark, on account of curtains drawn over all windows. It took Reith a few seconds for his eyes to adjust. But then he noticed there were four additional people in the room, apart from himself, Reza, and Vereinen. There was a man, about as tall as Reith, with a brown beard and short hair that matched. There was a woman a few inches shorter than the man with red hair tied back in a braid. And there were two small children, perhaps two and four years old, though Reith could not be certain.

"Hello," he said awkwardly.

"This is Reith," Vereinen said, point to Reith, "and Reza." He pointed to the dwarf.

"Why did you go into these poor people's house?" Reith whispered.

"I saw the older child looking at me through the window, so I knocked. They kindly let me in."

"We are afraid of the elves and the battle raging in our backyard," the woman said. "Vereinen told us you are here to help."

Reith looked at Vereinen. What help could they give? He and Reza had seen the size of the battle.

"We will do what we can," Reith said in reply.

"We have been stuck in our homes for three days now, as the battle continues," the man said.

Reith suddenly had a stroke of inspiration.

"How many in the town could fight if called upon? Spears, swords, bows, anything like that?"

"There are probably a few hundred who could fight, able bodied men and women who don't mind fighting," the man replied.

"I have an idea," Reith said. "Gather everyone in town who can fight at the other end of the town where our companions are waiting. Bring all the weapons you can."

The man, whose name was Gim, kissed his wife and children and pulled a sword, bow, and quiver from a trunk and followed them out into the street.

"Go door to door and get anyone you can. Send them out to get the other houses," Reith said. "We'll go map out a strategy."

"What are you thinking?" Vereinen asked as they walked back through the town.

"When we were on the roof, we were struck with the hopelessness of our situation," Reith explained. "We are so few, and the elven force is large. We needed more people."

"These aren't soldiers, Reith," Vereinen said gently. "You can't lead them into battle like they are. They'll be slaughtered."

"I know," Reith answered. "But they can help."

A short while later, nearly three hundred fighters from Palander filled the streets of the town. Gim stood near Reith, waiting for instruction.

Reith surveyed the fighters before him. Most were men his own age and older. Some were significantly older with gray hair. There were also several women. Most held bows. Some had swords, some had spears, and quite a few had various farming implements that would do for a weapon. Vereinen was right, these were not soldiers.

Reith held up a hand to quiet the crowd, and Gim yelled to get their attention. When it was quiet, Reith spoke.

"Let's divide up. Archers, over here with me, and

everyone else stand over there." The people split up into their respective groups. The archers outnumbered the rest by two to one.

"I think we can work with this," Reith said to Vereinen.

When everyone was settled again, he spoke up.

"People of Palander," he began. "You have been forced to hide in your homes. No more. For on this day, we take up arms to liberate our land and our people. We fight not just flesh and blood, but a Shadow."

At the mention of the Shadow, a shiver went through the crowd.

"What's a Shadow?" someone called out from the back.

"A Shadow is someone wholly given over to the evil of the Dark Powers," Reith explained. "But we are not alone," Reith continued. "The God of Light is on our side. The Guardians are on our side. Though we may be few, we are strong. We can end this war today and free ourselves from fear!"

He gradually increased in pitch and intensity as the speech went on, and at the end the crowd roared in approval.

"We will march for the battle," Reith began again. "When we are close enough, everyone who is not an archer will step forward and form a wall. Everyone with bows will stand behind the wall and will shoot arrows at the elves on my command. We fire together to do the most damage. We will force the elves to contend with us and split their attention. We hope this will be enough to give the king's army an advantage and bring the battle to a swift end. If the enemy charges us, we will fall back into the town, and keep hitting them with arrows. Now, let's go win our freedom!"

They marched through the streets of Palander, with

Reith leading the way on his horse. He was flanked by Dema, Ellamora, and Titus on one side and Vereinen and Reza on the other. The rest of the dwarves brought up the rear behind the company.

They reached Gim's house and the company split in two to round it and make for the open plain beyond.

"Good luck, Reith," Vereinen said. "I will wait here."

"See you soon, Vereinen. Be safe."

"You too, Reith."

Reith led them out, and as far as he could tell, they remained unnoticed by the elves. When he judged they were a sufficient distance from the elven army, he held up a hand and directed the archers to get in position, and the rest took their position in front of the archers, with weapons held out.

"Shoot high in the air, and shoot together," Reith called to the archers. "On my command!"

As one, the archers readied their arrows.

"Draw!"

The archers pulled back and aimed high in the sky toward their enemies.

"Fire!"

The first volley of arrows arched high in the sky. Before they had reached the pinnacle of their flight, Reith ordered more arrows on the string. These too were sent skyward.

Then the first volley hit the elves. Several of them fell as the arrows pierced them. Others glanced off helmets or shields and caused a mass confusion among the elves. They whirled around to see what had happened and that's when the second volley fell. More elves hit the ground, and the elves were in disarray. A third volley came down from the heavens, and though it did less damage than the first two, it still brought a few more elves down.

Elves were running about, and their captains and

commanders were trying to bring order. And then Reith saw him.

Solzar was astride a gigantic black horse. He was yelling instructions to his soldiers. Reith called for the next volley. Instead of aiming high like the others, he focused on Solzar. It was a long shot, and he had to aim above the Gray Man's head, but he had a chance.

"Fire!"

The volley went up and Reith's arrow went shooting out before it, lower than the rest. Reith tracked its flight and saw it going right toward its target.

But then Solzar held up a hand and snatched the arrow from the air like it was just a ball tossed to him. He looked at the arrow, then followed its shaft back. The cold, gray eyes found Reith's eyes. Solzar snapped the arrow shaft in his hand and tossed it to the ground in disgust.

Reith was simply too stunned to move. *How did he catch it?*

He came back to himself when Dema elbowed him in the ribs.

"What?" he asked.

"You haven't given the order to fire!" she yelled.

"Oh, yeah. Fire!"

Another round of arrows took to the sky.

"What happened?" Dema asked as she reloaded.

"Solzar caught my arrow."

"No way!"

"I wouldn't believe it, except I saw it. It was going right toward him and then he snatched it out of the air."

Reith gave the order to fire again.

The elves were now organized again, and several hundred were now marching toward them with their shields out. They did not present much of a target.

"Continue to fire at the main body of troops!" Reith called. "Three more rounds! Fire at will!"

Arrows went skyward, now in a more haphazard manner, spread out along the elven line. These last three rounds did more damage to the elves.

The approaching elves were getting close, so Reith gave the order to fall back.

They retreated quickly into the town. Reith and Reza climbed up on top of Gim's house again and trained their bows at the advancing elves. They shot arrow after arrow and managed to fell several of the elves as they advanced toward the town.

But then Reith's attention was drawn away from the advancing elves toward the main battle. Yells and shouts reached his ears and he looked up to see what was going on. The fighting was frantic where the elves had been who were advancing toward Palander. Human cavalry could be seen above the heads of the elves cutting a path through the center of the elven line. Reith saw Solzar organize his soldiers for a countercharge. But by then, the first humans had completely broken though the elven line, and the elven army was wholly divided. It seemed that all along the battle line, the humans were gaining advantage after advantage as the chain reaction of the elves line being cut in two reverberated across the whole battle. The elves halfway between Palander and the battle turned and rushed back to help their comrades.

"Charge!" Reith called to the defenders of Palander. Here was their advantage. Here was where the final stroke of the battle could be swung.

Reith and Reza practically jumped from the roof of the house in their haste to reach the ground and join the charge. He jumped on his horse and darted forward after his force. The townsfolk gave an almighty bellow as they leapt forward to vanquish their foes. Human soldiers from the king's army charged down toward them from the main battle and the elves in the middle simply threw down their arms in surrender.

Across the battle, elves had the same thought. Swords, spears, and bows were cast down before the advancing human army. Some elves ran for the forest, but most just sat and looked dejected.

There was one person who was not giving up the fight so easily. Solzar was still astride his horse and fighting furiously. His slain foes littered the ground around him and he taunted all. Several knights on horseback challenged him at once and he was able to repel all with a sword that moved as fast as lightning. Soon these foes too were on the ground before him.

Reith and the fighters from Palander reached the surrendered elves. Human soldiers surrounded the elves and began removing their weapons. Reith continued to the circle that was forming around Solzar.

"Enough of this, Shadow," came a rich and deep voice. Reith realized he was beside King Calmon. Calmon was dressed in the finest silver mail and held aloft a sword nearly as fine as the one on Reith's hip. He had a short beard and was sweating from the battle. Here was a king who fought his own wars.

"You can't defeat me," Solzar said in his cold, colorless voice. "I have strength you could only dream of."

"Solzar."

A different voice spoke this time, a voice Reith knew intimately.

"Solzar, please." Vereinen stepped between two soldiers, entered the circle and approached his former friend.

For once, the Shadow was at a loss for words.

"Solzar, surrender," Vereinen pleaded. "Lay down your weapons. Give up your hate. Forsake who you have become."

"I have become *somebody*," Solzar replied. "Why would I give that up?"

"Because deep down," Vereinen continued, "You are still that boy I became friends with all those years ago."

For the first time, a speck of color came across the gray countenance as red flushed in Solzar's face. Something about his countenance shrank and he sighed. He threw his sword to the ground and dismounted from the horse. He knelt to the ground, held up his hands, and said, "I surrender."

Just then, a guttural scream ripped through the air. Reith whirled around looking for the source. And then he saw it. Titus was breaking through the edge of the circle with his sword raised and murder in his eyes.

"This is for my father!" Titus growled and brought his sword down on the helpless Solzar.

But the blow never hit the Shadow. Someone dove between Solzar and Titus and took the blow. Vereinen's body fell, and he was dead before he hit the ground.

22

R eith was numb. He couldn't say or do anything. Others were moving around him taking care of business and things that didn't seem to matter at all to him anymore. Vereinen was dead, his master was dead, and the world had stopped for him and for him alone.

Reith dropped from the saddle and curled into a ball on the grass and sobs overtook him. He lost all sense of time.

The next thing he knew, he felt Dema's warm embrace. She did not say anything, as there was nothing to say. Not in the face of senseless death and violence. He lay there for some time until the sobs ceased and the tears dried up. Then he felt a tug and realized she was pulling him into a sitting position.

He looked around and noticed that they were relatively alone. The soldiers had all moved away. They were tending to their wounded and piling up the bodies for burial. The surrendered elves worked side by side with them as well. A few feet away from them, Vereinen's body lay just as it fell. It was hardly recognizable now with the wound and the blood. Reith looked away; afraid he would be sick. He noticed that Ellamora was standing near him too.

"Where's Solzar?" Reith asked Dema.

"King Calmon arrested him. Titus, too."

At the mention of Titus, rage washed over Reith and for a second, he wanted to go and kill Titus for what he had done. But just as soon as it had come, the feeling slipped away. *After all, what good would it do?*

"The king wants to see you, when you're ready," Ellamora said.

"I'm ready," Reith said, wanting to get as far from Vereinen's body as he could.

Ellamora helped Reith and Dema to their feet. Dema's hand found Reith's and Ellamora walked beside them. They walked across the battlefield toward the human army's camp. All around them, the remnants of the battle remained. Dead bodies littered the field. Fallen weapons and armor glimmered in the sunlight. Horses without riders ambled aimlessly.

They reached the king's pavilion, which was a large purple cloth tent. Two guards stood at attention beside it. They nodded for Reith and Dema to enter, but barred Ellamora's path.

"Just the humans," one of the guards said spitefully.

"She's with me," Reith said, not wanting to do anything without his friend at this point.

"She's an elf."

"I *said*, she's with me." Reith he drew his sword. He was going to fight these two guards, no matter what it cost him. The guards seemed taken aback by his sudden aggression. But then, from the tent, the king spoke.

"Let her be," King Calmon said calmly.

Ellamora was permitted to enter with Reith and Dema, and she shot a dirty look at the guards as she passed.

King Calmon's tent was sparsely furnished. The only luxury he seemed to have was a small wooden table behind which he sat. They stood before him and he surveyed them.

"I have been told you are a great general," the king said finally, looking straight at Reith, who blushed.

"I wouldn't say that, your highness," Reith stammered.

"From what your companion tells me," the king continued, gesturing to Dema, "you have proven most adept at surveying the situation and moving those under your command in the most efficient way possible. I have use for such men in my kingdom."

"Thank you sire," Reith said, not knowing what else to say.

"But onto other matters. Who was the man who stepped in front of Solzar? And why did he do it?"

At the mention of Vereinen, tears came again to Reith's eyes. He didn't know if he could speak without bawling again, so he gripped Dema's hand and squeezed it. She understood.

"Please, your majesty," Dema interjected. "If I may speak for him and tell the tale?"

King Calmon nodded in permission.

Dema spoke for several minutes. She recounted what she knew of Reith's life with Vereinen before Solzar attacked. She briefly described how they had met one another and their experiences in Crain and their trip to Sardis where they met Vereinen and what he had revealed about his relationship to Solzar.

Reith was only half listening to her. He tried to nod when appropriate, but he was mostly concentrating on not crying. He could not believe that Vereinen was gone.

When Dema had finished, King Calmon spoke again.

"That is quite the story, and I feel that I am only

hearing part of it. How you got from Sardis to here, and with the dwarves, I would very much like to hear. Someday. But in the meantime, I wanted to speak to you about another, urgent matter."

The king sighed and leaned back in his chair and put his hands behind his head.

"Something has happened that I am sure has not happened in all the history of Terrasohnen. But it would probably be easier to just show you. Guards, bring him in."

A few seconds later, they heard footsteps approaching the tent and the clink of chains. The two guards burst into the tent with a third man between them.

He was tall, with black hair that was beginning to gray. It took Reith a second to recognize him.

"Solzar!"

Quite the change had come over Solzar. His skin was no longer gray, but a rich tan. His eyes too had changed from gray to a shade like olive. They stared unseeingly, looking at nothing in particular. He was blind. But the biggest change of all was his entire aura. He no longer gave off a menacing vibe.

"As you can see," the king continued, "the Shadow is gone from Solzar. He is truly himself again."

Reith, Dema, and Ellamora looked on speechless.

"What happened to you?" Reith finally asked, staring into the new face of his old enemy.

"I can't explain it," Solzar said in a voice that was warm and bright, completely opposite his former voice. He turned toward the sound of Reith's voice, but he continued to stare without sight. "All I know is that while I was still wretched, Vereinen died for me. And that seems to have made all the difference. I came to myself on that battlefield. Vereinen's blood was spilled and my life began anew. I am sorry for the things I did and for who I was. I was young and so angry at everyone when I welcomed the Shadow into my life. But today, today I feel like I have woken from a dream, like I am spring coming out of winter, like the dawn after a long night."

"As you can see, it is the most peculiar thing," Calmon replied. "He is a new creature."

"So … what now?" Reith asked, not knowing what exactly to make of this situation. This man was standing here because Vereinen had given his life. This man was alive, the man who had killed so many people, while Vereinen, a good man, was dead.

"Oh, he is not a free man if that's what you are worried about," the king replied calmly. "No, he is in chains for his crimes, and will remain a prisoner until he dies. But he may still be useful to us. Solzar, tell our young friends what you know."

"There will be more Shadows," he said calmly. He shook his head in disgust. Reith wondered if he was genuinely against Shadows now, or if he was just pretending. But then he took in the entire change in Solzar, and he believed him.

"There already is a new Shadow in Kal-Epharion," Solzar continued. "He will come. King Koinas in Sardis is becoming a Shadow as well."

"Remus and Romulus are going to Sardis," Ellamora said with great concern. "They're going to overthrow their father."

"It will be a tall task," Solzar replied. "Time will tell if that was a wise decision or not."

"That will do, Solzar," King Calmon said coolly upon seeing the dirty look Ellamora shot the former Shadow. "Guards, take him away. Solzar, if your repentance is true, then we shall talk again on how you will pay off your debt with service to the kingdom."

Solzar nodded and the guards came in and took him away.

"Now, we must discuss the young man, Titus," Calmon said sadly.

"What do you mean?" Reith asked.

"He has broken the law. He attempted to kill a surrendered enemy. By law, his life is forfeit."

"You won't kill him, will you?" Dema asked, her temper rising.

"No, no, we won't kill him. We do not kill our prisoners," the king replied. "We believe the best in all and hope for change in even the worst murderers and villains. No, his freedom is what is required."

"He's just a kid!" Dema protested.

"You brought him to war. He's old enough to atone for his sins. The penalty must be paid."

"What if," Reith began, speaking as he thought, "what if Vereinen's death is for Solzar and for Titus. Titus never actually hurt Solzar. What if Vereinen's death saves Solzar from being a Shadow and saves Titus from being a prisoner for life?"

"An interesting notion," the king mused. "As I said earlier, we are in realms of justice never before seen in Terrasohnen. So here is what I will do. If Titus is repentant, if he is sorry for his actions, he shall go free. We place before him life and death. Let him choose."

"How will you do that?" Reith asked.

"A trial," Calmon replied. "I shall interview him and stand over him as judge, as I am required and entitled to be by the laws of my kingdom. If I deem he is repentant and earnestly is sorry for his actions, then he shall go free. If he holds onto his resentment or tries to justify himself, then he has rejected the chance before him. Does that seem fair?"

The three of them nodded.

"Very well, then. Guards, please bring me the other prisoner."

A minute later, Titus stood in the place Solzar had previously stood, and likewise, he was in chains.

"Titus," the king began. "You stand here an accused man. You entered the battle as a man, so your youth is no excuse for your behavior. You have broken the law against killing a surrendered enemy. What do you have to say for yourself?"

Reith looked at Titus and saw the scared boy he had first met by the river. But it was true, he had decided to join the battle, so he must face the consequences. But Titus looked scared. He looked toward Dema for affirmation, who nodded to him.

"I'm sorry, your highness," Titus said. "He killed my father, and I wanted to kill him."

"And how do you feel about the action you took now?"

"I didn't mean to kill the other man," Titus said, and tears came to his eyes. "I didn't mean to. I shouldn't have done it. I have blood on my hands."

He held them up as if to show blood dripping from them. The chains rattled.

"And how do you feel toward Solzar, the Shadow who killed your father?"

"He is no one to me, sire," Titus said, shaking his head. "Whether he lives or dies doesn't matter anymore. I have killed a man and must live with it. I don't want to kill anyone else."

Calmon surveyed the boy in front of him, then glanced to Reith, Dema, and Ellamora.

"I judge your answers to be true and of great merit," the king said finally. "So here is what will happen to you. You will accompany my army to Galismoor, and you will wear your chains the whole way as symbol of your crime. But when we reach the city, you shall be released and free to stay in the city or return to your home. Your debt is paid. Another has given his life for yours."

"Thank you, your highness," said Dema. "You are very generous."

"It is more than I deserve," Titus replied.

King Calmon dismissed Titus and the guards took him away.

"One last piece of business, before I send you on your way. Ellamora, do you know of trustworthy elves who could bring these captured elves safely to their homeland?"

"Crain is two or three days journey south of here, and Pallin and Laneras are trustworthy. Pallin commands a legion in Crain and Laneras is a close friend."

"Could we send for them?" King Calmon replied. "Would they come?"

"I think they would, if I went to them," answered Ellamora.

"Then you shall go at once," the king declared.

"We'll go, too," Dema and Reith said in unison.

"Dema, you may go with Ellamora," replied Calmon. "But I have need of Reith here. There is much I would like to discuss with him. We will not break camp until the elves are safely back across the river, so that gives us plenty of time to stay here and talk."

***

Within an hour, Ellamora and Dema were provisioned for their journey. Reith and Dema embraced for a long time before Ellamora cleared her throat to hurry them along.

"I will be back soon," Dema said.

"Be safe. I love you."

"I love you, too."

Dema and Ellamora mounted their horses and were soon out of sight. Suddenly, Reith felt very alone. Vereinen was dead and his two best friends in the whole world had left. Titus would have been a friendly face, but he was imprisoned. Romulus and Remus were marching toward Sardis many miles south. At least Dema and Ellamora would return soon with Pallin and Laneras. Reza and the dwarves were around, but he hardly knew them, despite his long travels with them. For a few days though, he would be mostly alone with himself and his grief.

For the sake of familiarity, he camped with the dwarves that night. They told stories around the fire, but Reith was only half listening. He knew Vereinen would have loved the stories. He laughed along with everyone else, but his laughter was forced.

As darkness fell, the cold ripped into him, chilling him to the bones. Dema's absence was felt even more now. He cried silent tears most of the night and barely slept. He felt weariness that had nothing to do with the lack of sleep. He felt an emptiness in his chest, like his very soul was being sucked out of him somehow. The night was darker and the cold was more bitter than any night he could remember, even the nights in the snowy mountain heights.

In the morning, he was again summoned to King Calmon's pavilion, and this time Reza was to accompany him.

The two of them walked through the camp, and Reith felt almost invisible. All eyes went to Reza as he passed. Humans and elves alike gawked at him. To his credit, Reza took all this in stride.

"I bet this is what you felt like in Darren Shahr," he said.

They arrived at the pavilion and had no trouble

gaining access. The guards barely even stared, thought Reith saw their eyes flit toward the dwarf with curiosity.

"Reza," the King began, "It is good to meet you. Tell me of your coming to this battlefield."

Reza briefly described the siege of Darren Shahr and the news Romulus and Remus were able to procure. He mentioned how he had volunteered to accompany Reith and the others and their travels through the mountains and down to the plain.

"Your courage and goodness are evident," the king noted when Reza completed the story. "May you be blessed by the Creator. I am glad you are here, Reza. I need dwarves and elves I can trust if we are to band together as peoples of Terrasohnen. There will be another Shadow from the east, and perhaps a Shadow already in the south and our races must find common ground and join together to fight for peace. What say you?"

"I agree, your majesty," Reza replied. "I was sorry that my queen did not send more troops to your aid. I was glad to come, if only to repay the debt my people owe Reith and his friends. If not for them, Darren Shahr would have fallen under the Shadow's control, and the entire eastern part of the world with it."

"We do not yet know if the rising Shadow in the south, King Koinas, has been subdued," the king said. "Word from Sardis would be welcome indeed. If he remains in power, we have to watch for threats in two directions. But whatever happens, Reza, do I have your word that you will work for the peace and prosperity of all Terrasohnen?"

"You can count on me," Reza replied.

"Good. Please make yourself as comfortable as you can here. We will not depart this battlefield until the elves are safely back across the river. Dema and Ellamora are fetching some friends to escort the elves back. You are dismissed."

Reza bowed and backed out of the pavilion, leaving Reith alone with the king.

"Did you need me, sire?" asked Reith.

"I do not," the king said. "But I would like to pass on a request from another. Solzar wants to speak with you."

"Solzar? Why?" Reith asked, stunned.

"He wouldn't say. That said, I will leave it up to you whether you see him or not. He is in chains and repentant, so you should be in no danger. I will send guards with you, of course."

"I will see him," Reith replied, still unsure as to why the former Shadow would want to see him.

"Very well," King Calmon answered. "Tell the guards outside of your desire and they will see to it."

A few minutes later, Reith approached a wagon that had become a makeshift jail. Guards stood beside it. Solzar sat calmly with his back against the wooden bars of his cage. All trace of the gray was still gone, and Reith found it difficult to wrap his head around the fact that this normal looking man in front of him had committed so much evil as a Shadow.

At the sound of Reith's approaching footsteps, Solzar stiffened in his cell.

"Who goes there?"

"Hello, Solzar," Reith said warily. "You wanted to talk?"

23

———

"Why did you summon me?" Reith asked.

"I asked for you because I wanted to talk about your sword."

"My sword?" Reith instinctively lifted a hand to place on the hilt and gripped it tightly.

"Don't worry, son," Solzar said with a laugh. "I do not want the thing anymore. I wanted to tell you about it."

"Why were you looking for it?" Reith asked.

"Because it is the Key to salvation for all of Terrasohnen," Solzar said simply. "It unlocks an ancient and great power."

"What sort of power, Solzar?" Reith asked.

"My masters," Solzar began with a shudder, "did not tell me. Probably in case I found myself in this very situation." He gestured toward the cage around him. "But from what they did tell me and what I deduced, that key unlocks something that will make the one who opens the lock nearly invincible."

"That is quite the power, indeed," Reith replied, not knowing exactly what to say.

"And you have the key," Solzar said. "But there is something you lack." He held up a small item between his thumb and index finger. It glinted and gleamed in the light. It was a ring woven of three metals: gold, silver, and copper, just like Reith's sword. "This ring is a map of sorts. It will lead you to the lock the key will fit."

"How does it do that?" Reith asked.

"It is said to grow warmer the closer the bearer of the ring and the key gets to the lock."

"But you didn't have the key, so it didn't work for you," Reith guessed.

"Correct," Solzar replied. "I could have been a stone's throw away from it, and the ring would remain unchanged. Here, take it." He stuck his hand through the bars and held out the ring to Reith, who took it from Solzar's fingers. It felt cold to the touch. Reith turned it over in his hand several times and inspected the craftsmanship. Then he slipped it onto his right ring finger.

"Now you have what you need," Solzar said. "I have no use for rings or swords. A key to get out of this cage is the only key I care to possess."

"Thank you, Solzar," Reith said, and he really meant it.

What a strange relationship this is turning out to be.

"I regret my actions," Solzar continued. "I am sorry, Reith, for the heartache I have caused you. I beg your forgiveness."

"I forgive you," Reith said automatically and was shocked to find that he actually meant it. He no longer held Solzar's past sins against him.

"Thank you, Reith."

"Why are you blind?" Reith blurted out before he could check himself. *How rude of me.*

"I don't really know," Solzar said slowly with great sadness in his voice.

"I'm sorry I asked," Reith said apologetically.

"No, no, it's fine," Solzar replied. "I have pondered the question myself since the battle. I have a hunch."

"Why do you think it happened?"

"I was in rebellion against the God of Light," Solzar answered. "I rejected the light and embraced, whole-heartedly, the darkness. I gave myself over to the Dark Powers. The light was repulsive to me. But when Vereinen gave his life for me, the darkness was extinguished and the light came flooding back in. It was too much for my eyes, which had for so long avoided the light. And so I am sightless because I forsook the light in my arrogance, greed, and cruelty."

"Do you think you'll ever see again?" Reith asked.

"The God of Light alone knows the answer to that question," Solzar replied. "Though, you could say that I see better now than I ever did as a Shadow. Everything is clear to me, in here." He pointed to his chest. "The eyes of my heart can see."

The next few days passed rather slowly for Reith. He was not summoned to see the king again, so he spent his time with the dwarves or by taking long walks around the camp by himself. On these long walks, he absentmindedly fiddled with the new ring on his finger. As he walked, he remembered the words he had heard repeatedly: *Fight for them. Then find me.*

As his fingers ran over the smooth metal of the ring, he wondered which part was next. The voice wasn't chiming in to give him the answer. Was it time for more fighting? Or was it time for finding?

He contemplated his next move. Dema and Ellamora would return soon, and then the elves would be taken home and the army would be free to move. He could accompany the king to Galismoor. He knew he must go north eventually to find what he was looking for. He thought back to the Shrine in the Free Isles and Onias' words. The key bearer was to travel north, across an inland sea, and follow a frozen river to the Temple of Ice. Was he to go north now? But he could also accompany Ellamora back to Crain or even go to Sardis. Or he could go with Dema to Suthrond. So many options were presenting themselves to him that he had a hard time discerning what he should do.

One morning, as he walked around the camp, he heard a commotion. Elves were approaching from the south. He ran through the camp and saw Dema and Ellamora riding toward him. Between them rode Pallin and Laneras. They all dismounted and there was a huge hug as Reith embraced them all. He found he was crying, though from joy or sadness, he could not say.

"Sardis belongs to Romulus!" Ellamora exclaimed when they all separated.

"The news reached Crain at almost the same time Ellamora and Dema showed up," Laneras said with a smile.

"What about Koinas?" Reith asked.

"He is imprisoned," Pallin replied.

"But he's not a Shadow?"

"Not yet," Laneras answered. "Who knows what he will become? But it's odd," Laneras said, a puzzled look coming across his face. "A man became a Shadow and then became unmade. Not exactly a book of instructions for dealing with others."

"Solzar and Vereinen were connected somehow," Reith said. "I don't think just anyone could die for a Shadow."

"Perhaps not, but it doesn't leave us any ideas going forward," Pallin replied.

"No, it doesn't," Reith agreed. "But I think it is time for you two to meet with King Calmon."

A short time later, Pallin and Laneras had finished speaking with the king, and arrangements were made for the elven soldiers to be escorted back across the river the next morning. After their meeting, Reith, Dema, Ellamora, and Reza were invited to meet with the king.

"I have special requests to make of each of you," the king said. "In this room are trustworthy, humans, an elf, and a dwarf, all of whom have risked much to bring peace to Terrasohnen. I would ask you to consider continuing your service to the world."

"What do you mean?" Dema asked.

"I mean that I wish you four to continue your work as ambassadors to the various kingdoms of Terrasohnen. If you are willing, Reith, I would have you go to the elves. Dema, I would have you go to the dwarves. And Ellamora and Reza, I wish for you to come to Galismoor to be ambassadors for your kingdoms here in my kingdom. Of course, these jobs would mean lots of travel back and forth from Galismoor to Darren Shahr and Sardis, so you would see each other fairly regularly. What say you?"

"I am honored that your majesty trusts me for such an important task," Ellamora replied. The other three nodded in agreement. "Do you need our answers now?"

"Not now," the king replied, "But soon. Hopefully by the morning, if you are able to decide by then."

"Let us talk amongst ourselves and we will decide by then," Reith promised.

"Very good," said the king.

Outside the pavilion, the four of them gathered together and weighed their options.

"What do you think?" Reza asked.

"It's quite the honor," Dema replied.

"I think I will do it," Ellamora said quietly. "I don't want to go back to Crain. At least not with Pryderus there."

"I am sure Romulus can depose Pryderus," Dema said. "But I am not sure about my course." She turned to Reith. "This would mean we would be apart."

"Yeah, it would," Reith said sadly.

"I also think I will accept the king's offer," Reza replied. "I would love to live in Galismoor and serve my queen in such a manner."

"I have to think about it more," Reith said. He looked at Dema and then down at the ring on his finger. His heart wanted to be wherever Dema was, and his soul wanted to find the mysterious voice. He didn't know what to do.

"Let's spend the day thinking," Dema suggested, "and then tonight we can come together and tell what we think."

"Yeah, that sounds good," Reith said. He and Dema hugged and kissed goodbye for now and went their separate ways to decide. Reith continued his loop of the camp he had begun earlier that morning.

As he walked, he prayed to the God of Light for illumination for his steps. He would love the ability to travel to Sardis and spend more time there. He would have a place of honor within the city and in his free time he could read and study and learn all he could, like he did under Vereinen. But Dema's face kept popping up in his mind. And often, the gold, silver, and copper ring would too.

He found a quiet spot away from the camp and sat down at the base of a tree. He closed his eyes and focused on breathing in and out slowly. After a while, the voice spoke again in his head.

Serve them. Fight for them. Then find me.

And in his soul, he knew exactly what he needed to do.

That evening, Reith and Dema met beside the fire to discuss their plans.

"I am going to Sardis," Reith said. "I do not know for how long, but that is where I am being sent."

"I decided to go to Darren Shahr," Dema replied. "But I will miss you so much."

"We will see each other," Reith said. "I will travel to you and you to me, and we can write letters. There will be official correspondence between the kingdoms now."

"I love you, Reith," Dema said, and she leaned in to kiss him.

When they separated, Reith whispered, "I love you too, Dema."

They held each other wordlessly all through the night, letting only their love for each other do the talking. As the sun rose, the elves began to gather for their trip back to their land.

Reith, Dema, Ellamora, and Reza went back to King Calmon to make their intentions known to him.

"I am glad you are all willing to serve," he said. "Here are your official orders, Reith and Dema. Your mission is peace and goodwill between all races. To that end, we will be creating a postal system between all the capital cities.

There are details in the scrolls. Ellamora and Reza, Reith and Dema will inform your rulers of what is going on and they will send you your own orders soon. But for the meantime, you are welcome to come to Galismoor with me and I will accommodate you within the castle."

"Thank you, your majesty," Ellamora said, with a slight bow.

They were dismissed so the king could see to the expulsion of the elven army. It was almost time to depart.

"Goodbye, my love," Dema said, squeezing him tight.

"Goodbye for now," Reith said. "I will see you again. And I will write as soon as I get to Sardis."

Reith rose and bid farewell to Ellamora and Reza as well before going over to Laneras and Pallin.

"Ellyn has been taking good care of your horse," Laneras told him.

"It will be good to see Ellyn, and Aspen again," Reith replied.

"Perhaps you can stay with us in Crain for a few days before you make for Sardis," Pallin suggested.

"Would Pryderus allow it?" Reith asked.

"I don't think we will have to worry about him much longer," Laneras said with a grin. "And now you're coming to town not as a refugee, but as a royal ambassador. If he harms you, he has King Calmon's army to deal with."

They rode south and came to Suthrond late in the day. The peach groves filled the air with a sweet smell and Heth came to meet them. Laneras and Pallin kept the army moving, so as not to disturb the people of Suthrond.

"Reith, I am so sorry to hear about Vereinen, you must be devastated," Heth said sympathetically. "Don't hold it against poor Titus."

"Titus is being treated very well by the king," Reith said. "And thank you. For everything."

"No, thank you," Heth said. "Your generosity is feeding us and making the land beautiful. These trees will stand for generations in monument to you."

Reith embraced the old woman. They held each other for a long time, before Heth pulled back, though she kept a hand on each of his shoulders.

"I am proud of you, Reith. You have come a long way." They hugged again and bid each other farewell. Reith mounted his horse and caught up with Laneras and Pallin.

Soon they reached the river and crossed it. Once more he was leaving his homeland. But this time, he was going by choice.

ABOUT THE AUTHOR

N. K. Carlson is a Storyteller living in the Panhandle of Texas. In his day job as a pastor, he tells divine stories of light and dark, good and evil. This vocation carries over into the writing of fiction, as the same themes are prevalent in his work. In addition to the book you are holding, he is the author of *Shadow and Sword*, which is Book One of *The Chronicles of Terrasohnen*. He is also the author of *The Things That Charm Us* and co-author of *The Smelly Gospel*. When he is not writing, he is probably reading, playing guitar, attending a sporting event, or spending time with his wife, Haley, and their two sons.